He became aware of footsteps on the path. They stopped at his door.

"You're Rabbi Small, aren't you? Of Barnard's Crossing?"

He peered nearsightedly at the speaker beyond the screen door, and although it was twilight he could see that it was a tall, attractive young woman of about twenty-five. Dark, wavy hair framed an oval face that at the moment was both hesitant and yet determined.

"Do I know you?" he asked.

"No, although you may have seen me around because I'm from Barnard's Crossing, too. I'm Joan Abernathy. I spotted you in the village yesterday. You drove up in the hotel limousine, so I figured you were staying here."

"I see. And what can I do for you?"

"I'd like you to convert me."

"I don't do conversions," he said.

BY HARRY KEMELMAN

FRIDAY THE RABBI SLEPT LATE
SATURDAY THE RABBI WENT HUNGRY
THE NINE MILE WALK
SUNDAY THE RABBI STAYED HOME
COMMON SENSE IN EDUCATION
MONDAY THE RABBI TOOK OFF
TUESDAY THE RABBI SAW RED
WEDNESDAY THE RABBI GOT WET
THURSDAY THE RABBI WALKED OUT
CONVERSATIONS WITH RABBI SMALL

CONVERSATIONS WITH RABBI SMALL

HARRY KEMELMAN

Fawcett Crest • New York

A Fawcett Crest Book
Published by Ballantine Books
Copyright © 1981 by Harry Kemelman

Published in the United States by Ballantine Books, a
division of Random House, Inc., New York, and in Canada
by Random House of Canada, Limited, Toronto, Canada.

Library of Congress Catalog Card Number: 81-1131

ISBN 0-449-24527-6

This edition published by arrangement with William Mor-
row and Company, Inc.

Manufactured in the United States of America

First Ballantine Books Edition: August 1982

To my wife, Anne

CHAPTER

1

The vacation in the mountains was Miriam's idea. With the children going to camp there was no reason why she and her husband, Rabbi David Small, had to stay in Barnard's Crossing all summer long. The Friday evening services ended in June and there were no holidays until the celebration of the New Year in September.

"There's just the minyan, and you're not needed for that," she said.

"Yes, but why do we have to go away?" Rabbi Small asked plaintively. "Barnard's Crossing is pleasant in the summer. We're at the seashore. People come *here* for vacation."

"People coming here can get a vacation," she pointed out, "but living here you can't. People call you and come to see you just because you're here and available. The only way you can get a real vacation is by going somewhere where you can't be reached. And you need a vacation. You haven't been sleeping well and you've been irritable. A couple of weeks in the mountains will do wonders for you. Now Gladys Shilkun was telling me about this perfectly wonderful hotel, strictly kosher—"

"A hotel!"

"They have cabins scattered throughout the grounds, each one separate," Miriam hastened to explain. "And they are furnished with a little fridge and a hot plate and some dishes so you can make your own breakfast or have tea in the afternoon without going up to the dining hall, where you get lunches and dinners."

"But what will I do there?"

"You'll rest. You'll sleep late in the morning. You'll take a walk through the woods. You'll have a chance to read and to work on your Vilna Gaon paper."

It wasn't that Rabbi Small really objected to taking a vacation; it was only that the idea had never occurred to him. So mid-June found him and Miriam at Hotel Placid in Grenardsville, ensconced in a small rustic cabin with a screened porch that looked out on the valley and the mountains beyond. He had feared that as a rabbi staying at a kosher hotel, he would be caught up in all kinds of activities that would interfere with his work on the paper he was writing, and had suggested that perhaps reservations should be made for Mr. David Small rather than Rabbi Small.

"Then you won't get the rabbinical discount," Miriam had pointed out. "Don't worry about it. When I call, I'll explain that you have important work to do and don't want to be disturbed." When, on arriving, she had been approached by the social director as her husband was registering at the desk, she had explained that her husband was there to work and did not want to be distracted by social activities.

He had winked at her and said, "Gotcha." Then cautiously, "But how about the daily minyan? Won't he go to that?"

"What time does it begin?"

"Well, the morning minyan, Shachriss, is at seven—"

"Then don't count on him. I want him to sleep late. Maybe Mincha, Maariv..."

"Gotcha." And another wink.

Later, at dinner, Miriam told her husband of the conversation. She laughed as a sudden thought struck her. "He kept winking at me, David. Do you suppose he thinks we're not married, that we are having an affair?"

The rabbi laughed. "Why would he think—" His eyes widened as she reached for a roll. "You're not wearing your wedding ring."

She looked at her hand, fingers spread, in dismay. And then she remembered. "Oh, I took it off to wash my hands and forgot to put it back on."

"Why did you take it off? Do you always?"

"Of course not. But, David, this is a very kosher place. There was one of those ring holders in the bathroom, so I thought I'd use it. Didn't you notice that they had a special cup for washing on the stand?"

"Come to think of it. Well, if you walk around without a wedding ring it's understandable. And you shouldn't leave things like that lying around in a hotel room."

"Oh, I'll get it right after dinner. Maybe I'll wear it on a chain around my neck, where it can't be seen, and let them gossip. It might be fun."

"That's all I need—to have people think I'm having an affair." But Rabbi Small smiled. He looked around the dining room and noted that fewer than half the tables were occupied. "It's certainly not crowded."

"It's early in the season," she explained. "I was talking to one of the guests. She said they always come at this time in June. In July and August she said it's mobbed."

He nodded. "Understandable. I suppose most of these people are from New York. The weather doesn't really get bad in the city before July."

The waitress, blonde, busty, and middle-aged, served

them the first course, a scoop of chopped liver on a lettuce leaf. Miriam took up a forkful and sampled it. "Oh, you'll like this, David. It could use a little more salt, though."

He tasted. "M-hm. I expect the food will be good. It usually is in these places." He looked around again. "They seem to be an older group."

She leaned back in her chair, the better to survey the other tables. "You're not kidding, David. It's an old-age home. Do you mind? It will be quiet and they won't be likely to bother you. You came here for a rest. Remember?"

"I don't mind. Oh, there's a young woman, the one with the red hair, two tables over."

Miriam turned casually and then leaned forward to whisper across the table, "She's sixty if she's a day. No, I'm afraid we're the youngest people here. I'm sorry. Maybe later in the season...The Shilkuns come up in August, I understand."

"I really don't mind," he assured her, and added, "if you don't."

She shrugged elaborately. "I didn't come to establish lasting friendships. Just not to have to keep house or cook meals and wash dishes and make beds for a couple of weeks is all I was looking forward to."

"But what will you do here all day?"

"Oh, they have a swimming pool, and there's a tennis court. Someone must play. Or I can just lie in the sun and do nothing. Don't worry about me."

The manager, who had been at the desk when they had registered and who now seemed to be in charge of the dining room, approached, smiling and rubbing his hands. "Everything all right, folks?"

"Everything's fine," the rabbi assured him. And then as the manager was about to turn to another table, Rabbi Small asked, "What do you do here evenings?"

The manager pursed his lips as he considered. "Well, there's the TV room, and the game room where you can play cards or checkers or chess. And let's see, Thursday nights we have a beano, and then some folks like to go into the village to the movies."

There was further amplification of the evening activities when the Smalls had finished dinner and were standing on the steps of the lighted veranda before plunging into the darkness along the gravel path that led to their cabin. They were joined by one of the guests, a short fat man with a gleaming bald head encircled by a halo of curly gray hair. He patted his considerable paunch with the palms of his hands, took a deep breath, and let it out in a low whistle. "Now that's what you call air, folks," he proclaimed. "Finest air in America. I've been all over. Ten years I've been coming here, and I say you can't beat it. Every now and then the missus says we ought to try one of the fancy places like the Concord or Grossinger's, but we always end up coming here."

"I imagine there's a lot more activity at those places," said Miriam.

"Activity, shmactivity," the man scoffed. "Lady, the air here is so full of oxygen that come nine or ten o'clock you can hardly keep your eyes open. Those places, young fellows go to meet girls, and vice versa. But if you're an old married man like me, what you want is rest. And believe me, this is the place for it."

After a couple of days the rabbi settled into the rhythm of the place. In response to long habit, he would wake up early, half past six or a quarter to seven, realize where he was, and luxuriating in the thought that he did not have to get up, roll over and doze again. Later, around half past eight, awakened perhaps by the smell of coffee perking on the hot plate, he would rise, recite his morning prayers, and then shower while Miriam prepared breakfast.

Afterward they would walk to the village about a mile away for the morning papers. They could have bought them at the hotel, but Miriam insisted that he needed the exercise.

At first the leisure he had at his disposal was actually counterproductive. On the assumption that he had all day free to work, he spent most of the morning reading the newspapers and the paperbacks that he had bought in the village. And in the afternoon, surfeited by a heavy lunch, he took a siesta. But before the end of the week, the inactivity palled. Immediately after breakfast one morning he resolutely set out his papers on the wicker table on the porch and began making notes.

"Aren't you coming down to the village?" Miriam asked.

"You go. I want to do some work."

When she returned about an hour later, her husband was still at work, his thick-lensed glasses pushed up on his forehead as he squinted at three-by-five cards. Miriam kept out of his way until noon, when she approached to ask if he was ready for lunch.

He leaned back in his chair and looked up at her lazily. "I'm not really very hungry," he said. "And they give you too much to eat up there. Would you mind going alone? Maybe you can get them to give you a sandwich and a bottle of beer for me. I don't want to stop right now. All right?"

"Oh, sure, David. Is it going well? I'm so glad. Any particular kind of sandwich?"

"Anything, anything at all."

Rabbi Small worked all through the afternoon while Miriam took a nap, washed her hair, did her nails, and then left him to go to the pool. Not until it was time for the evening prayers did he stop. He attended the minyan at the hotel and then waited in the lobby for her to join him so that they could have dinner together. Then they sat on the cabin porch watching the moon rise over the mountains in the distance as he talked of what he had done during the day.

"I feel that for the first time in years I've done a day's work," he said. "It's been so long since I've had a full day all to myself with no interruptions. It's nice."

"I'm so glad you're enjoying it," she said.

Then the telephone rang.

Miriam went inside to answer it. It seemed that she

was gone a long time, and when she came out, he saw that she was frowning.

"Who was it? Anything important?"

"It was Mother. Dad is in the hospital. He's going to be operated on tomorrow morning. I'll have to go to New York."

"The prostate?"

"Uh-huh. He'll be in the hospital for about ten days. And I'll have to be with Mama. She can't stay alone. I called the desk and they said there's a bus I can take at nine tomorrow morning. That's the earliest I can get away."

"What do you mean, I? We'll both go."

"No, David. It's not necessary. And there's no place for you to stay. I'll be sleeping with Mama."

"We could go to a hotel. Or I could sleep on the couch in the study."

"No, you'd just be in the way. And it would end up with Mama insisting on giving us the bedroom and her sleeping on the couch. And what would you do all day? What's more, if we're both there, Mama will feel she has to make meals for us. No, I'll go alone. Actually, it's just perfect our being here. I don't have to worry about how you're going to manage for meals the way I would if we were in Barnard's Crossing. You can make yourself some coffee in the morning. Or you can take all your meals in the dining room. And you'll be able to work undisturbed all day and half the night if you wish."

They continued to argue about it but in the end, when her husband agreed because it was obviously the most sensible plan, she said, "I'll go up to the hotel now and make the necessary arrangements."

"What arrangements?"

"Well, since I'm not going to be here for the next few days, there should be some reduction in our bill, shouldn't there?"

The next morning the rabbi got up when Miriam did, and because it was early enough, he attended the morning service at the hotel, and afterward she joined him

13

for breakfast in the dining room. They lingered over their meal until the manager came to inform them that the car was ready and waiting for them. They arrived early at the bus stop. As they paced back and forth in front of the one-story wooden shack that served as a waiting room, neither seemed inclined to talk. When the bus finally came, the rabbi helped Miriam with her bag and then stood at the curb smiling up at her and nodding reassuringly until the bus left. Then he walked home.

Although he tried to work, he found he could not concentrate. Finally he gave up in annoyance and picked up a paperback. Nor was it any better after lunch. He missed her presence, the sound of her movements in the cabin, the knowledge that she was within call. Late in the afternoon she telephoned to tell him that the operation had been successful and that her father was now in the recovery room.

"And you're all right, David? Did you get a lot of work done?"

"Oh, yes," he lied. "It's going well."

"That's wonderful. I'll call again tomorrow."

"Er, Miriam—"

"Yes?"

"I miss you."

After dinner he wandered into the TV room. The set was in the corner opposite the door, and facing it were half a dozen armchairs and a sofa, all of them occupied. He stood near the door and watched a hospital drama which concerned the problems of a brilliant surgeon who had become addicted to drugs. During a commercial an elderly woman on the sofa exclaimed, "Who knows what goes on in hospitals!" There were murmurs of agreement, and thus encouraged, she began to narrate what had happened to her when she was operated on for gallstones. Catching sight of the rabbi, she made motions of pushing over to make room for him on the sofa, nodding to him to indicate that there was a place for him. He smiled and shook his head and left the room.

He had no better luck in the game room. Four men were seated around a card table playing pinochle, slapping cards down on the table with frequent exclamations of triumph or disappointment. Although he knew nothing of the rules of the game, he watched for a few minutes. The players paid no attention to him, and after a while he sauntered out.

He returned to the cabin, thinking that perhaps now he might be able to work on his paper. But the only light inside the cabin came from the bed lamp, which did not quite reach the narrow table at which they breakfasted, and the cord was too short to reach the only other outlet. Up till now he had worked on the porch at a round, glass-topped, wickerwork table, but always in the daytime. At night, the only available light was the twenty-five-watt bulb in the porch ceiling.

He was tempted to go back to the hotel to see if he could borrow a lamp with a long cord, but finally decided that he really did not feel like working. He removed his jacket and kicked off his shoes and lay down on the bed to read. After a while he dozed off, and when he awoke he realized it must be late since the hotel was dark. It was after midnight.

Nevertheless, the next day when Miriam called, he assured her that everything was fine, that he had spent the evening working on his paper, and that it was coming along nicely.

"Are you sure?" she asked anxiously.

"Of course I'm sure," he answered indignantly. "I ought to know if I'm working."

"But you don't want to work too hard," she said soothingly. "Why don't you walk down to the village tonight and go to the movie?"

"Well, I'll see. Just don't worry about me. I'm getting along fine."

After dinner he sought out the manager.

"A lamp with a long cord? What kind of a lamp?"

"A floor lamp. I thought maybe from one of the vacant rooms..."

"I couldn't take a lamp from another room." He

15

sounded as though he had been asked to steal it. "I see you don't know very much about the hotel business. With us, we've got an inventory with the furnishings of every single room listed on a separate card. If we start moving things around, taking something out of one room and putting it in another..." He raised both hands ceilingward to express the unthinkable. "Look, you're going back to your cabin? Good. So I'll see if I can get hold of Maintenance, if he hasn't left yet, and maybe he can do something for you."

Although it was clear from the manager's tone that the likelihood was slim, the rabbi sat on the porch of the cabin and waited. He had just about decided that there was no use waiting any longer and was on the point of going in to change his shoes to walk to the village when he became aware of footsteps on the path. They stopped at his door.

"You're Rabbi Small, aren't you? Of Barnard's Crossing?"

He peered nearsightedly at the speaker beyond the screen door, and although it was twilight he could see that it was a tall, attractive young woman of about twenty-five, certainly not Maintenance. Dark wavy hair framed an oval face that at the moment was both hesitant and yet determined.

"Do I know you?" he asked.

"No, although you may have seen me around because I'm from Barnard's Crossing, too. I'm Joan Abernathy. I spotted you in the village yesterday. You drove up in the hotel limousine, so I figured you were staying here. I got the cabin number from the desk clerk."

"I see. And what can I do for you?"

"I'd—I'd like you to convert me."

He pushed open the screen door, saying, "Maybe you'd better come in," and motioned her to one of the wicker armchairs. "I don't do conversions," he said when she was seated. "It takes months and I don't have the time. I refer those who come to me for that purpose to Rabbi Bernstein in Peabody, who holds regular classes."

16

"Well, can I talk to you about it?"

"If you like. Tell me, why do you want to convert?"

"Why shouldn't I?" she asked, her low contralto voice insistent.

"Oh, there are lots of reasons why one should not convert to Judaism. The most obvious is that it involves assuming a burden that you don't have to. It's not easy to be a Jew."

"You assumed it."

"No," the rabbi said. "My parents assumed it for me. It was not an active choice on my part." He smiled. "And when I was made part of the Covenant, I was a week old, too young to do anything about it."

"After you grew up you could have dropped it," she said.

"There's a big difference between assuming a burden and dropping one that you already have," he said gravely.

"What's the difference? If it's undesirable, you don't take it on. And if it's something that's been wished on you, you get rid of it."

"There's stubbornness and pride. And then—"

"Pride in what?"

He shrugged. "Maybe just in carrying a burden. Here in America there's less of it now than there used to be. But even here, the Jew is aware that in many areas he has to be quite a bit better than the competition in order to make the grade at all. He's annoyed by it, angry at the unfairness of it, but he persists. Then if he succeeds, it's a source of pride." He saw that she did not understand and tried to explain. He searched the ceiling for an example. "When I was a youngster, an older boy would sometimes give a younger one a head start in a race. He would handicap himself—"

"Oh, that's done in sports regularly. The favorite horse is made to carry extra weight. And in golf the poorer player is allowed extra strokes."

"Indeed? And does the good golfer resent having to make do with fewer?"

"Of course not. He glories in it."

17

"Well, there you are."

"You mean that's all there is to it, stubbornness and pride?"

"There is also skepticism."

"Skepticism of what?" she asked.

"Of the usual alternative that is available," he said quietly. "In the Western world that means accepting Christianity, and we cannot because we are skeptical of the idea that an omniscient and omnipotent God, the Creator of the universe, would make use of a mortal woman to beget a human child; that because of Adam's disobedience we are all doomed to burn everlastingly except we are redeemed and achieve salvation primarily through faith in that child. To us that doesn't make sense."

"Not all Christians believe it either; not literally, I mean. They believe in it as a kind of symbolism. But surely, there must be something you do believe in."

Rabbi Small opened his eyes wide. "Of course there is. I was merely explaining why, over the years, we have chosen not to drop the burden we were born with. There is also a positive side. We think ours is the better way, even with the burden."

"Well, that's what I want," Joan said firmly. "I want the better way."

"But it doesn't apply to you."

"Why not?" she demanded indignantly.

"Because you weren't born to it. If you think our view, our way of life, is better, you can follow it. But you don't have to join us. You can have the best of both worlds. You could be the Righteous Gentile who has the same standing before God as the High Priest of Israel."

"Oh, I get it now," she said triumphantly. "I was told about it. You're supposed to discourage anyone seeking conversion. Three times, isn't it? Does this count as the first time?"

He shook his head. "My dear, it isn't like a lodge meeting ritual where you give the password three times. We don't play games. It is true that there is some

18

such rule, and in a sense it is typical of our religion since we try to spell out precisely how one should follow its principles. But we tend to discourage conversion because all through the Middle Ages it was illegal for Jews to convert Christians to their faith. And at all times there have been those who felt that it was unwise. In any case, there's no point to it."

"I don't understand."

Instead of trying to explain, he said, "I presume you want to marry a Jew."

"How do you know? Why do you say that?"

He eyed her shrewdly but remained silent.

The young woman blushed. "There is a man," she admitted.

"Aha! And he won't marry outside his faith."

"Not at all. He doesn't care."

"His folks, then. They want you to convert."

"They've never said anything to me."

"But?"

"And they're not the least bit religious. Although from what Aaron has told me, I imagine they would rather he marry a Jewish girl. That's only natural."

"They've been pressuring *him*, then? Nagging him? Perhaps quarreling with him about it?"

"Oh, they wouldn't try to pressure Aaron. It wouldn't do any good if they did. He would consider it an unwarranted interference with his rights as an individual."

"Then—"

"But I want to. If I'm going to share his life, I want to share his heritage, too."

"It's not as easy as that," the rabbi said. "You think you have only to declare your willingness and then undergo some sort of ceremony like a baptism, and you automatically become one of us."

"I understand there is instruction in the rituals and ceremonies—"

"To be sure there is that, but that's not what I meant." He sighed. "You are a Christian?"

"I suppose I am. We, my family, I mean, don't make

19

a big deal of it. I mean we're not—we don't belong to one of the evangelical or charismatic sects. We go to church sometimes—not often. These days we go to the Methodist Church when we go at all, but that's because we know the minister—"

"And you feel you should throw some business his way?"

She smiled. "Something like that. When we lived in Detroit we went to the Baptist Church. And before that we were Lutherans for a while."

"The theological differences between these churches, it did not concern you?" Rabbi Small asked.

"Not really. We'd belong to a church because my folks, mostly my aunt, felt we ought to. And we'd choose one that was convenient, and where the people seemed to be more or less like us."

"Equally disinterested?"

Joan laughed. "Just about."

"But when you changed churches," the rabbi insisted, "you must have been aware of a difference of attitude, of belief, of emphasis, in the sermon—"

"I don't suppose we listened very attentively," she said. "People don't, you know, not the way they listen to—to—well, to a lecture on some subject they're really interested in."

"I know," he said sadly.

"It's like this." She wiggled to get comfortable in her seat, as though she now felt at ease. "You join a church because your friends are members. I'm talking about Protestants now. Catholics are different. Or you notice the people who go there dress the way you do and talk the way you do. Sometimes the minister, especially if he's young, may be into something—"

"Into something?"

"Yes, you know, like the blacks, or the lettuce growers, or homosexuals. I mean he's worked up about some cause."

"Oh, I see."

"And if you're interested in it, too, you might go because of that."

"And then if he gets—er—into something else?"

"Some new thing, you mean? Well, if you don't agree with him, you might drop out. Or if you like him but don't agree with him, you might just put it down to his being a minister—"

"Like a special disability peculiar to the trade? An occupational hazard?" the rabbi suggested.

The young woman smiled. "Something like that. Ministers are supposed to get worked up about all kinds of things that other people don't get too excited over. Of course, if he tries to do something specific about it, like letting them use the church, or raising money for it, then there's apt to be a lot of talk and phoning back and forth by people who are upset. But it's always about politics or something that's in the news. I mean it's not theology. I mean, you don't expect a Methodist minister to talk against the Lutherans or the Baptists, or even against the Catholics."

"Or against the Jews?"

She colored. "Well, sometimes against the Jews. But not the modern Jews," she added hastily. "It would be around Easter, and it would be about the Jews of Jesus' time, about the Scribes and the Pharisees."

He nodded grimly. "That's one of the difficulties. Because Judaism as it is today is the Judaism of the Scribes and the Pharisees."

She was startled. "It is?"

He smiled faintly and nodded.

She looked at him doubtfully. "You're not trying to put me off again, are you?"

"No. But it does rather point up some of the difficulties, doesn't it? The same words mean one thing to you with your Christian background, and something else to us. You see, Christianity was a new and radical movement at the time, and radical movements are against the establishment. Well, the Scribes and the Pharisees were the establishment. If the movement succeeds, as Christianity certainly did, then the meanings and connotations that it ascribes to certain terms and concepts are crystallized and become the official

21

meanings. But while the movement succeeded, the establishment also persisted—down to the present day. It's us. So the terms *Scribes, Pharisees*, which in Christianity suggest smug complacency, pettifogging legalism, self-righteous hypocrisy—those terms in Judaism refer to a group of saintly men, profound thinkers, men whose lives were dedicated to setting up a system by which God's will might be done."

She thought a moment and then nodded slowly. "I understand. I realize that I have to make certain mental adjustments in changing from one religion to another."

"Ah, but ours is not even a religion in the sense that you know the word." He leaned back in his chair. "You are twenty-four? Twenty-five?"

"Twenty-five."

"Then you probably know someone who converted to Roman Catholicism—"

"A roommate of mine at college married a Catholic boy."

"And she told you about it? It probably involved attending a class for several months, probably run by the Passionist Fathers, or is it the Paulists? Unless she came of a strong Puritan or Calvinist family, it probably was not difficult. Certain principles she may have found hard to swallow, like the infallibility of the Pope, the doctrine of purgatory, the indulgences. But even these were approached by a series of logical steps—and the Catholic Church is nothing if not logical—so that she couldn't help but accept the conclusions arrived at. If she had any doubts, she kept them to herself, perhaps with the mental reservation that her doubts were her business, or even that she might come in time to believe. But she already believed the broad outlines of the theology. It was a matter of adjusting to the interpretation of a passage from the Gospels here and a different twist there. And you probably thought that converting to Judaism would not be very much different, except that you might be asked to replace the person of Jesus with the person of Moses in your thinking.

22

And since you are not strong in your faith, it did not seem difficult to switch from a man who lived two thousand years ago to one who lived three thousand years ago. Well, it's not like that. Judaism is not a faith. It does not call for an oath or even an agreement to believe in a set of principles. Belief is not a test at all. Nowhere in the Bible are we called upon to believe."

"But I don't understand. You must believe something."

"Yes, but it is not a test." He shook his head in vexation. "The difficulty is that even when we use words that mean similar things for us and for you, they don't mean the same things. We have taken your words like *prayer, religion, sin*, in an effort to communicate, but they don't mean the same thing for us as they do for you. And it is not much better when we retain our own words. You equate them to a word of your own and assume it is the same thing. But it isn't. For example, you call me *Rabbi* and you assume that I'm the same as a minister or a priest, that *rabbi* is merely our word for the person with the same function. But it's not. You assume that our synagogue is an institution like your church, but it's not. You assume—"

"But isn't the synagogue a place where you go to pray?"

"It's a place where we go to *daven*, which is not quite the same as pray. It's a place that traditionally we used for individual study, which makes it a kind of library. And where a learned man would teach those less learned, which makes it a kind of school. And where we come to meet about communal affairs, which makes it an assembly hall. And where the stranger in town who has no money and no place to go might be bedded down for the night. And where if he came on a Friday afternoon, just before the Sabbath, he would be invited by one of the local people to the Sabbath meal that night, and—"

"But those are all things that have to do with religion. The study and the teaching, they're all connected with religion, aren't they?"

He smiled broadly. "If I gave you some money to pay a bill for me, and on the way you lost it, would you be liable for the money?"

She was bewildered by the sudden change of subject. "Why—I don't know—I suppose it would depend. I mean, what's that got to do with it?"

"Well, that's the sort of thing I might be teaching at the synagogue," he said, smiling with satisfaction. "In fact, it *was* the subject of discussion a couple of weeks ago in a class I conduct at our temple."

"But that's law, civil law."

He nodded. "That's right. The law of agency. But with us it's a matter of religion. With you it's something to be handled by a lawyer. With us it's a matter that would be presented to a rabbi to decide." He grinned at her. "Want some more?"

He took her silence for assent. "Electricity," he announced. "What is the nature of an electric current? What happens when you talk on the telephone, or press a button to summon an elevator to your floor, or talk through a public address system? That's a rabbinical concern. It's connected with the whole subject of working on the Sabbath. Or anatomy. I am presumed to be able to examine the entrails and viscera of birds and animals and determine if an observed anomaly indicates disease. Or chemistry. There is a chemical that is fed to young roosters which interferes with their sexual development and renders them capons. That is a concern of the rabbi. He must decide if this makes them ritually unclean and hence unfit to eat. The doctor prescribes medicine for his patient, but if the patient is a devout Jew he might come to me to inquire if he might take it, and I might have to find out from the doctor or the druggist just what the medicine contains and how the drug is derived in order to determine if it comes within the rules governing kosher foods."

She looked at him doubtfully, as though she suspected he might be pulling her leg. "Does that happen very often?" she asked.

"To me? Never! None of my congregation is that

concerned or that observant. But I did once have to pass on whether a member of my congregation could take his medicine on the Day of Atonement when we are expected to fast. And my grandfather, who was an Orthodox rabbi in New York, served on a Board of Kashruth. He was frequently called upon by the licensed slaughterers to determine the nature of some anomaly, a spot on the bladder or the lung of the carcass of a cow, and to decide if it was ritually clean and hence fit to eat."

"Anything else?" she asked.

The rabbi thought he detected a hint of sarcasm. "That might come within my jurisdiction? Oh, lots of things. I am expected to have some knowledge of astronomy as it affects the calendar. And I'm supposed to have some knowledge of accounting since disputes which I might be called upon to settle might be concerned with business. On the other hand, there are functions that the priest and minister have that I don't concern myself with. I don't hear confessions, for example. And if one of my congregation told me he had sinned, I might talk to him about it, but I would not impose a penance on him, even if he were willing, and I'm not empowered to absolve him of his guilt. I do some counseling because I am furnished with information from various social agencies that could be useful. If someone came to me with the problem of what to do with an elderly, senile parent, I am able to help by directing him to the proper social service agency or by furnishing him with a list of rest homes. If all he wanted was a sympathetic ear, I would be available, but only the way some friend might be. I suppose I get quite a bit of it because I *am* available. On the other hand, I might suggest he see a psychiatrist or a marriage counselor. And of course, I have no special inside track with the Almighty. I might be asked at some public affair to recite a blessing, give the invocation, some such thing. And I do. But it has no more strength, no more validity, than it would if done by any member of the congregation."

Night had fallen, and it occurred to the rabbi that the presence of an attractive young woman sitting with him in the darkness while his wife was known to be away might be misconstrued. People had been passing by on their way to and from the hotel, and while he thought he might be imagining it, it seemed that some of them had slowed down to stare. Over the years, as the rabbi of Barnard's Crossing, a small suburban community in Massachusetts, he had developed a sensitivity to the dangers of gossip.

Rabbi Small rose leisurely to his feet. She looked up and, misinterpreting his intention, said, "Oh, I've taken so much of your time—"

"Not at all," he reassured her. "I just thought perhaps you would care for some refreshment. I think there's some ginger ale in the fridge." Without waiting for her to answer, he went inside, and then called out from the kitchenette, "There's ginger ale and some cold milk. Or I could heat up some coffee if you prefer."

"No, ginger ale will do fine," she called back.

CHAPTER

2

Rabbi Small rummaged in one of the cupboards and found a tray on which he set the bottle of ginger ale and a couple of glasses. At the door, momentarily balancing the tray in one hand, he snicked on the porch light, and then in the glare of the single naked bulb overhead, he set the tray down on the wicker table and motioned her to help herself.

"Oh, thank you." Joan filled her glass, then drew a pack of cigarettes from her purse and asked, "Is it all right if I smoke?"

"Go right ahead." He looked around, spotted an old flowerpot in a corner of the porch, and brought it over to her. "You can use this as an ashtray."

She offered him the pack, but he shook his head. "I had to give it up. It was too hard smoking all week and then stopping for the Sabbath, so I cut it out entirely."

She puffed reflectively and then said, "I gather that

a rabbi is not a religious leader in the usual sense, that he's a teacher and maybe a kind of executive director of the community. But you do have certain purely religious functions, don't you? You do give sermons like the minister and the priest, and you direct or supervise the religious services, don't you?"

He shook his head. "I do here in America largely because of the example of your clergymen. It is not traditionally part of the rabbinical function, neither the giving of sermons nor the directing of the service. The order of the service is set and any adult, that is, any male thirteen years of age or older, can conduct it. If a stranger appears at one of the daily services, we're apt to ask him to lead the prayers as a matter of courtesy. As for the giving of sermons, by tradition I am required to give only two a year, on the Sabbaths before Passover and the Day of Atonement, and they're not really sermons in the usual sense of the word. They're more like dissertations on the Law."

She was nonplussed, but doggedly tried again. "Ministers and priests do things like marrying people and burying them. They confirm young people and they christen babies. Don't you do those things?"

"I certainly don't christen babies," he said.

"Oh, I guess you wouldn't christen them, but you know what I mean."

"Name them? I have nothing to do with that. If it's a girl, the father comes to one of the synagogue services when the Torah is read and arranges to be called for one of the portions of the Reading. In the blessings which are pronounced at the time, one is for the child, who is mentioned by name. If it's a boy, he's named when he is circumcised by the *mohel*, the one who performs the operation, in one of the blessings he recites."

"But that's you, isn't it?" Joan asked. "I don't mean you personally, but it's a rabbi who does the circumcising, isn't it? Because I went to one. You call it a Brith? This girl friend of mine invited me. Everyone there referred to the man who was doing it as the rabbi."

"The term is used loosely, I'm afraid," he said. "Here in America he is usually a doctor, an M.D. Frequently it's done in the hospital by the obstetrician, if he's Jewish. Actually, it's the function of the father of the child because Abraham did it to his son, Isaac. Part of the ceremony, in fact, consists of the father handing the knife to the *mohel* with a request that he act for him."

She brightened as she remembered something. "Well, about a month later Doris invited me to another party, a Pid something."

"Pidyon Haben," he supplied. "'The redemption of the son.' It's only done for the first one, and only if it's a male. 'Whatsoever openeth the womb.'"

"Why only if it's a male?" she demanded, bristling.

"Well, it goes back to the time when the firstborn male was pledged to the service of God in return for the Hebrew firstborn being exempted from death when all firstborn males were slain, the last of the ten plagues, on the night of the Exodus from Egypt. Originally these firstborn males constituted the priesthood, but later the function was taken over by the tribe of Levi. Did you go to the party?" he asked.

"No, I couldn't make it. But Doris told me something about it, about the ceremony, I mean. She said her husband hands the child over to the rabbi, who then asks him if he wants him to keep it or if he wants to redeem it. So then the father says he wants to redeem the child and he gives the rabbi some money and takes the child. No?" as the rabbi shook his head.

"No. The child is given to a *kohane*, a priest, someone with the surname Cohen or its cognates, Kahn, Kagan, Katz. That last is an abbreviation of *kohane tseddik*, which means 'righteous priest.' Those, by the way, are among the few truly Jewish names. Names like Goldstein, Rosenbloom, aren't. And not all people who bear *those* names, the kohanic ones, I mean, are *kohanim*— that's the plural. The grandparents of a friend of mine who is named Cohen got the name from the clerk at the immigration center who assigned it to them because he found the Russian one they presented unpronounceable. And there are also *kohanim* whose names do not indicate their priestly affiliation."

"And they're not rabbis?"

"No, they may be plumbers or accountants or lawyers or grocery clerks. But they are all presumably descendants in the male line of Aaron, the brother of Moses. In the days of the Temple, they functioned full-time as priests, offering sacrifices at the altar and so on. But now their functions are vestigial—"

"Oh, they do other things besides—"

"Yes, vestiges of their former functions. On holidays that don't happen to fall on a Sabbath, they bless the congregation with the priestly blessing that you are no doubt familiar with because the Church took it over. 'May the Lord bless thee and keep thee; may He make His face to shine on thee—'"

"Oh, is that where it comes from?"

"Uh-huh. It kind of points up the nonliturgical function of the rabbi, doesn't it? Inasmuch as it is not he but the *kohanim*, all those who are present, who bless the congregation. The *kohane's* sacerdotal function is also indicated in the restraints which are imposed on him. He is not supposed to marry a divorced woman, for example. And in Israel, where all marriages come under the jurisdiction of the rabbinate, anyone with a kohanic name would not be permitted to marry a divorced woman unless he could prove, and it wouldn't be easy, that he was not really of kohanic descent."

"Even if he weren't religious?"

"That's right. He's also not supposed to be in the vicinity of a corpse, which tends to restrict the activities of the rabbi who happens to be a *kohane*, because his congregation expects the rabbi to participate in the funeral ceremonies."

"Well, that's what I meant. You *do* bury people."

"But not in the sense that you mean it," he protested. "I am not necessary, and my function is not sacerdotal. I merely act as a master of ceremonies. Usually I deliver a eulogy because—because the family expects it. But that's all. And it's almost the same as my function in the marriage ceremony. I'm not really necessary, not in any priestly or religious sense. I might have to inquire as to whether both parties are Jewish and free to marry, but that's legal and investigative. I also draw up the marriage contract, which is obviously legal. Convinced? Oh, yes, you mentioned confirmation. Well, that's not really traditional with us. The Reform and Conservative wings of Judaism, influenced by the Church, have incorporated it. But the Orthodox have not."

"Isn't the Bar Mitzvah a confirmation, and don't the Orthodox have that?"

The rabbi shook his head. "It's not a confirmation, and even the ceremony is not necessary. When a boy is Bar Mitzvah it means only that he has reached his thirteenth birthday and is now an adult and hence responsible for his own actions. For the girl, the age is twelve, by the way. That's all there is to it. He's called up to read from the Scroll or to have a portion read in his name because as an adult he can now be counted as a part of a minyan. But if he isn't called up, if there's no ceremony at all, he's still Bar Mitzvah and would be if he never entered a synagogue. The party that usually follows is a—well, a birthday party."

"Then it isn't a confirmation at all," said the young woman.

"The sad truth is that over the years, here in America at least, it had the effect of being just the reverse."

"I don't understand."

"Well, the idea of confirmation is a rededication to the religion, which with us would mean further study. Here, it usually means the end of the youngster's religious study. In most cases it means that he does not return to the religious school. In any case, while the rabbi may make a little speech, give his blessing perhaps while resting his hands on the boy's head, it's all hocus-pocus. He isn't necessary and his presence is not required."

Her lips trembled as she tried to restrain a smile. "You'll forgive me, Rabbi, but you say you're not necessary for this and you're not necessary for that, and the things you're supposed to decide, you're almost never asked to. Then why do they pay you? They do pay you, don't they?"

"Yes, they do, and in comparison with the pay of priests and ministers, rather well. I suppose that, too, is an indication of the essential secular nature of my position."

"How do you mean?"

"Well, I suspect you people pay your priests and ministers very little because you feel that they have been called to their mission by God and have no choice but to serve. But since we make no such claim, our salaries are determined on the basis of supply and demand. Does a synagogue or temple need a rabbi? Not really. In the ghetto towns of Russia and Poland it was the community rather than the synagogue that hired the rabbi. But here each synagogue is apt to want its own. Basically, the function of the rabbi in America is to guide his congregation in our tradition."

"You mean you teach them to be Jews."

"You get to be a Jew by being born one," he said flatly. "If you're born of Jewish parents who have not made public disclaimer or converted to another religion, then you're automatically a Jew. You see, we are a tribe, an ethnic group, a people claiming descent from Abraham and Sarah, and in a sense Judaism is the way of life, religion if you like, of our tribe."

"But what if someone was born a Jew but didn't believe in your religion?"

"He'd still be a Jew," said the rabbi, "unless he actually converted to some other religion."

"That doesn't make sense," she protested. "I can see that you can't choose your race, of course, but it would seem to me that your religion is something you *can* choose, that in fact you have to if it is to have some meaning."

"It is confusing," he admitted, "and in a general way, you're right. But it's a little different with us. We are not terribly concerned about private thoughts or private doubts. There's no way you can know about them. I suppose the most religious person has at one time or another had spells of agnosticism or atheism. But when a Jew publicly and formally converts to another religion, or marries in a Christian ceremony, then he is regarded as not only having given up his religion, but as having opted out of the tribe as well, renounced his citizenship, so to speak. That's not logical, I admit, but it is the result of a long, unhappy history. If his parents are devout and highly observant, they might very well go through the mourning rites as though he had died."

"But if—"

"Look at it this way. Suppose this same son of highly observant parents married a girl who was nonobservant, who was agnostic or atheistic although of Jewish parentage. His parents might consider it a terrible misalliance, as a millionaire might consider it a misalliance if his son married one of the maids. He might disown him. He might order him from the house. He might from that time on refuse to see him or speak with him, let alone with his wife. But he would not mourn him as dead."

"And if he converted you would no longer refer to him as a Jew?"

He shrugged. "We might." He smiled. "Especially if he had done something which would make us inclined to claim him. Just as some Christians might refer to him as a Jew if he had done something reprehensible. More likely we would refer to him as 'of Jewish parentage.' That's the usual formula."

Then what you're saying is that not only do you have to be converted to the religion, but you also have to be adopted by the tribe."

"That's right."

"But there must also be some doctrine, some code, some set of beliefs that you all subscribe to."

"Not that *we* have to subscribe to, just that the convert has to. With us it's assumed. The basic principle is that there is only one God. Everything else derives from that."

"Oh, monotheism. We agree with that."

He shook his head. "No, we mean it in a different way. We mean that He is one and alone and unique, without beginning and without end. He has no family and there are no intermediates who have special access to Him. I guess that's one thing that we all believe in."

"Even the atheists among you?" she asked with a smile.

But he nodded gravely. "Even the atheists. There is a kind of affirmation in their denial, for it is the existence of the one God that they deny. Two gods or a family of gods, they don't even consider."

"I suppose," Joan said, "you are referring to Jesus as the son of God and the Virgin Mary. Well, enlightened Christians nowadays don't believe that either, not literally. Not even some of my Catholic friends."

"Are what you call enlightened Christians really Christians then?" he asked.

She considered. "Well, of course, in the sense that they believe in Christian ideals, like—like being decent and kind and helpful to one's fellow man."

"Oh, all civilized people believe that. Probably all primitive people do, too. What is it that makes it Christian?"

"Well..."

"Is it the belief that though we are born sinful, we can be saved and go to heaven only through Jesus?"

"Oh, not necessarily in believing in him as the son of God who decides who goes to heaven and who goes to hell, but in following his teachings." She leaned forward confidentially and said, "I'm not an expert, of course. I mean I'm no theologian or anything like that. I expect you know a lot more about it than I do. But my understanding is that Christianity is supposed to be an advance on Judaism, its fulfillment, or the next step anyway. The 'turn the other cheek' business, for instance. Maybe it's more than most people can do, but it's a kind of ideal that they should aim for. And the business of heaven and hell, well, of course, I don't believe in people floating around just playing harps.

34

That would get pretty dull after a while, I imagine. And people roasting on a spit, that's just as bad the other way. But it stands to reason that nasty, wicked people have to be punished. It would be terrible to think they could get away with it. And all the nice, decent people, some of them have a terrible time. There has to be some way to make it up to them. That's reasonable, isn't it?"

"If you can believe it," he said with a shrug. "We can't. But if Christianity is an advance, why do you want to take a step back?"

She looked at him reproachfully as though he had set a trap for her. Then she smiled. "It does seem silly, doesn't it? But then I attended a symphony concert a couple of weeks ago. It was all modern music by composers I had never heard of. I'm not terribly knowledgeable about music, but the people I was with are. I mean, they really are. According to them, what I was hearing was a great advance over traditional music. But I still prefer Mozart and Beethoven."

He nodded in appreciation of her quick recovery. He eyed her speculatively. "Tell me about this young man you're interested in," he said.

She brightened immediately. "Aaron? His name is Aaron Freed. Do you know the Freeds?"

He shook his head. "Are they from Barnard's Crossing?"

"No, from Salem, just over the line. But they have a lot of friends in our town. I thought you might have met them. I've known Aaron for about half a year. I met him at a party. He's tall and lanky and not terribly good looking, but I was attracted to him from the beginning."

"What was it that attracted you?"

She sat back and considered. "I don't know, except maybe that he seemed more—more purposeful than any of the other men I knew. Maybe it's because he's a scientist. He teaches and does research in physics at M.I.T. I hadn't met any scientists before and I got the feeling that his work had a special importance. I mean,

35

he wasn't engaged in selling or promoting things. I made no bones about liking him. I mean, I didn't pretend to be indifferent. You know, the usual little maneuvers in the battle of the sexes. It seemed out of place with him, like using baby talk with a child genius. I know now that it wouldn't have worked with him."

"Yes, some men resent it."

"Well, I didn't try it. He called me the next night and practically every night after that. Within a week we knew we wanted to marry."

"That was quick."

"It was enough. We were both sure," she said simply.

"You knew he was Jewish?"

"Oh, yes."

"And he knew you weren't?"

She laughed. "With the name Abernathy?"

"You discussed it? The difference, I mean?"

She shook her head. "Not really. He asked me if I minded and I told him I didn't. And I asked him if he minded, and he said my religious beliefs, like my politics, were my personal and private business."

"Nevertheless, you want to change?"

She nodded slowly.

"Because you think it will make for a better marriage?"

"For that, and because—" She blushed. "Well, you Jews have been so successful—managing to survive through all the centuries even though you are scattered all over the world. And you've done so well in—oh, all kinds of pursuits, in science and medicine and law and literature and business. It's usually assumed that it's a matter of genes, that because of the difficulties you people have had to face only the best survived. But it occurred to me that it might not be that at all, that it might be a matter of what you believe, the ground plan you operate on."

"You told Aaron that?"

"Uh-huh."

"And what did he say?"

"He laughed at me. He said it didn't apply to him because he had no religion."

"I see. And your folks, how do they feel about it?"

"Well, my aunt wasn't crazy about the idea."

"I mean your parents."

"My aunt is my parents, or at least one of them. She brought me up. My mother died when I was very young, and she took over."

"And she's been with you ever since?"

"That's right. She's the only mother I've ever known, and I think of her as my mother."

"And she's opposed to the marriage because Aaron is Jewish?"

"Uh-huh. You see, she's the churchgoing member of the family. Occasionally Dad goes, but it's only to humor her. He has no interest in such things." She laughed. "He considers them women's concerns. So when she sent me to Sunday school he didn't object as he might have if I had been a boy. He and Aaron get along very well together, but Auntie is—well, disappointed."

"And it doesn't bother you that she is disappointed?"

"Sure it does. I don't want to hurt her. But if you never did anything that displeased your parents, you'd never become a person in your own right."

The rabbi chuckled. "Curiously enough, according to rabbinic law there are only two conditions when a child may disobey his parents: one is if they order him to sin; the other is in choosing a spouse."

"Really? Then I'm all right as far as Jewish law is concerned. I don't suppose that would make it any easier for my aunt, though."

"What do you call her? How do you address her?"

"Auntie, Aunt Jane, sometimes just Jane. It depends on the circumstances."

"And your mother, you don't remember her at all?" he asked curiously.

She shook her head. "I was an infant when she died. While making no secret of it, Dad rarely spoke of her to me, I presume so as not to complicate my relations with Auntie. I think the first time was when I had to fill out some form which called for the mother's maiden name. Her name was Admore, Sarah Admore."

"Admore?"

"Uh-huh. British, I presume. It was in London that they met. Once when my father was going to England on business and I asked him if he planned to look up the Admores, he laughed and said there weren't any. So I don't know."

"Interesting. And how about Aaron's folks? How do they feel?"

"Well, I'm sure they like me as a person. They had me to dinner a couple of weeks after I met Aaron. And I've been there any number of times since."

"But you did say that Aaron told you that they preferred a Jewish girl."

"Oh, yes, but it's got nothing to do with religion. I can understand that. It's like an Italian marrying a Polish girl. His folks, and hers too, would object even though they are both Catholic."

"Do they know that you're interested in converting?"

"No. When I mentioned it to Aaron, he was opposed to it."

"To your converting, or to your telling them?"

She laughed. "To both." She tried to explain. "You see, he doesn't believe in religion, not in any religion. But the one you're born in becomes a kind of social habit. You may practice it, but it doesn't mean anything. However, if you undertake to make a change, then you're making a—a positive act."

"I see. And he doesn't want you telling his folks because that would be compounding the error."

"That's exactly his attitude. And besides, it wouldn't make any difference because it's my ethnic origin rather than my religious beliefs they object to. I mean, if I were born Jewish, they wouldn't care what I believed."

"I see. You know, I would like to meet Aaron someday."

"You can very easily," she answered quickly. "He's

here in Grenardsville with me. I could bring him over—"

"I'm completely free evenings," the rabbi offered.

"How about tomorrow night?"

"Fine. About the same time would do nicely." As she rose, he said, "You're both staying in a hotel here? I didn't know there was another."

"There isn't. I'm a counselor at the Y camp on the lake. I used to do it for the whole summer when I was in college. Now I just come up during my vacation. And I arranged for Aaron to come, too. He's helping out in the Boys' Division, coaching basketball."

"And what kind of work do you do the rest of the year?"

"I'm with American Designers. We design office layouts and furniture." She laughed. "Aaron calls me a designing female. And of course I am. All women are, aren't they?"

"Well, if he's not too busy—"

"Oh, believe me, he'll be glad of the chance. We're pretty busy during the day, but there's nothing to do evenings."

Rabbi Small opened the screen door and waved as Joan set off down the gravel path. As he let the door swing to, he saw the social director strolling by and called out to him, "Nice evening."

"Right on," said the social director, and winked elaborately.

CHAPTER

3

The next day, right after five when the long-distance rates change, Miriam called to say that she had seen her father, and that although he had spent an uncomfortable night, he was now feeling better. "And the doctor said everything looks fine."

"Oh, that's great. You explained why I wasn't there?" the rabbi asked anxiously.

"Of course. He didn't expect you in any case. After all, it wasn't a party he was having. Did you manage all right?"

"Oh, sure."

"Was it lonely? You can go up to the hotel, you know. There's something going on all the time in the evening."

"Oh, I was all right." He hesitated. "Someone came over to see me, someone who wants to be converted, a—a young woman."

"Really? Someone from the hotel?"

"No, she's working at the Y camp. She's from Barnard's Crossing, too. She saw me getting out of the hotel limousine when we went to the bus, so she inquired at the hotel."

"I see. Is she attractive?" Miriam asked, a little too casually, he thought.

"Huh? Attractive? Oh, I guess so, sort of. Why do you ask?"

"No reason." Then after a pause, "Except that if we're recruiting a new member for the tribe, it might as well be a good-looking one."

"Yeah, I suppose."

Back in his cabin after the evening meal, the rabbi found himself wondering if the young woman would come. He had worn a tie and jacket for dinner, and now was changing to an open-neck sports shirt. He had no sooner tucked his shirt into his slacks when he heard a knock on the porch door. Hurrying out, he was surprised and a little disappointed to see that it was not Joan Abernathy, but a tall, thin young man with a high, narrow forehead, long aquiline nose, and a jutting chin.

The rabbi looked at him inquiringly.

"Rabbi Small? I'm Aaron Freed."

"You're—"

"Joan said she told you about me."

"Oh, yes, of course. Come in." He opened the door and stood aside for him to enter. "Isn't Miss Abernathy coming?"

"She had something to do in the village and I said I'd meet her here. I walked over, but she has my car and should be along shortly. I came a little early because—well, because I wanted to make sure you understood the situation."

"So?" The rabbi raised his eyebrows.

"Oh, we plan to get married," he went on hastily. "That's settled. I don't know what she told you, but I just want you to know that her converting is not a necessary preliminary."

41

"So she said. However, I find myself thinking how your folks feel about it."

The young man shrugged elaborately, and then amplified the gesture by saying, "I can't say that they're crazy about the idea."

"You mean they disapprove. And it doesn't bother you?"

"Look, Rabbi, their attitude is completely irrational and I refuse to be governed by it. My folks are not concerned with what Joan believes. They can't be since they themselves have no beliefs. It's because she wasn't born Jewish. Now if she converted, she still wouldn't have been born Jewish, so what's the point?"

"When you say they have no beliefs, you mean they are not observant?"

"That's right. Oh, on the High Holy Days they put in an appearance at the local temple, and my father went to say Kaddish when my grandfather died, but they don't go to pray or anything like that. And other than that, nothing. And it's not because they don't know what they're supposed to do. When my grandparents were alive, my mother kept a kosher house— kosher meat, two sets of dishes, the whole bit. Otherwise the old people wouldn't have eaten at our house. I went to the religious school until I was Bar Mitzvah. That was because my grandfather was living with us at the time and he insisted on it."

"And the school had no effect on you?"

The younger man smiled and shook his head.

"Well, even as a practical matter, it might be important. For example, if you should happen to go to Israel— Why are you smiling?"

"Because I very well might," Aaron replied. "I'm negotiating now to do some research work in Rehovot next year. Are you saying it would make a difference if my wife were gentile?"

"Well, an observant Orthodox colleague, perhaps someone from Bar Ilan University, might refuse to drink a glass of wine in your house if he thought your wife might have poured it."

"You're kidding."

"No. It's an ancient prohibition based on the supposition that the wine might have been intended for idolatry."

"So I'll serve Coca-Cola." The young man dismissed the matter with a wave of the hand. "Look," he said, "I've always tried to live my life according to what I thought was right. I refuse to be bound by ancient superstitions. I don't avoid walking under ladders and I have no hesitation in sitting down thirteen at table. I hope you won't take offense at my frankness, but I regard religion, all religion, as myth and superstition."

"Opium for the masses," the rabbi murmured.

"No, Rabbi, I'm not a Marxist. My view is simply that religion is outmoded science. That is, it offers explanations for physical phenomena. But science has proved that those explanations are not true." He flung out a long arm. "Where did man come from? Well, the best answer they could come up with a few thousand years ago was that a god created him out of a handful of earth. But then Darwin came along and gave us the theory of evolution, and we have a whole host of data from various disciplines—archaeology, anthropology, biology, chemistry—to prove it. You *do* believe in evolution, don't you, Rabbi?"

"Oh, the proofs are incontrovertible."

"Okay, then. The same thing happened with the origin of the earth, and the sun and the moon and the stars. Modern astronomy can give rational explanations for them. There are differences of opinion, of course, but they are all in the same ballpark. And the idea that a god created them in a day or two is not. Geology can explain the physical appearance of Earth, the mountains, the rivers, the seas, and the continents. And at a lower level, maybe a million miles lower, the social sciences—psychology and sociology and economics—are beginning to understand the reason for man's behavior, for his happiness and his unhappiness, for his success and failure." He sat back in his chair and smiled complacently. "You see, I am a strict rationalist."

"Well, so am I," said the rabbi.

"You are?" Aaron was startled. "But how can a rabbi be a rationalist without being a—a—"

"A hypocrite? Because mine—ours—is a rationalist religion. We are expected to use the minds we are endowed with. There are no mysteries about which we are forbidden to inquire. I don't deny that some Jews have a mystical approach to the principles of our religion. I presume their minds and imaginations work that way. Mine doesn't. Perhaps because I have no capacity for it. From time to time in the course of our history, mystical elements have crept in. Usually it is the result of the influence of the religions of people among whom we live, the Persians, the Babylonians, the Greeks, and more recently, the Christians. Sometimes these elements have even been incorporated into our religious services. But I don't have to subscribe to them. As a matter of fact, I don't."

"Well, that's a new one on me. Still, you believe in God, don't you?"

"Oh, certainly."

"Well, that's a mystical concept," said Aaron triumphantly.

The sound of hurrying footsteps on the path outside, followed immediately by the appearance of Joan at the door, prevented the rabbi from answering. The two men rose to greet her. She held up her face to Aaron to be kissed and said, "Have you been here long?"

"No, just a few minutes," he answered.

"Has he been behaving himself, Rabbi?"

"Oh, admirably," said the rabbi. "He's just been challenging my belief in God."

"It doesn't surprise me. Aaron doesn't believe in anything except atoms and molecules," she explained.

"Not just atoms and molecules," the young man corrected. "Only in real things."

"What, not interested in hypothetical particles?" asked the rabbi.

"Oh, sure," said Aaron, "but they're on the way to becoming real. Actually, their reality has been determined deductively and it's only a matter of time before it is demonstrated. All kinds of discoveries are made the same way—the planet Uranus, for example, and the element helium."

"Well, that's the same method that's used to justify the belief in God," said the rabbi. "The unity and order in the universe—"

"But you don't need God for that," Aaron objected. "You can posit the same thing from the laws of physics. Newton's laws of motion and Einstein's theory of relativity explain the movements of the stars and the planets. Modern astronomy goes a long way toward explaining the origin of the universe."

"Yes, but finally, where does it get you?"

"It gets us back practically to the beginning of things. That's where it gets us. You'd be amazed at how close to the actual beginning modern theory takes us." Aaron held up his hand with thumb and forefinger an inch apart. "The big bang theory brings us that close to the actual beginning."

"Trace the universe back to a single exploding star," the rabbi retorted, "or even to a single exploding atom, and you're still no further ahead. You still have to explain the origin of that one atom."

"But you're in the same fix, Rabbi. You have to explain where God came from." Aaron grinned. "It's a standoff."

The rabbi grinned back. "Not quite. Because your science has brought you to an impasse where something has to come from nothing, which is impossible according to the rules of your game, like working out an equation and coming up with an answer of four equals zero. That indicates that the original equation was wrong, which means that you've got to rethink your premises. According to your system you have reached a dead end. But in our system there is no such impossibility because we say the universe was created by God, who by His very nature precludes explanation. He always existed. He had no beginning and He has no end. By definition."

"Oh, come on, Rabbi." Aaron flung himself back in his chair. "All you're doing is taking what you call my impossibility and calling it God."

"Not at all," said the rabbi. "I'm just attacking the problem from the other end."

"How do you mean?"

"Well, you are looking at the situation as it stands now and you say this was caused by that, and that in turn was caused by something else, bits of reality that you track down one at a time in the hope that when you get enough of them, you'll be able to present an all-embracing theory. Man developed from some monkey-like creature coming down from the trees onto the grassy plains, and the monkey in turn developed from some creature being forced to take to the trees and so on. When the sticky question comes up as to how a mindless creature produced one with a mind, your anthropologist takes refuge in the concept of interminable time. In several million years anything could happen. The biologist traces life back to the one-celled organism and then he reaches his sticky point, explaining how life could derive from lifeless chemicals. And he takes refuge in the same concept of interminable time. If there is plenty of time, then somewhere the right chemicals will combine in the right quantities to produce life. It's a little like the monkey that would produce all the works of Shakespeare if he pecked away at a typewriter long enough."

"But—"

The rabbi plunged on. "You do the same thing in geology with mountains and lakes and oceans and earthquakes, and in astronomy with stars and planets and galaxies."

"And you? What do you do?" Aaron managed to interject.

"Oh, I start from the present as you do. But seeing the order and harmony of the world about me, I make an intuitive leap and posit that this grand design is—

by design, which means a designer, which implies a mind, which suggests a God."

"What you're doing is—"

"I'm suggesting a different system to explain the reality that yours can't, just as the Einsteinian system offered explanations for phenomena that the Newtonian system couldn't."

"What reality?" Aaron asked.

"The universe," replied the rabbi promptly, "which all men instinctively feel manifests a grand design."

"But science has proved that this so-called grand design is merely the working out of immutable laws," Aaron said with exasperation.

"So what? Do you think it detracts from the concept of God that you can show that the stars and the sun and the moon evolved rather than that they were fixed in the heavens all at once? Or that it detracts from Him that man evolved over billions of years from a bit of slime rather than that he was created complete in a single day? On the contrary, it enhances His greatness, and we are grateful to science for enlarging Him in our minds. What's more, these immutable laws you talk of, we established them as a governing principle long before there was a concept of science in the minds of men."

"You did?"

The rabbi nodded vigorously. "We did when we established Him as a God of justice, in Genesis, in the story of Abraham arguing with God over the destruction of Sodom and Gomorrah. If you remember, God had announced that He was planning to destroy those cities and Abraham said, 'Shall not the God of justice deal justly?' Which is to say, is not God bound by His own rules? And God accepted the limitation."

"Isn't that where Abraham bargained Him down from fifty virtuous men to ten?" asked Joan.

"That's right," said the rabbi. "God agreed not to destroy the cities if there were fifty, and then forty, and thirty, and finally ten."

Joan laughed. "I remember a minister once saying that it showed that Jews dickered even with God."

The rabbi smiled. "It's true. Maybe it's because we have a Covenant with Him that we feel we can argue with Him and even call Him to account. Our tradition shows quite a bit of it. There is the story of Jonah, for example. It's also implicit in the Book of Job. More recently, Reb Isaac of Berdichev, a Chassidic saint, actually called Him to a Din Torah, which is like summoning Him to appear at a rabbinical court for trial in a suit of breach of contract. And in *Fiddler on the Roof*, Tevye demands to know why God could not have made him a rich man. That's why we find it hard to understand the Christian rationale for Jesus as a necessary bridge between man and God. We've never felt any difficulty in addressing Him directly."

Aaron, who had been leaning forward in his chair with his chin cupped in his hands and his elbows resting on his knees, now straightened up and said, "Look here, Rabbi, your position is that God is bound by His own laws with respect to man. Is He also bound with respect to other things?"

"Of course. Our idea of justice is universal, and that means the universe and all things in it," the rabbi replied.

"Are you perhaps hinting that this is the basis for the law of cause and effect, Rabbi?"

"More than hinting. I'm asserting it."

"But what do you gain by attributing it to God?" asked Aaron.

"We gain meaning and purpose for the universe. These may be of no importance to a mindless thing like a stone or a tree or even to the lower animals, but to man they are all-important, because without a felt purpose life is meaningless."

"A man can have an individual aim and purpose," Aaron pointed out.

"Then one aim is as good as another," retorted the rabbi, "and there is no scale of values, no right or wrong, no good or evil, only perhaps pleasant and unpleasant sensations. Can you organize society on that basis?"

"Oh, come now," Aaron protested, "you don't need a God to organize society. All you need is to show that it's better for everyone if it is organized."

"And how are you going to show it?" the rabbi challenged. "How would you go about proving, for example, that honesty is the best policy, or even necessary? Would you take a poll? And would the powerful members of the community feel the same way about it as the weak ones? How about the wealthy and the poor?"

"And with a God?"

"Ah, then you can assume that there is purpose in the universe, and man, the one portion of it that has understanding and freedom to determine his own course of behavior, can choose to further that purpose or try to obstruct it. Then you can have a code of law and of ethics and morals that transcends the interests of individual members of the community and the conditions of the moment."

"How about Russia?" asked Joan.

"What about it?"

"Well, they don't have a God. Officially they are atheist. And they have an organized society."

"That's right," Aaron chimed in. "They have a society and a code of law, without a God to give it sanction."

"Then what does give it legitimacy?" asked the rabbi. "What is its sanction?"

"The good of the group, I suppose," Aaron answered. "They have laws against theft and murder and so on because these things are bad for the people as a whole, for the society, for the group."

"I doubt it." The rabbi shook his head. "Which group? One's immediate family? Or one's village? Or one's age peers? Or the state? Or the Communist world in general? One's loyalty to one group frequently runs counter to one's loyalty to another group of which one is also a part. And it's not hard to see how a crime might help one group while it hurt another. The safety of a small rural village might be assured by the murder of a commissar from the city who had just finished an inspec-

49

tion. No, I can't imagine that it is loyalty to the Soviet Union that keeps the Russian law-abiding."

"What then?" asked Aaron.

The rabbi shrugged his shoulders. "Some of it may be fear of the authorities. But mostly, I think, as it is for most people, fear of God. Behind the legal code issued by the government, which most of them certainly have not read, is the knowledge, the felt certainty, that some actions are wrong. Not merely illegal, but wrong. And that kind of feeling can come only from something outside, beyond, the government. And that can only be God."

Aaron pointed a long, bony finger at him. "You know what you're doing, Rabbi? You're setting up a system and then filling up all the holes and cracks with a concept you call God. Then if you're challenged to explain this God, you say He is unknowable and unknown."

"Isn't that what you do in your science? Let X equal the unknown. Then you go on to use it in your equations just as though it were a regular number."

"You mean God is X?"

"Sure. Why not, if it helps you form your equation and arrive at a solution?"

"Maybe you've got something there, Rabbi," Aaron said. "And then again, maybe you haven't. Because we use X in order to find its value. That's what the equation is for: to solve for X. But according to you, God is by His nature unknown and presumably unknowable. So He can't be X. It's pointless."

The rabbi nodded, not the least put out. "I see. I was never very good at math. Well, when we say that He is unknown and unknowable, we mean that we can never know the full nature of His being. But that doesn't mean that we have no understanding of Him at all. We can make certain logical deductions about Him from the mere fact of His being."

"Such as?"

"That as the Creator of the universe, He is unique."

Aaron considered. Then he nodded slowly. "All right.

50

There's no point in having two or more. I suppose that any being capable of creating half a universe would be able to create a whole one."

"Precisely. And would you grant that He is a sentient being with purpose?"

"I suppose He would have to be," said Aaron. "Otherwise the creation of the universe would be merely an accident and it would be pointless to have Him at all."

Joan cleared her throat and the rabbi turned to her and said encouragingly, "Yes, Joan?"

"Well," she began uncertainly, "doesn't it say somewhere in the Bible that He created man in His image? I mean, wouldn't that mean that He looks like us?"

"Yes, it does," said the rabbi approvingly.

"You believe that?" demanded Aaron.

"I do," said the rabbi. "Oh, not in the sense that He has two arms and two legs. But I believe we resemble Him in that, like Him, we alone of all creatures have mind and will. In that respect, as a sentient being, He created us in His image. Our religion, all religions, are based on it."

"How do you mean?"

"Because mind can communicate with mind, however limited the one and infinite the other. If it weren't for that, there would be no religion. Do you follow that, Joan?"

"I—I think so." She turned to her fiancé. "How about you, Aaron?"

"I'm a physicist, not a metaphysicist. I have to think about it." He leaned forward, bracing his elbows on his knees and resting his chin on his clenched fists. Finally he looked up and said, "Suppose I accept the creation of the universe by a God as a working hypothesis."

"Fine," said the rabbi. "Then will you grant that He is one?"

"Sure. There's no point in more than one. I've already admitted that."

"And that He is sentient?"

"Okay. I've admitted that, too, because there's no point without it. Anything else?"

"I suggest that He is a God of justice."

"Is that a guess, Rabbi, or are you offering it as a logical deduction?"

"Let's say a logical inference. Because if He is one, then there is no other god to disagree with Him, or argue with Him and make Him change from His original course. So if He has decreed B should follow A, then B will always follow A. A given action will always produce a given effect. Isn't that what justice is all about?"

Aaron considered and then nodded. "All right. But where does it get you? The whole point of a working hypothesis is to explain observable phenomena. What is there in our regular experience that is explained by your hypothesis?"

The rabbi flung his arms wide. "You yourself said it: causality," he announced triumphantly. "The law of cause and effect. He is the God of the universe and His justice applies to all things in it."

"Hmm." Aaron lay back in his chair, his long legs outstretched. He pressed his bony hands together, palm to palm, and rested the joined index fingers against his lips as he considered the rabbi's argument.

Joan glanced at her fiancé, and seeing that he was absorbed in thought, turned to the rabbi. "In this course in anthropology that I took, the prof claimed that each society chose or created its own gods, rather than the other way around."

The rabbi nodded. "Yes, but in this case it works out the same in the end, whether the idea of justice as the greatest good leads to the idea of one God, or that the idea of one God leads to the idea of justice as the greatest good."

"I don't quite follow," said Joan.

"It's like this," said the rabbi. "If a people think of beauty as the greatest good, then they would develop a multiplicity of gods because beauty takes many forms. If power were considered the greatest good, then the idea might be symbolized in a hierarchy of gods with perhaps one who ruled all the others. If love were the greatest good, then there would probably be at least two, probably male and female, the lover and the object of his affection. But if justice were regarded as the most desirable thing, then you would naturally be led to the doctrine of one God because the concept of justice calls for a single arbiter or referee. So it's possible that the concept of one God followed rather than preceded the concept of justice as the greatest good."

Aaron raised his head. "Why does a general abstract concept have to be embodied in the form of a god or gods in the first place? Why did early man have to crystallize his ideas of love and power and justice in the form of gods?"

The rabbi laughed. "On the basis of my experience in counseling, I'd say it was probably the result of an attempt to explain personal misfortune."

"How do you mean?"

"Well, people come to see me about all kinds of troubles, about a son or a daughter or a wife or a parent or a neighbor. Almost invariably, I sense that the underlying thought is, why me? The son is in jail; the daughter is involved with some rascal; the wife wants a separation. But I always get the feeling, and more often than not it is actually expressed, that what is bothering my visitor is bewilderment that it happened to *his* son, or *his* daughter, considering how good a father he had been. When I go to visit the sick I am apt to encounter the same thing. Why did it happen to *me*? So I can readily believe that in the dawn of history when man was first becoming aware of himself, the attitude was even more pronounced.

"Imagine a band of primitive men making their way through the forest. One of them steps on a loose stone and twists his ankle or breaks his leg. After he gets through swearing, my guess is he'll be thinking, why did this happen to *me*? As he broods darkly over his misfortune, the thought will occur to him that some member of the band, perhaps someone he has quarreled with, or perhaps one of those laughing at his misfortune, pushed the stone into his path as he passed ahead in order to do him an injury. But if that's out of the question because he is alone, he may assume that a spirit put it there, perhaps the spirit of the rock."

"Why wouldn't he attribute it to just bad luck?" asked Aaron.

"Because the concept of luck, good or bad, is a pretty sophisticated idea if you think about it. It calls for an intuitive understanding of the random principle and the laws of probability. Cause and effect is comparatively easy. A child can understand it. If he is naughty, he is slapped. If he cries, he gets fed. It's easy to see that B is caused by A, or at least that A leads to B, or is followed by B. Even that X is caused by A plus B plus C. But when we talk of luck, we are talking about an effect which is the result of so many factors that we can't calculate them or even list them. It's not for no reason at all that when we are walking together *your* hat blows off your head and rolls in the gutter, and mine doesn't, but because of a sudden gust of wind caused by a car driving by as a house door opposite opened as you raised your head as, as, as...

"It's easier to blame someone. And if there is no obvious someone, then you posit a someone unseen, a spirit, especially if the bad luck happens more than once. Here is the leading hunter of the tribe. Just as he is about to shoot, his bowstring breaks. He restrings his bow and as he is lining up another target, he steps on a dry twig and the game is startled and leaps away, and he comes back to camp empty-handed. And it was the same the day before and the day before that. We would say he was having a run of bad luck, but he doesn't think that way. He knows only that it is so contrary to his normal experience that it must be that something or someone is working against him. And since he can think of no natural thing, then it must be something supernatural. He may come to this conclusion on his own, or it may be the explanation he gets from the wise one of the tribe."

"By the wise one I presume you mean the shaman or medicine man," suggested Aaron.

"That's right."

"But by the time the tribe had a medicine man they would already have had a body of belief or superstition, wouldn't they? What would make him the medicine man or the wise one?"

The rabbi shrugged. "He might be someone who had managed to stay alive to what appeared a great age. Or he might be unusual in some other way, perhaps subject to epileptic fits, or spells of insanity. Or he might be someone so ugly as to make others afraid of him. Throughout the Middle Ages the witches who were hunted down were merely ugly old women who lived by themselves. Once it was noised around that they had special powers, they were apt to assume them because it gave them a sense of importance to be thought able to summon spirits."

"Yes, but how would primitive man, medicine man or anyone else, get the concept of a spirit in the first place?"

"Oh, that's not too hard to understand. A man dreams of someone he knows is dead. He wakes up and the person is not there. Or it could be when he's gone without food for a few days and his mind wanders. All right. He's seen the person, spoken to him perhaps, and yet when he awakens, or when he focuses his eyes on the spot where the person appeared to be standing, he is gone. So unlike his comrades in the camp, he appears to exist at certain times and not at others. He is different. He can suddenly appear seemingly from nowhere and disappear inexplicably. But since his body is known to have been buried, it must be something else—his essence, his spirit."

"All right. Go on."

"Well, the wise one would assure our unlucky hunter that he was the victim of some mischievous or wicked spirit. He might give him a charm which he could wear around his neck, or an incantation he could mutter at appropriate times. This would control the evil spirit in the same way a nose ring controls a fractious bull. Of course, this is magic, not religion.

55

"Now when you multiply these spirits, when there is a spirit of the path and a spirit of the tree and a spirit of the forest and of the campfire, you begin to sense relations between them. They are not all evil spirits; some of them may be neutral or even benign, in which case the purpose of the incantation is to call their attention to you and help you. The relations, the connections and interactions, between the spirits naturally tend to mirror those of the things themselves. Take the sun and the moon, for instance. One disappears from the sky as the other appears. So it is easily assumed that one is chasing the other, and then to posit that the sun, the stronger, is a male pursuing the female moon. Or a river might be thought of as a male nourishing and fructifying the field through which it flows, which would be female."

"When does it become religion?" asked Joan.

"Ah, well, as the spirits take on personality, the tendency is to deal with them as persons, as very powerful persons. If you are looking for help from a powerful person, the strong man of the tribe, for example, you don't mumble incantations at him. You ask him; you implore him; and you usually offer something in return—food, work, or submission. When you approach the spirits in that way, then they become gods, and magic becomes religion."

"Why is it magic if you force and religion if you ask?"

"Because asking implies a being who has a mind to understand your need, and a will to help you if he wishes. Furthermore, the act of asking is an admission of his strength and your weakness. A bolt of lightning is a blind force that can strike anywhere, but the god of lightning, or the god who hurls the lightning, can be beseeched to strike your enemy, or at least not to strike you."

The telephone rang and the rabbi got up to answer it. As he went to pick it up, he called out, "It's probably my wife, from New York."

Aaron looked inquiringly at Joan for confirmation and said, "I guess we'll be running along, Rabbi."

"Oh, all right."

"And can we come tomorrow?"

"Please do." And then into the receiver, "Miriam? How's Dad?"

When she had finished reporting on her father's condition and the events of the day, she asked, "Did she come again tonight, David? Is she there now?"

"No, they've just left."

"They?"

"Uh-huh. She came with her young man, an Aaron Freed."

"What's he like?"

"Oh, he's a bright young man, about thirty, I'd say. He arrived a little before she did, so I was able to talk to him alone for a few minutes. He came early on purpose in order to explain to me that as far as he is concerned Joan doesn't have to convert; that he considers all religion a lot of old-fashioned, superstitious folderol that has been superseded by science."

"Oh, one of those. Offensive?"

"No, but condescending."

"He wasn't really objecting to your converting her, was he?"

"No, but—"

"Then what difference does it make?"

"It makes a lot of difference."

"Why? You think he might keep her from sticking to it?"

"I'm not interested in her. If she wants to convert, she'll have to go to Bernstein's class in Peabody. I just agreed to discuss it with her."

"Well, then—"

"It's Aaron I'm interested in. Him I would like to convert."

"But he's Jewish."

"Sure, but like so many of our bright young people, he equates Judaism with other religions, and these he considers just superstition. I hate to see him throw away his heritage because he doesn't know what it is."

"So how did it finally end? Did you convince him?"

"No, but he did ask if they could come again tomorrow night."

"You're not going to let them monopolize your time, are you, David?"

"Oh, no fear of that. I can't work in the evening anyway. To tell the truth, I enjoyed fencing with him. It was stimulating."

As they made their way to the hotel parking lot where she had left the car, Joan asked, "Well, what do you think of him?"

"Oh, he's all right." Then in a burst of generosity, "I guess he's a pretty bright guy."

"But were you convinced?"

"Convinced?" He laughed. "Lord, no. You've got to understand, Joan, that all these guys, ministers and priests and rabbis, have a line of argument that they've worked out and polished up over the centuries."

"But if it's logical and reasonable—"

"It appears to be—on the surface. It's only what you'd expect. You've got to examine it closely to find the flaws. It's new to me, so I've got to think about it."

"But you do want to come back, don't you?"

"Oh, sure. Look, it's a more interesting way of spending an evening than arguing with Bill Chatterton over why Tony Baggio doesn't hit more baskets than he does, which is what I was doing last night."

CHAPTER

4

When Joan and Aaron came the next evening, the rabbi was on the porch awaiting them. No sooner were they seated when Aaron said, "This is tricky stuff for me, Rabbi. I'm used to dealing with figures rather than words. For instance, you equated justice with the law of cause and effect. But they're not really the same thing. In the physical world causality is demonstrable, but it isn't in the actions of men. And certainly not in the value system that's incorporated in the idea of justice. Certainly the wicked aren't always punished for their crimes and the good properly compensated for their virtue—not in this life. Of course, I suppose you'll reply that they are in the next world, in heaven or hell, but—"

"We don't really believe in heaven and hell," said the rabbi quietly.

"We don't?" Aaron was incredulous.

"Isn't it in the Bible?" asked Joan.

"Not in our Bible," said the rabbi. "It's a New Testament concept. Oh, we've flirted with the idea from time to time, under the influence of prevailing philosophy. But even then it was a rather vague notion, never carefully spelled out."

"And yet, when my grandfather died," Aaron said, "my father went to the synagogue every morning and evening to say Kaddish. I remember one terribly snowy winter morning when my mother suggested he pass it up, and Dad said, 'No, I've got to go. It's the least I can do for my father, as I expect Aaron will do it for me.' Now doesn't that show that my father, at least, thinks there's an afterlife and that his prayers were helpful to his father? Isn't it part of our tradition to recite the Kaddish for the dead?"

"And when the time comes, do you think you will?" asked the rabbi gently.

Aaron reddened and then laughed shortly. "My father is in his fifties and is in pretty good shape." Then defiantly, "Yes, I think I probably would."

"Why? Because you think it will ease his passage to heaven or help him through purgatory; that it's a kind of mass for the dead?"

"Well, I don't believe in those things, but—I mean, if he expects it, if I were to promise to—well..."

"Did you ever read the Kaddish?" asked the rabbi.

"I suppose I must have read it in the prayer book one time or another."

"If you did, it would probably surprise you because there's no mention of death in it. Rather it is a doxology, an elaborate glorification of God. 'Magnified and sanctified be His name throughout the world' is the way it begins. It goes on to ask that His kingdom be established on earth and ends by asking for peace for all Israel. Not a word about the deceased or about death. And by the way, the prayer is in Aramaic rather than Hebrew."

"Then—"

"Another interesting thing about the mourner's Kaddish is that it is recited only in a public service, that is, when there is a minyan present. It is never recited when the mourner prays by himself at home. Furthermore, whereas we normally mutter our prayers silently, this prayer is said aloud. Now, taking those three elements together—that it is in praise of the greatness of God, that it is said aloud, and that it is said by the mourners only in a public service—should indicate its true meaning and significance. In effect, the mourner is making a public affirmation of his faith in God even though he has just been deprived of someone who is near and dear to him. We *do* have a prayer for the dead, one where we actually mention his name, but it is said only at the graveside and during the memorial service that is performed on certain holy days during the course of the year. And by the way, the Sephardim, those who come from Spain, don't go in for it; only the Ashkenazim, those from Eastern Europe."

"Then what you're saying is that when my father went to the synagogue so faithfully every day, morning and evening, for a whole year—"

"Eleven months and a day."

"All right, eleven months—that he wasn't really doing anything for his father?"

"Not really."

"Did he—does he know that?"

"I'm sure he does."

"Then I don't see why—"

"Because it's an old custom and custom takes on the force of law with us, as it does with most people. It's our way of expressing our respect and love for the departed. And because it is expected of us by our parents, we feel we have a commitment to that effect. I suspect it also helps to assuage some of the guilt feelings that children usually have about their parents after they're dead."

Joan said, "But Aaron's grandfather, according to Jewish law or tradition or whatever it is, he just dies? I mean, that's it?"

"He lives on in Aaron's father," said the rabbi, "and in Aaron, and in Aaron's children when he begets them.

He also lives on in the memory of his family and his friends and all those who knew him."

"But why not a life after death?" Joan insisted. "Why don't you believe it? It solves the problem of rewarding the good and punishing the wicked."

"But it raises more problems than it solves," said the rabbi. He leaned back in his chair and laced his fingers behind his head. "When I first came to Barnard's Crossing, I was a city boy. I had lived in apartments all my life; when anything had to be done in the way of repair, one notified the building superintendent or the janitor and he took care of it. In Barnard's Crossing, where people live in their own houses, they tend to do things for themselves. Once, when I wanted to put up some bookshelves, a neighbor suggested I do it myself and offered to lend me the necessary tools. In the course of doing the job I learned a great truth, and that is that if you make the tiniest error in the angle in sawing a board, it is magnified enormously at the other end. If your cut is off by just the width of your pencil mark, it can mean that the other end of an eight-foot plank can be off by as much as an inch."

"Naturally," said Aaron. "It's like the spokes of a wheel. They're close together at the hub but inches apart at the rim."

"It's the same in cutting out a dress from a pattern," Joan said.

"Really? Well, it's also the same in one's thinking," the rabbi said. "You make one little mistake at the beginning and it leads you farther and farther afield. When my neighbor saw the first results of my carpentry, he consoled me by saying the cracks could be covered with a strip of molding. I confess I've been suspicious of molding ever since. I always wonder if it's covering up a crack due to a mistake in the original cutting." A sudden thought occurred to him. "Is that the reason for lace and trimming on a dress?" he asked Joan.

"I don't think so," she said doubtfully. "If you don't

cut it exactly according to the pattern, it just doesn't hang right."

"Oh? Well, that's what happens in our thinking; it doesn't hang right. You pull it at one point, and it hitches up at another. If every man is to be rewarded or punished according to his deserts, the obvious question arises if there shouldn't be a distinction between the truly saintly man and the one who is merely slightly more good than he is wicked. And of course there's the same situation on the other side. So you cover that crack with a bit of molding. You posit a series of hells as in Dante's Inferno. Or you set up another institution, purgatory, where those who are insufficiently saintly are purged of whatever evil there is in their natures. According to Catholic doctrine, there is a kind of bank in which the surplus of sanctifying grace which a saint achieved is deposited in a treasury of merits on which the less saintly can draw for their own salvation. It's one of the advantages that the Church offers its members. But then the individual sinner isn't really getting all that's coming to him, is he?

"Then there is the question that the very concept of hell, and purgatory too, raises. Hell is a place of terrible punishment. Who presides over it? Who inflicts it? It can't be God or Jesus because of the Christian doctrine of love as the greatest good. The idea of either engaged in torture and torment is unthinkable. So you give the job to an angel, Satan. But angels are—well, angelic. It's hard to think of *them* as engaged in that kind of work. So you offer the explanation that Satan was a wicked angel. He had revolted against God and was cast out of heaven for it. But that suggests that if an angel could commit evil in heaven, then it can't be a completely virtuous society. And presumably, if an angel can go wrong there, then certainly a mortal soul can. So do you then have another day of judgment for another afterlife?"

"Yeah, I see what you mean by covering the cracks

63

with molding," said Aaron. "By the way, what happened to the bookcase?"

"It wouldn't stand straight; it leaned. I finally had to screw it to the wall with an angle iron, but it holds books," said the rabbi resignedly. "How about your dress, Joan?"

She laughed. "I fussed with it for a while and then put it aside and never wore it."

The rabbi nodded. "You were lucky. My bookcase— I had to change the place where I had intended to set it so that I could attach the angle iron to the wood of the door frame. And that meant that I couldn't open the door to its full width. Then I had to move my desk, which meant that I didn't get as good light from the window. I'm afraid that when we make an initial mistake in our thinking, the effect is more like my bookcase than like your dress, Joan. We don't discard it. Rather we keep it and it affects our thinking on other things. The Christian doctrine of an afterlife and heaven and hell, for example, destroys the concept of free will."

"But Christians believe in free will," said Joan.

"Do they?" asked the rabbi. "What do you mean by free will?"

"Why, the freedom to choose—"

"To do what?" he fired back at her. "To turn right or left at the corner? To have eggs or cereal for breakfast? The lower animals have that kind of free will. The donkey can choose to crop the grass at his feet or move a few steps to where it appears to be greener."

"No," said Joan, "it means that man can choose to do good or he can choose to do evil."

"Can he?" The rabbi canted his head to one side. "Can he when he knows he is under the eye of an all-seeing God 'who observes the fall of the sparrow,' and who will reward him if he does the one and punish him if he does the other? Is that free choice? Think of the rat in the laboratory maze. If he goes down one path, he gets an electric shock. If he goes down the other, he gets food. Two or three runs and he soon learns which path leads to what. Does he have free choice? Because thereafter he always chooses the food to the electric shock, does that make him a good rat? Would anyone steal if he knew that a policeman were watching and would be certain to arrest him? To have free will one must be truly free to choose."

"Do Jews believe in free will?" asked Joan.

"Very much so," said the rabbi.

"Then how do you work out proper punishment for the wicked? You say there's no hell in the Bible. Doesn't it deal with the subject at all?"

"Yes, in the Book of Job. And the answer is that the sun shines just as brightly on the wicked as it does on the good, but that evil carries with it its own punishment and virtue is its own reward." He could see by their reaction that the answer was disappointing. "It has the merit of being realistic," he added.

"But it's not very satisfying," Joan observed.

"Isn't it? Well, let's think about it. What do we mean by evil? Fire and flood and sickness and accident are all unpleasant things, so I suppose you could call them evils, but they don't count in the present context because we can't do anything about them. They are among the facts of life like growing old and eventually dying. Nor are we really concerned with the evils resulting from an error in judgment or from a momentary indecision. These are normal to the all-too-imperfect human. I ask you to consider instead those occasions when you are presented with a choice of actions, one of which you know is wrong, and you do it anyway. What is it that makes it wrong for you and why do you have to think about it? Because you would not normally do it. Why not? Because you consider it beneath you. Well, if you then go ahead and do it, usually for some personal advantage, the punishment is certain and immediate. It drops you to the level that you formerly regarded as beneath you. It diminishes you. It makes you smaller. It is no longer beneath you because you have lowered yourself to do it, so your status as a person is now lower than it was. And, mind you, it's rarely limited to just that one action. That action may admit

65

a whole range of changes in attitude, associations, life-style."

He leaned back in his chair and looked from one to the other as though inviting a remark or a question. When they remained silent, he went on, "I don't go to the movies very often. The last time was several months ago. It was a gangster film, about a man who killed for hire. In a series of flashbacks it was established that he came of a respectable family, and indeed had served as an altar boy as a youngster."

"Oh, yes, we saw it," said Aaron. "He'd give the local church ten percent of his fee after each killing."

The rabbi nodded. "Yes, that's the one. It wasn't clear whether he gave the tithe in retribution for his crime, or to ensure good luck on the next one, but the general impression was that the killing did not weigh too heavily on his conscience. However, it is shown that he came to his state of professional detachment only after a series of what might be called agonizing appraisals of his situation."

"Yeah, like when it shows him after his first score," Aaron said.

"Score?"

"Yes, the first burglary. That's the term they use."

"Oh, yes. On that first escapade he carried an unloaded gun. You remember it showed him removing the bullets from the cylinder just before setting out. Obviously, although capitulating to the demand that he take part in the burglary, he is still unwilling to risk having to murder. But then, as he made other scores—scores?—his scruples diminished, and his standards of acceptable conduct were correspondingly lowered to the point where he not only became capable of murder, but even came to specialize in it. And then we come to the climax of the story, when he was ordered to murder his own brother, the FBI man. I don't remember why he was chosen. Was it the sadism of his superiors, or—"

"It was because the big shots thought he was the

only one who would be able to get close enough to make the hit," Aaron offered.

"That's right. Although I seem to recall that they were amused or at least appreciative of the irony of the situation. Well, the point I want to make is that by a succession of wickednesses over the years he had been diminished to the level where he was no longer a person with normal feelings and emotions, but a mere tool to be used by someone else for pointing and shooting a gun. Punishment? He punished himself and that by his own free will. It's like—like—look here, imagine a fine machine, perhaps a measuring gauge capable of great accuracy. You get a spot of dust on the mechanism and it doesn't render it completely useless, but it does interfere with its accuracy, perhaps at the second or third decimal place. Well, that's what evil does. Each voluntary evil act is like a speck of dust on a fine mechanism. And you get enough of them, and the mechanism *does* become useless."

"And I suppose a good deed would be like a spot of oil on the works," Aaron suggested.

The rabbi smiled. "Something like that." Then he frowned. "No, that's not quite right. I'm afraid my analogy breaks down at that point because your idea suggests that the machine when new has a certain capacity which the drop of oil permits it to maintain. But the human machine is not like that. It has the capacity to grow, to increase in refinement. So the virtuous act would not be a spot of oil on the mechanism which would merely maintain its pristine accuracy, but a sort of special adjustment which would increase its performance, perhaps to another decimal place. Or you might think of a seedling, and virtue the water that makes it grow. In that respect virtue would bring its own reward, again through the exercise of one's free will."

There was a moment of silence, and then Joan asked with some exasperation, "Then where does it all come from?"

"Where does what all come from?" asked Aaron.

"Evil. Where does it come from? I was always told it was from Satan. You've poked fun at the idea of his being a fallen angel. So where does he come from?"

"He doesn't. He doesn't exist. Not for us, except as a folklore character perhaps. He appears in the Book of Job, for example, but that is a poem and he is obviously being used as a poetic device."

"Then—"

"Where does evil come from? It comes from God, the Origin and Creator of all things, both what we consider good and what we consider evil." The rabbi sat back and said easily, "If you think about it, in common experience, there is no such thing as unmitigated good or unmitigated evil. Good comes out of evil and evil comes out of good. War is evil, but along with the rape and murder and plunder there is heroism and self-sacrifice and comradeship. There is destruction, but there is also invention and scientific discovery which is of value in peacetime. On the other hand, think of the advances in medicine which practically eliminated a host of children's diseases, which is an obvious good. But this in turn led to rapid increases in population which culminated in starvation and famine, which is not. That's the metaphysics of it. According to traditional Jewish psychology, everyone has a good inclination and an evil inclination, the one drawing him toward good and the other toward evil. Which is just another way of saying that we have free will."

"Is that what all Jews believe?" asked Aaron. "I mean, is that the official view?"

"You should know," the rabbi answered almost reproachfully, "that there is no official point of view. We have no Pope or hierarchy that establishes dogma. The Orthodox, Conservative, and Reform segments all have different ideas of what Judaism is. And in the Orthodox segment, the ideas of the Chassidim differed so markedly in certain particulars from those of the others, the Mithnagdim, that for a while, at the beginning of the Chassidic movement, the rabbis on one side excommunicated the rabbis on the other. In a sense, I suppose, each Jew is his own Sanhedrin, his own supreme court. Nevertheless, there is a consensus on the most basic principles. All Jews believe in strict monotheism. All Jews believe that God is primarily a God of justice. All Jews believe that man has free will. Now within the framework of those few basic principles, there are various answers to secondary considerations that—"

"But heaven and hell," Aaron insisted.

"All right, that's a case in point. They're not mentioned in the Bible. Under the influence of surrounding religions the heaven and hell doctrine gained some acceptance among Jews. You see, there are styles in ideas just as there are in other things, and that idea was in style at the time, just as nowadays it seems not to be in style. A people suffering under the repression of the Roman occupation of their country, and later on during the Middle Ages, even more from the hostility of the Christian Church, would be prone to welcome the pleasant fantasy of an afterlife where all scores would be settled."

The rabbi smiled ruefully. "You see, while we claim to be a nation of priests, we are not a nation of philosophers. The prophets envisioned an eventual glorious resurrection, but it applied not to the individual but to the nation. The Messiah would come and Judea would rise again and be a light unto the nations. I might point out that this would take place not in heaven, but right here on earth. We never really developed the concept of heaven as a place outside the real world, someplace beyond this planet. The nearest we ever came to it was the Garden of Eden, which presumably is somewhere here on earth."

"Complete with the Tree of Knowledge?" asked Aaron, smiling.

The rabbi smiled back. "I don't know. Man, having once eaten of the fruit of the tree, was presumably doomed. I don't see how he could un-eat it."

"But how about the individual?" Joan asked. "Wasn't there any thought of personal salvation?"

"Ye-es," the rabbi said. "And curiously the idea developed primarily among the Pharisees. It followed from their certainty that God was a God of justice. But there was considerable disagreement as to just what would happen, and a coherent schema was never worked out. Did it apply only to the righteous? Or were all subject to resurrection and a life after death? And what of the wicked? Was the mere act of dying sufficient retribution for their sins in this life? Or did they undergo some form of purgatory, and for how long? Was it just the soul that was reborn, or was it body and soul together? All kinds of theories were promulgated, especially among the mystics. None of it, I might say, had any justification in the Scriptures."

"But what do most Jews believe?" Joan insisted.

"It's hard to tell. We don't issue questionnaires on personal beliefs. My guess is that Reform Jews and most Conservative Jews, and probably a large number of Orthodox Jews, believe that death is the ultimate end of the individual, except insofar as he lives on in his children and in the memory of friends. But you can't tell about these things with any certainty. There's no way of knowing how much Jews are influenced by the surrounding and pervading Christianity. They might absorb it from the general culture around them, and not having thought about it too much, they might assume that it was part of Jewish doctrine as well. And they might be inclined to accept it because it's an easy and pleasant doctrine to hold if you don't think it through to its logical implications."

"How about Orthodox Jews?" asked Aaron.

"Well, with them it's pretty much an article of faith because the Pharisees, the expounders of the Oral Law, approved it. But since no clear and explicit plan was ever worked out, as in Roman Catholicism, for example, my feeling is that for most of them it's just a comforting thought that everyone ultimately will get his just deserts. However, I must admit that when I was in Israel, I found that some of the extremely devout were very particular about being buried on the Mount of Olives because according to the legend they would be the first to be resurrected with the coming of the Messiah. One unpleasant effect of this belief is their violent opposition to autopsies. That's partly because for them an autopsy constitutes a desecration of the dead, but also because one or more organs might be missing and hence not available come the resurrection. In fact, there was an outbreak of vandalism directed against the houses and apartments of pathologists of the Hadassah Hospital."

"By the same people who stone automobiles on the Sabbath?" suggested Aaron.

The rabbi nodded. "I suppose."

There was a moody silence, finally broken by Aaron. He stretched out his long legs and thrust his hands into his pockets. "You know, Rabbi," he drawled, "I had an Indian graduate student working with me a couple of years ago. He was a Buddhist. They don't believe in heaven and hell either. They have a doctrine of reincarnation which serves the same purpose, though. If you've been wicked, then in your next reincarnation you drop one or more notches in the social scale. Say you were a prince, and wicked; then in your next reincarnation you might be born a poor commoner, or an untouchable. Or you might even be reborn as one of the lower animals, a dog or a monkey, if you had been very wicked. And of course, it works in reverse, too. So a saintly commoner would be reborn as a prince. Now it seems to me that none of the objections you made to Christian doctrine would apply. I mean, it doesn't call for a Satan or a heaven and hell—"

"But I'm sure you see that there are other objections," the rabbi said.

"Like what?"

"That prince, for one. Since he was presumably the result of thousands of previous reincarnations which finally brought him to his present eminence, he ought to be a saint. So, too, all other men of authority, wealth, and power. And there is no indication of it. And how about those who were reborn as one of the lower animals. How does a dog or a mouse rise on its next re-birth? Is it by being a good mouse?"

"All right, all right." Aaron grinned. "I should have asked Singh about that. I guess I wasn't too interested."

But Joan was still thinking about the rabbi's interpretation of the film. "How about the Boss and the other big shots?" she asked.

"The Boss?"

"Yes, in the movie. I see what you mean about the main character, but how about the one who gave him his orders? He didn't agonize about having somebody killed."

"Because the story wasn't about him," Aaron said.

"You don't suppose he was born that way, do you?" the rabbi said. "If he had been, would he have been allowed to grow up? In comparison to an ordinary man he was a dwarf, a Lilliputian."

"But he didn't feel that, or know it, or care," she protested. "And neither did his friends and associates. To them he was the Boss."

"So what?" demanded the rabbi. "He was nevertheless, and so were his friends. And I'm not so sure that he wasn't aware of what he had become. He must have been aware of a world beyond his immediate circle. He was certainly aware of the common desires for respect, loyalty, affection, and he knew that for him all that was available was the cheap imitation which had to be bought with money."

"Then how about someone like—like Hitler?" she persisted.

"What about him? Do you think there are special rules for perpetrators of massive evil? That they are in a different category? It doesn't take a giant, not even a wicked giant, to do great evil. An idiot child playing with matches can kill a whole theater full of people. Hitler devastated Europe like—like the Black Death in the Middle Ages. So you might say that he had shrunk to the status of the germ that caused the plague." Turning to Aaron, he added, "And being reduced to a microbe doesn't take a reincarnation. The transformation takes place in this life and is the result of one's own choosing."

"Is that all you can say about Hitler and the Holocaust?" demanded Aaron, suddenly angry. "That the death of millions was compensated for by one man, or a few, shrinking to the size of microbes? Is that your idea of justice? Is that the action of a just God?"

The rabbi shook his head. "Wickedness always injures. That's what makes it wicked. The Holocaust was the work of men, not only of Hitler and his group, but of all the others who contributed. You could include the German Communists who chose tactics over principle and refused to join with the Socialists to prevent the Nazis from coming to power. And the Russians who made a pact with Hitler. And those throughout Europe who collaborated with him even after he had overrun their countries. It was the work of men, so how can you blame God for it?"

"Or it could indicate that there is no God," Aaron retorted, "or at least not one who cares."

"Or that it is hard to face up to the fact that we are imperfect creatures in an imperfect world," said the rabbi, "and that we frequently use our great gifts of mind and free will to perpetrate great wickedness. Of necessity, that's the other side of the free will coin. On the other hand, it's also one of the glories of the human condition, for we can improve, we can grow." He smiled. "How about some ginger ale?"

CHAPTER

5

As he sipped his drink, Aaron observed, "What you're really saying is that when you do something wrong, your conscience bothers you and—"

"No, I'm not," said the rabbi promptly. "Conscience is something else again. It's second-guessing one's behavior. Some people seem to have a special talent for it, or at least seem to be more bothered by it than others. I myself am comparatively untroubled by it. Miriam, my wife, on the other hand, is always worrying about something we did or failed to do. 'Did we pledge enough?' 'Do you think I was inconsiderate?'" He chuckled. "She also worries when we leave the house whether she locked the front door and whether she remembered to shut the bedroom windows against the predicted rain. No, I'm talking about using your mind to make a free choice to commit an act which you normally regard as beneath you. In doing it, you automatically slip down a notch to the level of the person for whom that kind of action is standard. Your conscience may reproach you and it may not. But you will always know that you have dropped to a lower level. You can't dodge that."

"All right," said Aaron, "but what makes it Jewish? Is it in the Bible?"

"It's not spelled out, of course, but it's implicit in what *is* in the Bible."

"How so?"

"Well, if we are free to choose our actions, and if we have minds to understand what we are doing, then a just God, having indicated by giving us commandments that He is concerned about our behavior, must have machinery for rewarding our virtuous choices and punishing our wicked ones; that is, our obedience or disobedience to His commandments. Now those concepts—a God of justice, free will, mind, concern for our behavior—they *are* in the Bible. A day of judgment or heaven and hell are not."

"How about death as a punishment?"

The rabbi shook his head. "It can't be an individual punishment because it is visited on everyone. Death is presumably the punishment for the race as a whole for Adam's disobedience. But actually it's an aspect of life in general and, because man alone is aware of it, part of the human condition. The same is true for sickness and poverty. The Book of Job, as well as common observation, indicates that these can happen to the most virtuous. Similarly, the wicked can be rich and powerful and healthy. But if they are wicked, they are small, low, whatever else they are. And they know it. The reward and punishment are inescapable, and they fit the deed exactly."

"All this is kind of new to me," said Aaron. "Let me see if I'm getting it right. The usual idea is that since God is just, then virtue should be rewarded and evil punished. But since they obviously are not, then there must be an afterlife where they are." He looked inquiringly at the rabbi, who nodded encouragingly.

"All right," Aaron continued, "but since there is no evidence that there is an afterlife—"

"And the very concept inhibits free will," the rabbi prompted.

"You mean the business of not stealing when a policeman is watching. Right. So, since you can't use an afterlife and the heaven-hell idea to dispense justice, you offer the explanation that we dispense justice to ourselves by growing or diminishing as a result of our free choice of action." He canted his head and added in grudging admiration, "Well, at least it's completely rational."

"M-hm."

"But look here," said Joan excitedly, "how about the idea that the individual doesn't really have freedom of choice? I mean, he may do things because of the environment he grew up in, or the genes he was born with."

Aaron added, "Then you certainly wouldn't want a heaven and hell, because it would be a gross miscarriage of justice to punish someone for something that he was programmed to do."

"Apart from the fact that we are all conscious of having free will," remarked the rabbi. "However, the doctrine, which was called predestination, was held by a number of Church Fathers—St. Paul, St. Augustine, Calvin. Basically the reasoning is that since God is omniscient, then He must know everything past, present, and future, which includes the knowledge that John Smith will go to heaven and Mary Jones to hell."

"Why do you have the woman going to hell?" Joan demanded indignantly.

"That's the rabbi's male chauvinism peeping out," said Aaron. They laughed, and he went on, "I'll admit that your explanation is rational, but it seems to me that you're kind of free and easy with the Bible. You pick and choose the portions that serve your purpose."

"Of course," the rabbi admitted. "Doesn't everyone with available evidence? Every judge, critic, philosopher, scientist? The Bible from our point of view is a communication from God to Moses and from him to the people of Israel. That means that God's infinite intelligence spoke to the finite mind of Moses. Obviously, only a tiny fraction of God's communication could come through to him or be understood by him. Then the resultant highly limited and imperfect transcription had to be transmitted to a host of other finite minds and adjusted to their understanding. So the result is that much of it comes through as folklore, myth, fable, legend, symbolism."

"And the miracles, how do you treat them?" asked Aaron. "Do you rationalize them, too?"

"How do you mean rationalize them?"

"Oh, you know, the usual. That the walls of Jericho fell because of a timely earthquake, or that the Red Sea parted because a new planet crashed into our system. That sort of thing."

"Not at all." The rabbi shook his head vigorously. "It is not one of the tenets of my religion that I am required to accept every myth, legend, and fable as factually true. Our attitude is that we were given minds to use. We have no thought control."

"Well, Christians don't either," said Joan stoutly. "At least Protestants don't. Catholics might because they have this index of books that they're not supposed to read, but—"

"They've now given it up, too," said the rabbi. "But there is still the requirement of faith that all Christians are called upon to exercise: faith in Jesus as the son of God, faith in him as the savior whose grace saves you from hell and admits you to heaven. With many Christian sects faith takes precedence over everything else, over a virtuous life, over good deeds. It is the essential test of whether you go to heaven or not. And what is faith if not control of the mind? Or as someone put it, 'believing what you know ain't so.' We don't have to believe the miracles in the Bible as Christians have to believe the miracles of the New Testament."

"Why are they bound and we not?" asked Aaron.

"Because the intent of the two sets of miracles is

77

different. The miracles in the Bible do not prove anything. It is a God who is performing them, and by definition a God can do anything. The intent is not to prove His power; that's assumed."

"Then what's it for?"

"I suppose to show His special care of the Jewish people. It doesn't take a miracle for slaves to revolt and make good their escape from their oppressive masters. It has happened countless times in the course of history. Similarly, no miracle was necessary for the fall of Jericho. No wall is impregnable, and the walls of Jericho could have been breached by the skill and courage of the attacking army. And if no miracles had occurred, it would not mean that the Lord was not with Israel. He could have shown His special care of His people by inspiring them to extra effort and gotten the same results. But the miracles serve to demonstrate the point to the most simpleminded, so it's quite possible that they were invented for that reason.

"The miracles in the New Testament, however, are something else again. There, it was an ostensible man who was performing them, and they are adduced to prove that he was a God. To believe them enables you to believe that he was a God. Not to believe them is to doubt his divinity. They are his claim, really his sole claim, to divine origin. If you believe that he walked on the water, and fed the multitude with a few loaves and fishes, and raised Lazarus from the dead, then you might believe the miracle of his birth and of his resurrection after death and that he is a God. If you don't believe the miracles, then you must conclude that he was a man, perhaps a very good man, even a saintly man, but only a man, who lived and died some two thousand years ago. Of course you might feel that what he said manifested extraordinary wisdom, and you would then perhaps consider yourself a Christian in the same way that people consider themselves Marxists or Freudians. You might join a study group engaged in discussing his ideas, but I don't think you'd pray to him for help in your present problems."

But Aaron persisted. "Some Jews believe in the miracles and in the literal truth of Genesis, don't they?"

Rabbi Small laughed. "Oh, sure. When I was in Israel, I visited the Mea Shaarim quarter of Jerusalem. That's one of the extremely Orthodox sections in the city. I talked with one of the residents about the Six Day War, and he said, 'We here in the quarter told our young men who were going off to fight not to rely on miracles. Instead, we urged them to recite the Psalms.'"

Joan and Aaron laughed and the rabbi looked pleased. Then Joan said tentatively, "You—er—you spoke of God's special care for the Jews. That suggests that the Jews are the Chosen People. Do you believe that?"

From the look that passed between them, he sensed that they had discussed it between themselves. He smiled benignly at them. "That bothers you, the phrase 'Chosen People'?"

"It bothers a lot of people," said Aaron. "It shows a kind of chauvinism that most people resent."

"And yet Christians had no compunction about taking it on," the rabbi observed wryly.

"How do you mean?"

"Well, Christian theory does not deny that the Jews were the Chosen People. Their view is that with our failure to accept Christ, we lost our status, and Christians, the New Israel, became the Chosen. But actually, the idea in one form or another is common to many nations and peoples. The ancient Greeks had the idea that they were unique, that they alone were civilized. All other nations were barbarians, by which they meant originally that they uttered sounds like *ba-ba* rather than proper speech like Greeks. Even more, the Athenians thought of themselves as the chosen of the Greek world as indicated in that famous speech of Pericles. The Romans had their *Pax Romana*. The British felt it was their duty to assume 'the white man's burden.' In modern times the United States feels that it is its function to bring democracy to the world—"

"Just as Russia feels that its function is to convert the world to Marxism," Aaron added.

"Right." The rabbi nodded. "In the present instance, our tradition holds that God chose us, and that we voluntarily assumed the burden of obeying His commandments. Which means in effect that we agreed to be bound by a higher moral and ethical standard than that of the surrounding nations. Now a skeptic or an atheist might say that it was a monumental delusion on our part, that there was no god involved, and that we assumed this ethical standard on our own. All right. He can doubt or deny the first part of the proposition, that God chose us. But he cannot deny the second part, that we assumed the burden. That is historical fact. Or you might say we chose to be the Chosen."

He leaned back in his chair. "Indeed, there is a story in our tradition to the effect that God offered His law to all the other peoples of the world first. That is, He offered each of them the opportunity to be the Chosen. And only when they had all refused did He come to the tiny, powerless Jewish nation. I can only add that most Jews feel that life would be a lot easier if we had not been the Chosen. They recognize it as a voluntary assumption of the burden of a higher ethic. It's the point I made when you first came to see me, Joan."

"But *you* don't deny the first part of the proposition," Aaron urged.

"No, I'm not an atheist. Besides, it doesn't make sense. Why would a people, a small, powerless people at that, assume a burden that they didn't have to? That's even harder to believe."

"Well," said Aaron, "it's a lot harder for me to believe that God, a being of infinite magnitude, talked to a mere man like Moses, or—"

"It's your scientific training that's at fault," the rabbi said with a smile. "It imposes certain limitations. If you had worked in the humanities, in literature, for example, it would be no problem at all. Converting myth and fable and symbol to underlying truth is normal to the discipline. How did God talk to Moses and Abraham and all the others the Bible says He spoke to? Well, God is certainly a sentient being. He has mind, intelligence. And so have we. One intelligence can communicate with another intelligence however disparate the two may be. We manage to communicate with infants, and to a degree even with the lower animals—cats, dogs, horses. Mind seems to reach for mind. We believe He made a covenant with us. A covenant is a contract, and in law we say a contract is a meeting of minds."

"Yeah, but how—between an infinite God and a finite man?"

The rabbi shrugged. "You struggle with a problem for days and can't seem to make any headway. Then it comes to you suddenly, intuitively. In telling about it afterward you might say, 'It came to me out of the blue,' or you might say, 'I had a brainstorm,' or 'I had a hunch.' In a more primitive and more God-oriented society a person might say instead, 'I had a vision,' or 'I heard the voice of God telling me what to do,' or 'God spoke to me.'"

"Are you saying that all intuitions come from God?" Aaron demanded.

"No, I'm merely offering it as a possibility."

"But if inspiration or intuition all comes from God—" Joan began.

But the rabbi cut her off quickly. "I don't say all of it did, or any for that matter. Merely that it is a possibility."

"But if you believe that God communicates with man," said Aaron, "you must have some theory as to how it's done."

"All right, let me give you a possible—er—ah—scenario. I understand that in the early days of radio, people used to stay up half the night twiddling the knobs of their homemade sets in an effort to tune in some distant broadcasting station."

"Ham radio operators still do it," said Aaron. "This

friend of mine has made contact with people halfway around the globe."

"Is that so? I didn't realize it was still going on. Now suppose you think of the mind as a kind of broadcasting station, but also capable of receiving—"

"Sure. Two-way."

"Two-way? Yes, I suppose that would describe it. Then you can imagine the mind of God as a station of infinite capacity operating twenty-four hours a day. And our own minds would be pictured as tiny local stations operating for relatively short periods. I assume that most of the messages that any small station would receive would come from other small local stations."

"Excuse me, Rabbi, but the large station would tend to drown out or override the small station."

"Oh? Then perhaps my figure is not a very good one."

"Well, the large one could be operating on a higher frequency. Then it would work out all right," Aaron said good-naturedly.

The rabbi nodded gratefully. "Very well, then most of the messages, that is, the ideas, the intuitions, the inspirations, that any one mind would receive would probably come from the minds of other men. But these small stations differ one from another. They may be wired in a different way?" He looked hopefully at Aaron.

"Sure, they can have different hookups."

"Hookups?"

"That's right. Different circuits. My friend is always buying new equipment."

"I see. So when the conditions are just right, a local station can sometimes tune in the super-station. But even then the message will probably not come through clearly. There will be fading and static. And most of the stations will tune it out in annoyance. But one or two will be interested in that higher-frequency signal and might try various hookups in an effort to bring it in clearly. Do you understand?"

"Those are the religious people, aren't they, Rabbi?" asked Joan. "Is that what you're trying to say?"

"And the special hookups are prayers, I suppose," said Aaron.

"Not necessarily," the rabbi said. "Those few who are interested in the signals from the super-station hope to acquire information, knowledge beyond what can be learned from normal channels, a clue to ultimate truth and reality, perhaps."

Aaron smiled. "But that would include scientists and researchers?"

"Of course. And writers and artists and philosophers and—"

"The hookup could be a scientific experiment?" suggested Aaron.

"Certainly. Or it could take the form of prayers, study, or meditation. Or of mortifying the flesh by various ascetic practices. Or by alcohol or drugs or—"

"By drugs?"

The rabbi shrugged noncommittally. "Sure. Some American Indian tribes use peyote, a form of mescaline, in their religious ceremonies. I'm not suggesting that all of these ways are efficacious, or that any of them are. We just don't know. But always, and everywhere, man has tried to make contact with gods in all kinds of ways. In early primitive times, one method was to try to incorporate them in oneself by ingesting them. An animal, or even a human, was delineated as the manifestation of the god and was then sacrificed and eaten. That was involved in the worship of Adonis and also of Osiris. Some anthropologists have suggested that our various Sabbath and holiday feasts derive from that primitive concept; and, of course, there is the Christian celebration of the mass, in which the body and blood of Christ are consumed. Some try to make contact with the Godhead by abandoning the world of men and normal society and have gone into the desert to live, or retired to a monastery. Others, thinking that it was their own flesh that stood in the way, have starved themselves, or gone in for flagellation and even mutilation of the body. Yoga, meditation, sexual orgies are some of the other methods."

"Well, what's the Jewish method?" asked Joan.

"Since we assume that in the Bible we have God's word, our tradition inclines us to study—the Bible, the commentaries on the Bible, the commentaries on the commentaries, and ultimately, since it is all of God's truth that we are trying to learn, study in general. The attempt to make direct and intuitive contact with God is mysticism, and generally speaking we don't go in for mysticism. We are satisfied that He has given us commandments, instructions, which help us to live in this world, to enjoy it, to improve it if possible, to—"

"Then what good is it?" demanded Aaron. "If you have a God who is unknowable in the first place so you don't know if you're making contact with Him or not, and it doesn't make any difference because, being omniscient, He knows your need and won't help you in any case because He's bound by His own rules of justice—then what use is He to me? What good is that super-station to me if I can't radio it for help when I need it?"

"Well—"

But Aaron continued. "Take these evangelical preachers you see on TV. *I* can't profit from them because I can't believe any of it. But at least they offer those who do believe something definite. They say, 'Let Jesus come into your heart and your troubles will disappear.' I assume it works for some people because they're always reading out testimonials. But you offer nothing. So even if I accept your religion as true, what good does it actually do me?"

The rabbi nodded amiably. "That's a legitimate question. And the answer is that religion is not static. It changes; it develops; it evolves. Originally, as you suggested, it was primitive man's science, offering explanations for the world around us. But that function of religion disappeared when astronomy, chemistry, physics, and biology offered us better explanations. Another function of religion is to provide us with a Father who is stern but just, and yet loving and forgiving. But as a Father, He can also be called on for help in an emergency."

"And you believe that?" demanded Aaron.

"*I* don't," said the rabbi simply. "While that picture of God as the rewarding and punishing Father is seen again and again in the Bible, I think we have outgrown it in the same way we have outgrown Genesis as a factual account of the creation."

"But other Jews—"

"Oh, sure. Many Jews, especially the Orthodox, believe it as a dogma, just as some still believe in the biblical account of the creation. One segment of Orthodoxy even opposes the establishment of the state of Israel on the grounds that our expulsion from the Holy Land and our dispersal were God's punishment for our sins, and that it is impious to interfere with His will by trying to make it on our own instead of waiting for His agent or messenger to bring us back. This chastising Father doctrine has the merit of making the misfortune that befell us reasonable and understandable. If nothing else, it assuages the vexation of unmerited suffering. Job suffered as much from the thought that his punishment was unmerited as he did from the misfortune itself. And he repudiated the imputations of the friends who came to console him that he must have sinned secretly."

"I know the story, of course," said Joan, "but I've never actually read the Book of Job. How does it come out?"

"Ah, that's very interesting," said the rabbi, "particularly since it is generally assumed that the book is included in the canon because it represents the Jewish view on the subject of misfortune and punishment. God answered Job with a series of rhetorical questions— 'Were you present when I made the world? Do you know what supports the earth? How I keep the sea separate from the land? Who finds food for the lions? Who feeds the ravens?'—the whole point being to contrast the mind that is responsible for the immensity and complexity of the universe with the minuscule mind of man.

In effect God was saying that since man cannot possibly understand all the conditions, it is presumptuous of him to question the fate that has been meted out to him. Job admitted his error and was restored to his former prosperity. Now I read that as signifying that there is no discernible correlation between virtue and good fortune, or between evil and misfortune. The good man doesn't necessarily prosper or the wicked one necessarily fail to. It's a matter of luck."

"That's not very satisfying," Joan observed.

"Isn't it? Would you rather have the rewarding and chastising Father with all its implications?"

"What implications?"

"The implication that when a man is poor or sick or otherwise unfortunate it must be because he is wicked."

"Oh, that. I was thinking more about someone you can pray to for help. Don't you believe in the power of prayer at all?"

"Not in the sense that your question implies. Certainly not in the New Testament sense of 'Ask and it shall be given.' In the privacy of one's mind, one may say anything, of course. In times of great stress or affliction even a confirmed atheist might express a fervent hope, or issue an anguished cry for help to—to the universe perhaps. And within that analogy of all minds as two-way radio stations, conceivably there might be a response: perhaps a sudden intuition on the part of the attending physician, or an unexpected concern on the part of a friend or ally, or even the sharper focusing of one's own capacities. In retrospect it may seem to have been a stroke of extraordinary luck approaching the miraculous, or an answer to one's prayer.

"Some Jews feel that way about the Six Day War. But the efficacy of that kind of prayer is not a tenet of our religion. In our congregational services we recite set prayers, most of which are blessings or glorifications of God. There is little petitionary prayer in our religion, and what there is, is largely in the form of general requests for life and peace for the community. In the Orthodox and Conservative congregations the prayers are recited in Hebrew, and the fact is that the great majority don't know the meaning of the words they are mumbling. In the Reform movement the prayers are recited in English—here in America." He laughed. "When I was in Israel, I met some American tourists who had gone to the Reform synagogue in Jerusalem, assuming that the service would be in English. They were quite disappointed and a little indignant when they found that it was entirely in Hebrew. They hadn't realized, or perhaps had forgotten, that the Reform principle is to hold the service and recite the prayers in the language of the country. And inasmuch as the language of Israel is Hebrew, the service was in that language."

"Well, it makes more sense to know what you're saying," said Joan.

"Do you think so?" The rabbi looked at her quizzically. "I wonder. The way in which Jews recite their prayers, inaudibly and as rapidly as they can, obviously too fast to absorb the meaning of the text, suggests that the exercise is more probably an aid to meditation."

"Something like a mantra?" suggested Aaron.

"Perhaps. In any case, there is no sense of a petition or request for special consideration. Our concept of God as an omniscient God of justice tends to minimize that tendency. For if He knows all before making His judgment, why should He change it? Certainly, completely foreign to our tradition is the kind of thing that is seen in that charming bit of calendar art: the little boy in his nightshirt kneeling at his bedside, praying for a pony or a bicycle. It's simplistic to be sure, and yet typical that the Jewish equivalent to the Christian 'Give us this day our daily bread' is 'Blessed art thou, O Lord...who brought forth bread from the earth.'"

"Then, like Aaron, I say what good is it?" asked Joan, bewildered. "Of what use is your religion to me, or your God, for that matter, if I can't call on Him for help when I am in need?"

"Yes, Rabbi," Aaron said, "you seem to be saying that God set the universe in motion and then washed

His hands of it and let it operate by itself. I seem to remember from a philosophy course I took as an undergraduate that the idea was developed in the eighteenth century. It was called—er—"

"Deism. No, Judaism is not Deism. We are convinced that in creating the universe, God had a plan or purpose and that He must be interested in how it is working out. Let's go back to that scenario I gave you of the broadcasting station. That suggests the idea that God is so interested that He broadcasts truth and knowledge and understanding every minute of the day and every day of the year. He is constantly interested and concerned. And presumably the more of it we can absorb, the better, the healthier, the wiser we will be.

"If life on this earth were completely happy and pleasant, if there were no sadness, no affliction of any kind, we might never think of God and we would feel no need of Him. Our need is because of the pain and suffering, the hardship and disappointment. Now, we cope with it in various ways. I mentioned some of them: analgesics like drugs, alcohol, sex, gluttonous feasting; or counterirritants like asceticism, flagellation, and mutilation. There are also the psychological solutions embodied in doctrines like the Christian one to the effect that this world is merely a gateway to the next where there will be no pain and suffering, only ineffable bliss—for those who qualify. Islam also offers a heaven, one of quite earthly and mundane pleasures, and needless to say without any of the penalties that pleasure is apt to exact on earth. The pains of this life the Muslim bears with patience since it is his fate, Kismet. The Christian Scientist goes further; he denies that there is pain. He regards it as a delusion. On the other hand, the Eastern religions have evolved techniques for blotting out the pain, and in place of heaven, the Buddhist looks forward to another reincarnation where he hopes life will be easier."

"Well, what's wrong with them if they work?" asked Aaron.

"What's wrong with them is that they all represent

a flight from reality of one sort or another, and in the long run that never works."

"Then what do Jews do?" asked Joan.

"Ah, we did an unusual thing. We chose to *face* reality and accept it. We recognize that our world is imperfect and as a result offers much in the way of hardship and bitterness and vexation. We bless God for whatever good He has given us. And as for the bad, we bless Him for that, too. 'The Lord giveth and the Lord taketh away; blessed be the name of the Lord.'"

"But how does that help the individual?" demanded Aaron.

"How does your science help him?" retorted the rabbi. "How does it help to know that disease is caused by germs or viruses?"

"Oh, come on, Rabbi. That's pretty obvious, I should think. If you know the cause of a disease, you can set about finding a cure or a means of prevention."

"Right. That's the value of science, and that's also the value of our religion to us. When something unpleasant happens, we do not shrug our shoulders and say it is Kismet, nor do we say it is a delusion, nor yet that it is characteristic of this world and that we needn't be concerned because this is only a temporary stopover on the way to the real world to come. Anything bad or unpleasant we say is probably wrong, and perhaps need not be. We have no magic words that call down the lightning on our enemies, or that can cure cancer in our friends. If we are sick and in pain, we accept it for what it is and see a doctor. If we see a wrong, we try to rectify it. Since for us this is the only world there is, we try to make it a better place."

"Is that why there are so many Jews in radical movements?" asked Joan.

"Probably. And in philanthropy and medicine and science and law."

"And yet I never noticed that any of the radicals I knew were particularly religious," said Aaron dryly.

The rabbi smiled. "No? Well perhaps it expresses itself negatively, not in what they accept, but in what they refuse to accept; in their skepticism rather than in their faith; in their doubt that an observed evil is a law of nature and must continue. Where do you suppose your own scientific skepticism comes from? Do you think you were born with it? That it was in your genes? Or did you, perhaps, acquire it in your father's house?"

"My father has no religious beliefs that I've ever been aware of," Aaron said flatly. "None that he ever expressed to me."

"Are you sure?" the rabbi demanded. "Because our religious system not only calls for believing certain things, but also in not believing other things." A thought struck him. "I suppose that's the modern application of the commandment against worshiping idols because there isn't much idol worship in the biblical sense these days. So, in nonobservant Jewish households, while much that we believe is perhaps never mentioned, it is usually pretty clear what we do not believe."

"I never thought of that," Aaron said.

CHAPTER

6

Aaron had risen and walked over to the end of the porch, whether merely to stretch his long legs, or because he wanted to isolate himself momentarily from the other two while he considered the rabbi's suggestion. Now he turned abruptly and said, "All right, Rabbi, suppose I accept your analogy of the broadcasting station as a working hypothesis. Here is God broadcasting away, and people all over the world from the beginning of time catching snatches of the message accidentally, or by deliberately trying to tune in. Then why wouldn't they all come up with the same answers? The message is the same, isn't it?"

"It is and they do," the rabbi replied. "In all societies that we know anything about, the same things are considered wrong: incest, murder, theft, adultery, lying. There are different ways of controlling them or punishing them, but they are always held to be wrong, evil."

"But they could have all been evolved out of common observation that these things tend to destroy the fabric of society," said Aaron.

"You mean there might have been a period when murder, for example, was normal, and then they noticed that the tribe or the band was growing smaller, and then put a stop to it by passing a law against it? Possible, but rather unlikely. And how about incest? It is taboo even among peoples so primitive that they have not as yet established the connection between the sex act and the birth of children. Are you suggesting that somewhere along the line the shaman said to the elders, 'Gor has been bedding with his sister, Plik, and all her children are idiots, so it might be a good idea if we forbade brothers to sleep with their sisters'?"

Aaron laughed. "I assume that it was the result of a natural disinclination."

"Why? You don't find it among the lower animals. How did it develop among humans?"

"Didn't the Egyptian pharaohs always marry their sisters?" asked Joan. "Seems to me I read that somewhere."

"I suspect that was more ceremonial than actual," said Aaron. "Right, Rabbi?"

The rabbi shrugged. "Or it could be the exception that proves the rule, something so outrageously contrary to custom as to establish the pharaoh in the minds of the people as a different order of being entirely."

"All right," said Aaron, "then let's get back to my original question. If the source is the same, the message would be the same. And if the message is the same, why would Jews be different?"

"I suppose you might say that the Jews were lucky in having grasped the major truth that there is only one God. Everything else followed from that." He frowned as he fished for an analogy. "When you lecture, do all your students take down the same notes?"

"Obviously not, but—"

"And if it were a large lecture hall," the rabbi pressed on, "and the acoustics were bad, I presume those in the front rows would get a lot more than those in the back. And some are more attentive. And some have a little more interest in the subject, or are more knowledgeable. Any of these will make a difference. And when you think of the areas of agreement among all cultures of what is right and what is wrong, as opposed to the areas of disagreement, then I'd say God's message or His instructions have come through rather clearly. Although the Ten Commandments, for example, are usually thought of as purely Judaic code, the fact of the matter is that the last half, all the *Thou Shalt not*'s, are followed by all cultures. It is only the first half that is distinctly Jewish."

"But Christians accept the first half," said Joan.

"I wonder," said the rabbi. "The first commandment is 'I am the Lord your God who brought you out of Egypt where you were slaves. You will worship no god but Me.' Now Christians believe in the divinity of Jesus Christ as the son of God, not in the sense that we are all God's children, but in the literal sense of having been begotten by God on the Virgin Mary. He is not regarded as a prophet like Moses or Mohammed but as a divine personage sharing the Godhead with his father."

"But he is not supposed to be a separate god," Joan protested. "As I understand it, Christian doctrine regards him as a manifestation of the Triune God."

"Yeah, but isn't Jesus the one you pray to?" Aaron asked. He turned to Rabbi Small. "How did they come to develop something as complicated as three gods in one?"

"I suppose because originally it was a purely Jewish movement."

"You mean it started among the Jews? What difference would that make?"

"Well, if it had been a pagan movement, then it would have been relatively simple to add Jesus to the hierarchy of gods as the Romans did when they made gods of some of their emperors. Or if there had been no strong commitment among Jews to the doctrine of the one God, Jesus could have been offered as an alternative, or an adjunct. You see the problem. For the Jew there was only one God, so Jesus had to be offered and promoted as a part or an aspect of Him." He paused and then said, "I wonder if you realize how bold and radical the doctrine of one God was at the time. It must have invited all kinds of distrust, even hatred and enmity, the first anti-Semitism."

"But why?" asked Joan.

"Because primitive people respected each other's gods. While they may have been convinced of the superiority of their own, they assumed as a matter of course that other gods were also powerful, especially in their own territories. When they left their homes to travel in foreign parts, they were careful to make obeisance to the local gods in whose land they found themselves. Even when they conquered a country they did not abolish the gods of the people they subjugated. Rather, they incorporated them in their own pantheon and adjusted their theogony accordingly. Thus, while Zeus was definitely an Achaean god, his wife, Hera, was in all likelihood the goddess of the aborigines of the Peloponnesus which they took over. So was Athene.

"But because of the first commandment, the Jews could not participate in this free and easy arrangement. Not only did they not permit the worship of other gods in their own land, but they even denied that any others existed—anywhere. Theirs was the one God and there were no others. And as if to add insult to injury, there was no representation or statue of Him because of the second commandment against making a graven image. So from the point of view of the ancient world, they were a godless people, and one moreover that refused to accept the benefits of the gods when they were offered them. For centuries the idea of one God had been dinned into them by their teachers and their prophets. They had suffered for it, but they had stubbornly clung to the concept in spite of the ridicule of the rest of the world."

"Or because of it, I bet," Aaron remarked.

The rabbi nodded. "Not unlikely. The Maccabean Revolt had begun in their defense of it—"

"Yeah, I remember that story from Sunday school," said Aaron.

"And you probably also remember the apocryphal story of Hannah and her seven sons."

"Yeah, she let each of them be killed rather than let them sacrifice to an idol. Isn't that it?"

"That's right. The historicity of the story may be questionable, but the point is that its plausibility was accepted."

"You mean people thought it might very well have happened," said Joan.

"M-hm. It was a heroic act, but from their point of view not insane, or even unreasonable. So you can see that the early Church could not claim that Jesus was a god in his own right as they might have done in Greece or Rome or Egypt. To Jews in the land of Israel he could only be presented as an aspect of God, His son, or His Messiah. And by the time Paul had succeeded in reorienting the Church to the gentile world, the pattern had been set."

Aaron chuckled. "I can well believe that the stubbornness of the Jews might well have annoyed the people of the ancient world. I'm trying to think of a modern parallel—"

"You don't have to. They provoked a similar response all through the history of Christianity. Right down to Vatican II the official Christian attitude has been that the Jews are stubborn and stiff-necked in refusing to accept the divinity of Jesus. And the fact that he was one of ours made it all the more reprehensible. To this day most Christian theologians take the point of view that Judaism is not a separate religion from Christianity, but rather a primitive form of it. Blindness or spite presumably keep us from taking the next logical step. The more liberal among them admit that we have suffered over the years at the hands of the Christian Church, but very few are prepared to accept *our* point of view that not only are the two religions separate and distinct, but are even doctrinally in opposition to each other."

"Isn't every religion doctrinally in opposition to every other?" asked Aaron.

"Not really, at least not in the same way. Buddhism, Shintoism, and other Eastern religions are different systems altogether. Islam, which is based on the vision and prophecy of Mohammed, is different from Judaism, but not in opposition to it. It holds to the doctrine of one God with Mohammed as His servant, from their point of view the last and the greatest of His prophets. We don't happen to agree, but it doesn't run counter to our basic ideas. But Christianity is something else again. Its relation to Judaism is like the two figures in that Swiss barometer. When one goes out, the other comes in. If God is one, as we claim, then there is no room for a second deity in the form of Jesus. On the other hand, if Jesus is a god, then our God cannot be one and unique."

"I get it," said Aaron. "Those two religions not only disagree, but they also contradict each other."

"Right."

"And since they're both referring to the same concept..."

"There's an impasse," the rabbi finished for him.

Aaron nodded seriously. "I suppose that basic contradiction must bother Christians from time to time when they stop to think about it, and our clinging to the original doctrine serves to point it up. I can see that it might not endear us to them."

"I think that's a fair summary of the situation," the rabbi agreed.

"I've never thought of it that way," Joan protested.

"No, but I'll bet your minister has," Aaron shot back at her. "How about the next commandment, Rabbi? Anything there to cause confusion?"

"Not for us. It's the commandment forbidding the making of images. The prohibition is obviously against the making of idols which would then be worshiped, rather than against the arts of painting and sculpture.

96

Nevertheless, we Jews tended to avoid representational art altogether, and it's only in recent years that we've developed any artists of note. But that commandment seems to have provoked considerable controversy in the Christian Church. The flat, two-dimensional icon of the Orthodox Church was based on the conviction that only three-dimensional representation, representation in the round, was forbidden. And one of the objections of Protestantism to Roman Catholicism is that the sculptures in the Catholic churches and in innumerable shrines constitute idol worship. Or course, knowledgeable Catholics are quick to point out that it is not the statues themselves that are venerated or worshiped, but the persons whom they represent; that the statues are obviously merely pieces of wood or stone or clay, but that they serve to concentrate and focus the mind of the worshiper."

"But simple folk in primitive communities don't always make the distinction between the clay statue and what it represents," Joan said.

"And plenty who are not so simple," said Aaron. "How about all those people who have St. Christopher medals dangling behind their windshields to protect them from motor accidents? It's all too easy to confuse the symbol with what it stands for."

"The easiest thing in the world," the rabbi agreed. "We have not been entirely exempt from it. During the Middle Ages some rabbis went in for amulets and talismans which they distributed to ward off sickness or bad luck. And even now, some think of the mezuzah as something of the sort."

"What's a mezuzah?" asked Joan.

"It's a little oblong box that is mounted on the door—" Aaron began.

"Oh, yeah, your folks have one on their door."

The rabbi explained. "It contains a little scroll of parchment on which are written the verses from the Bible which begin, 'Hear, O Israel, the Lord is our God and He is One.' And it goes on, 'And you shall love your

97

Lord with all your heart and all your soul and all your might. The commandments which I give you this day you will remember and teach them to your children. You will keep them in mind in your going out and your coming in, at work and at rest. You will bind them on your arms and on your forehead as a reminder, and write them on the doorposts of your houses and your gates.' It's like tying a string around your finger to remember something."

"Then how does it get to be an amulet or whatever?" asked Joan. "Oh, I know. Some Jewish girls wear little gold or silver ones as lockets. Is that what you mean? They think they bring good luck?"

"No-o, I don't think they do really. My impression is that girls wear them to show they are Jewish. They are also apt to wear a Star of David for the same purpose. That doesn't bother me. I was thinking of something else. I was thinking of some of the extreme Orthodox who should know better." He smiled as he leaned back in his chair and stretched out his legs. "I was walking down Fifth Avenue in New York one day when I was accosted by a young man who asked if I were a Jew. When I said I was, he handed me a flier which had been issued by some organization that was dedicated to the preservation of the sanctity of the mezuzah. There was a bit of instruction on the proper way to affix it to the door frame. And then it went on to explain that it was important to check the mezuzoth in one's house periodically to make sure that the ink had not faded or the parchment frayed because then it would be useless. There was even a phone number that one could call twenty-four hours a day if one were uncertain and wanted an expert opinion. It also went on to say that many mezuzoth were being sold in which the scroll was of paper instead of parchment and on which the verses had been printed instead of written by a scribe with a quill. These, needless to say, were completely useless." He spread his arms, palms upturned. "Why? If it is a reminder, won't it remind if it is printed? In Israel I heard a story in the same vein.

What's significant about it is that the man who told it to me, a Chassid, was convinced it was true. A friend of his had gone to his rebbe—the leader of his particular sect," he explained in an aside to Joan—"to ask his advice. After half a dozen years of marriage his wife had not conceived, and they were childless. The rebbe told him to go home and check the mezuzoth throughout the house. He did as he was bade and discovered that in one of them the word for *children* had accidentally been left out by the scribe, or perhaps had faded. I've forgotten which. He replaced the scroll with another and nine months later his wife gave birth to a fine baby boy."

He joined in the laughter that followed his story, and then said, "Now that's magic, not religion. If it can cause a barren woman to conceive, it is an idol, a pagan god like those swollen belly figurines that anthropologists are always digging up which may have been made for the same purpose. If it is efficacious only when prepared in precisely the proper form of approved materials by an accredited scribe, and useless when the same message is printed on paper, then it is not the message that is important, but the thing itself. And its efficacy, I presume, is that it protects the household against misfortune like the *lares* and *penates* of the Romans."

"All right, then how about the Torah Scroll?" asked Aaron. "It seems to me that we pay honor to the physical Scroll. We march it around and people kiss it. Isn't that the same kind of thing?"

The rabbi pursed his lips as he considered. "No-o, I don't think so because we don't use the Scroll that way. We carry it around the sanctuary and as it passes down the aisle, people reach forward to touch it with their prayer shawls which they then put to their lips as a sign of love and respect for the Law. The purpose of the procession is to bring the Scroll from the Ark where it is kept to the reading desk from where it will be read. It is used only as—as a book. It is never used to perform magic. In biblical times, to be sure, in the days of the

99

prophet Samuel, an attempt was made to use the Ark containing the tablets of the Law in that way. In a battle with the Philistines, the Ark was brought up by the Israelites to help them overcome the enemy. But the result was that the Israelite army was badly defeated and the Ark was captured, suggesting that the Lord resented the Ark's being put to such a use. I don't know of any other cases. No, all things considered, we've been remarkably free of that sort of thing. By and large, I think we have tended to obey the second commandment. Yes, and the third one as well."

"What's the third?" asked Joan.

"That's the one about taking the name of the Lord in vain, isn't it?" Aaron offered.

"That's right."

"Does that mean not swearing by His name?" asked Joan.

"Yes, and a lot more. It means—" The rabbi remembered something and began to chuckle. "When I first came to Barnard's Crossing to take up my duties as rabbi—the second or third day, in fact—a member of the congregation came to see me. He told me he was happy I had come, that he was happy they had chosen a young fellow like me—I was not yet thirty at the time—rather than 'some old geezer with a beard' as he put it. I assumed it was a courtesy call to welcome the newcomer and that he would leave shortly. But he settled back in his seat and began to talk about himself, and I sensed that he had something else in mind. When he mentioned that he was in the insurance business and that his agency was extremely successful, I thought the purpose of his visit was to sell me insurance, and I began to frame a polite refusal. But no, it wasn't that. 'I just bought a new car, Rabbi,' he said, 'and this time I decided to go whole hog—you'll pardon the expression—and get a Cadillac.' I murmured something about being happy for him. And then it came out. 'So what I'd like from you, Rabbi, is that you give it your blessing.'

"'Oh, I can't do that,' I said.

"'Why not?' he demanded.

"'Because I'm not in the blessing business.'

"'You mean it's against your principles?' He was honestly puzzled.

"'It's against my religion,' I said.

"'You mean there's some law against it?'

"'That's right,' I said. 'The third commandment: Thou shalt not take the name of the Lord in vain.'

"He was disappointed, and I imagine hurt. After he left, it occurred to me that I might have suggested that he could recite a *shechayanu*."

"What's a *shechayanu?*" Aaron asked.

"You don't know? It's a blessing which we make when we finally achieve something we have worked and hoped for. 'Blessed art thou, O Lord...who has kept us alive and brought us to this moment.' But of course, that was not what he wanted. He wanted a charm that would preserve the car and its passengers from accident and injury. Or that I call God's attention to this particular car and have Him put it on His list of cars that are not to be damaged."

His listeners chuckled appreciatively. Joan said, "My aunt is always saying, 'Bless me.' Would that be contrary to the commandment?"

"It's not in accordance with *our* tradition and practice. We have blessings for all kinds of things. They follow a regular formula: 'Blessed art thou, O Lord, King of the universe, who'... et cetera, et cetera. On arising, for preserving us through the night; on washing, for commanding us to wash; on breaking bread, for bringing bread from the earth. In effect, they are means of giving thanks for various things we receive. With us, the blessing is never an idle expression of piety. That would be taking His name in vain. With us it is always specific. When the observant Jew gives thanks to God for having brought forth bread from the earth, he then chews on a piece of bread. When he blesses God for having created the fruit of the vine, he then takes a sip of wine. Otherwise he would feel that he was

101

taking the name of the Lord in vain. Do you understand?"

"I—I think so," she said.

"It might not strike you as terribly important," the rabbi continued, "but it had a tremendous effect on our religious practice."

"Really? How so?" Aaron asked.

"Well, it limited our piety, or rather our religiosity. We are required, for example, to pray three times a day. There is no virtue in praying six times a day, which is quite different from the situation among Christians. In some monasteries and convents the priests and nuns spend almost all their waking time in prayer. To us, that is unthinkable. A priest, after hearing a confession, might require the penitent to recite ten Hail Marys. To us, this makes no sense."

"Then what does a pious man do?" asked Joan. "I mean a really pious man. You know, someone who is considered practically a saint."

"I understand. Well, for one thing, he would be of the world. He would be kind, generous, concerned. He would engage in good works, in improving the lot of his fellow man. He—"

"Yes, but that's all, well, secular. I was thinking of religion. You said he wouldn't pray more than he was required to. But I imagine all observant Jews do that. What would make him different? What would he do that would show that he was more concerned with God than were other observant Jews? Would he be ascetic? Would he be celibate? Would he fast?"

"Oh, no. We regard fasting and asceticism as scorning the good things that God has provided for our pleasure and enjoyment. As for celibacy, our view is that the unmarried man is incomplete. 'Male and female He created them.' Besides, there is the injunction to be fruitful and multiply. No, none of these would indicate piety. I suppose with us it would be study. Whereas the pious Christian would spend his time in prayer and fasting in an effort to come closer to God, the pious Jew would pursue the same goal through study. It is a religious obligation that is enjoined on all Jews. The kind of man you're talking about would do a lot more of it."

"What kind of study?" asked Aaron, interested.

"Well, traditionally it was study of the sacred books, the Bible, the Talmud, the various commentaries, because these were either the word of God or interpretations of it. In studying them, Jews were trying to understand what God expected of us. But nowadays we realize that His truth can also be found in the laboratory and in the observatory. My own personal view is that the studies of an Albert Einstein had the same religious significance as the studies of the Vilna Gaon, one of the greatest of our Talmudists."

Aaron rubbed his hands gleefully. "Ah, now we're getting someplace. I don't know how big a guy the Vilna Gaon was, but I get the general drift of what you're saying, and I like it."

The rabbi smiled. "I thought you might."

"The lights in the hotel just went off," Joan remarked. "It must be late."

Aaron glanced at his watch. "Hey, it's after midnight. We'd better be getting back, Joan. Gosh, Rabbi, I didn't mean to keep you up so late. I—"

"Quite all right, Aaron. I enjoyed it."

"And tomorrow night?"

"I'll be expecting you."

"That was quite a session," Aaron remarked as they made their way to the car.

"What do you think?" she asked anxiously. "I mean, are you convinced now that I should go ahead with conversion? That it's worthwhile?"

"Look, Joan, that's entirely up to you."

"Well, I'm going through with it," she said stoutly. "As soon as we get home next week, I'm going to see this rabbi in Peabody and make the necessary arrangements. But are you—I mean, does it make sense to you, what the rabbi said?"

"Ye-es. But it's different for me than it is for you."

"Why is it different?"

"Well, my background is different. As the rabbi said, Judaism not only calls for believing certain things, but for not believing other things."

"So?"

"So I guess that the second part, not believing certain things, I've had all along."

"Well, it's not that different for me. Dad is pretty skeptical. If it weren't for Aunt Jane, I would have received no religious education at all. And what I was given probably didn't take too firm a hold because of Dad's attitude."

"Maybe that's why your dad and I get along so well."

"Yes, he likes you." They rode for a while in silence, and then Joan said, "What if—suppose Rabbi Small convinced you. What would you do?"

"What do you mean?" Aaron asked.

"I mean would you go to the daily prayers? Would you start eating only kosher food and all that kind of thing?"

"I doubt it."

"Then what would you do?"

"I don't know. I don't know how my newfound religion would express itself. I probably wouldn't know until it actually happened. I suppose I'd be more tolerant and understanding when next I happened to enter a synagogue. Maybe I'd feel different about myself. I just don't know."

Early the next evening Miriam called from New York. After giving news of her father, who was doing as well as could be expected, she asked, "Did she come again last night, David?"

"She? Joan? Yes, she came with Aaron. They didn't leave until around midnight."

"And you talked the whole time?"

"What do you mean I talked? We all talked. Well, I suppose I did do most of it."

"Wasn't it—isn't it tiring?"

"No, I enjoyed it. You know you always learn more by teaching than by studying. As you try to explain,

104

all kinds of ideas, analogies, examples, occur to you that you hadn't thought of before, and they shed a new light on your own views. To tell the truth, I found it quite exciting."

"But have you convinced him? That's what you're after, isn't it?"

"Well, he certainly didn't say, 'You've convinced me, Rabbi.' He listens. He asks intelligent questions. He raises objections—seriously. Even if I succeed in convincing him, I don't expect him to come here to the hotel to participate in the minyan."

"What do you expect?"

"I don't know. I've never tried to convert a Jew to Judaism before, although I suppose that is essentially my job in Barnard's Crossing—converting Jews to Judaism I mean. But I don't feel I've been terribly successful at it. Maybe I'll do better with an individual than with a whole congregation. We'll see."

"They're coming again tonight?"

"They asked to. Maybe that indicates I'm making progress. Then again, maybe it just means that they prefer an evening of talk to the movie in the village."

CHAPTER

7

Joan and Aaron came a little earlier that night, and almost before they sat down, Aaron said, "As I understand it, you say the change in the first commandment by the Christian Church came about because of the logic of the situation."

"Right."

"Then wouldn't the other commandments have been affected?"

"They were. You can never change just one thing. The second and third were also altered. You see, the appeal of Jesus was that he bridged the immense gap between the infinite God and the lowly finite creature man. Here was a being seemingly like themselves whom people could see and touch and whom they could ask for help in their misery. Well, that was all right for the generation in which he lived and which knew him. But what of succeeding generations? As the years pass, fact becomes history, and history becomes fable or old wives' tale. How do you convince later generations that there ever was such a human manifestation of the divine? Well, the best way is a picture or a statue of him, even though it seems a clear breach of the second commandment. Furthermore, it helps to promote faith if the believer is encouraged to call on Jesus frequently, although that tends to weaken the third commandment against taking the name of the Lord in vain. Having made a change in the first commandment, they had to make corresponding changes in the other two that dealt with the Godhead."

"How about the Sabbath?" asked Aaron. "That's the next commandment, isn't it? Doesn't that involve God?"

"In a way. We rest on the Sabbath because presumably God rested on that day. Sociologically, that was a revolutionary idea at the time."

"This book I read," Joan said, "claimed that the Sabbath was originally a pagan holiday to celebrate the four quarters of the moon."

"It's quite possible that they marked the different phases of the moon by some sort of religious ritual," the rabbi admitted, "but I doubt if it took the form of a day of rest. We know that because the surrounding cultures ridiculed the Jewish Sabbath. They said it showed we were a lazy people who insisted on one day of rest in seven, which was unthinkable at the time."

"The Jews did it because God was supposed to have rested on the seventh day, having spent the other six creating the universe," Aaron said. "Doesn't that strike you as an astonishing bit of anthropomorphism, Rabbi? The idea of God's being tired and having to lie down to rest?"

The rabbi smiled easily. "Sure. But there's a great deal of anthropomorphism in the Bible. It's all part of the effort to transmit complex philosophical ideas to unsophisticated minds. In this case the reason was perhaps to ensure obedience to a commandment that was bound to be resented."

"Why would it be resented?" asked Joan. "Why

would people resent having to take a rest once a week? Did they *want* to work all the time?"

"Ah, I see you've forgotten the rest of the commandment. Just a second. I'll get a Bible and read it to you." He rose and strode into the cabin to reappear a moment later with a much dog-eared Bible in hand. He riffled the pages. "Here it is. Freely translated, it says, 'Observe the Sabbath and keep it holy. Six days you will work, but the seventh is a day of rest dedicated to Me.' Now get this. 'On that day no one is to work, neither you, your children, your slaves, your animals, nor the strangers who live in your land.' Now do you see why the commandment might be resented? While no one would object to taking a day off once a week, giving a day off to one's household, to one's servants and slaves, was something else again. That was from Exodus. There the commandment goes on to give God's resting as a reason for the Sabbath. But the Ten Commandments are repeated in Deuteronomy, and there we are given a different reason for the Sabbath." Again he riffled the pages. "Here's how it goes in Deuteronomy. 'Your slaves must rest just as you do. Remember that you were slaves in Egypt and I, your God, rescued you by My power. That is why I command you to observe the Sabbath.'"

"Yes, I can see why that would be resisted," Joan said, "and also why you call it revolutionary."

"You know, Rabbi," Aaron said, "there's a *non sequitur* there."

"How do you mean?"

"Well, the Exodus commandment, even though it involves the ridiculous idea of an omnipotent God having to rest, is at least logical. It says, 'I rested on the seventh day, so to be like Me, you must also.' But in this Deuteronomy one He says, 'I took you out of Egypt so you must rest.' What's one thing got to do with the other?"

The rabbi nodded. "Good point. The important clause is not 'I, your God, rescued you. . . .' That's really a modifying clause. The important clause is the first one,

'Remember you were slaves in Egypt.' What it means is, 'you remember that when you were slaves in Egypt, you had to work all the time and were not permitted to rest, and how you resented it. So you must not treat your own slaves in the same way. Therefore you must let them rest one day a week, too.' The two passages show a distinct shift in emphasis. In Exodus, God says, 'I rested so you must, and incidentally your slaves, too.' In Deuteronomy, He says in effect, 'Because you know how bitter slavery is, you must let your slaves rest one day a week, and of course, you, too, will rest.'"

He leaned back in his chair and said, "I wonder if you realize the full significance of that wording in the commandment."

"How do you mean?"

"Well," said the rabbi, "when I was in college, freshman hazing by the sophomores was fairly common. Although it was abolished in many schools, I believe some may still have it, military academies, for example. The point is that the system continues because the freshmen become sophomores the following year and it seems only natural that they should visit on the new freshmen what they suffered when they were in that lowly state. That seems to be the natural course of things. Now the point I want to make is that the commandment enjoins us not to mistreat the servant and the slave for the very reason that we were ourselves slaves and so know what it entailed. Again and again, throughout the Bible the point is made that the stranger must be treated properly, 'for you were strangers in a strange land.' And you might say that is the basic lesson of our most important holiday, the Passover, when we recall the period in our history when we were slaves in Egypt."

Aaron asked, "So why did the Church change the Sabbath to Sunday?"

"That I think was Paul's doing, in his campaign to turn the Church from the Jews and focus it toward the gentile world. Obviously, the less association with its Jewish origin, the better. Since Sunday is the first day of the week, however, the rationale for making it a holy day had to be changed. What's the point of resting *before* you have worked and gotten tired? So it became the Lord's Day, on the assumption, I believe, that Jesus was born on a Sunday. Of course, in practical terms it doesn't make too much difference as the weeks succeed each other. If you normally start work on Monday and work a six-day week, you look forward to Sunday as your day of rest, rather than thinking of it as the beginning of the next week. That, by the way, was one of the changes that the Reform synagogue introduced, having the Sabbath on Sunday rather than on Saturday. Naturally, more traditional Jews felt that it was copying the Christians, which the Reform synagogue flatly denied. They insisted that it was intended only to make it easier to maintain the Sabbath since the six-day work week was practically universal at the time."

"Well, it does make sense," said Joan. "If you have to rest one day in seven, it would seem sensible to do it on the one day which was a non-workday anyway."

"Our Sabbath is not merely a day of rest, though," said the rabbi. "It is more than that. It is also a holy day. It has been said that not only did we keep the Sabbath, but more important, that the Sabbath kept us. That is usually taken to mean that we maintained our character and our life as a nation by adhering to our special practices. But it was more than that." He stopped as he considered how best to explain. "Look here: one of the chief reasons for the rapid rise of Christianity was that it gave the poor and the oppressed of the Roman world the hope of redressing their wrongs in a future world. Well, we Jews have nothing like that. But we have the Sabbath. On the Sabbath the Jew is transformed. Think of the Jew in the crowded ghetto, poor and fearful, despised and oppressed. But on the Sabbath he becomes a prince. He bathes and puts on his best clothes and goes to the synagogue to greet the Sabbath with the joy with which one makes ready for the arrival of a bride. Afterward he goes home to the

Sabbath feast. The house has been especially cleaned and the table is set with the best the family can afford. Candles are lit, and the food consists of special holiday dishes. There is always meat and wine and fine white bread.

"The holiday which begins at sunset Friday continues until sunset Saturday. It is not merely that one does no work on the Sabbath. More important, one divorces oneself from all the cares and worries of the workday week. Those twenty-four hours are a period of joy; sadness and sorrow are not permitted to obtrude. Even the mourner, recently bereaved of a loved one, may not mourn on that day. So, if you consider the trials and tribulations that were the common lot of the Jew, an unwelcome stranger in foreign lands through most of his history, the Sabbath provided him with relief from worry and tension one day in seven. In that sense, by giving him some measure of psychological relief and release, the Sabbath can be said to have preserved the Jew."

"Yes, I guess that's different from our Sunday," Joan said.

Either because he was impatient with the rabbi's explanation or because it invoked pictures long forgotten, Aaron said brusquely, "How about the next commandment?"

"The fifth, 'Honor thy father and mother.'"

"Anything unusual about it? I mean, do we Jews interpret it in some special way that's different from everyone else?"

"I don't know," said the rabbi simply. "I just don't know enough about family relationships in other early societies. In some primitive tribes where property descends through the female line, the husband comes to his wife's village to live. The education and training of the male children are not the responsibility of the father but of the mother's brother. Does the son then show the same respect to his father that he probably does to his mother? Or in societies where polygamy is common, or where the child might be the offspring of a concubine, does he accord his mother the same respect that he shows his father? I just don't know. It may be that this one, like the negative commandments that follow, was quite generally accepted by all peoples. On the other hand, it may be that the reason for the commandment is that normally people do not honor their parents."

"How do you mean?" asked Aaron.

"Oh, it's normal to love your parents, maybe even to like them. It's a lot harder to honor and respect them. They're so hopelessly old-fashioned for one thing." He laughed. "A young man who was having a bit of trouble with his parents once said to me, 'This may shock you, Rabbi, but I don't have much respect for my father.' I'm afraid I shocked *him* when I answered, 'Of course not. Most people don't. That's the reason for the commandment.' From my observation we begin to lose respect for our parents at about the age of five. That is when we form peer groups and the mores of one's peers constitute the ultimate wisdom. At least, that's when my Jonathan began telling me that I didn't understand. We begin to recover our respect for our parents when we ourselves become adults, say in our twenties." He sighed. "I guess I've got a number of years to go before Jonathan begins obeying that commandment."

They laughed in sympathy. Then Aaron said, "So it means that at most only five of the Ten Commandments are unique with us."

"Yes, I would say so."

"So if Jews differ from other people because they obey four or five more commandments—" Joan began.

"Oh, there are a lot more that we obey," said the rabbi.

"There are?"

"Six hundred and thirteen, according to our tradition."

"Six hundred and thirteen!" She was aghast.

"Of the Written Law," he went on. "In addition to all that are included in the Oral Law."

She stared at him, her face showing blank dismay.

He smiled at her. "The number six hundred and thirteen is more rhetorical than actual. There are supposed to be three hundred and sixty-five negative commandments and two hundred and forty-eight positive ones. But there is considerable disagreement as to just what verses constitute the six hundred and thirteen; there is a good deal of duplication, for one thing, and many of them apply only to a special segment of the population, such as the priests, or to special situations that no longer apply, such as the commandments governing sacrifices."

"Well, that's a relief," she said.

"Perhaps the important thing is to understand just what a commandment is," the rabbi continued.

"Why, it's an order, something someone tells you to do, and you have to do it. Isn't that it?" Joan said.

"That's right, but there are implications in the word that should be understood."

"You mean that it has to be from a superior to a subordinate," suggested Aaron. "Otherwise it's not a command, but a request."

"That's right," said the rabbi approvingly.

"And it's got to be something that's within the capacity of the person to do," Aaron went on eagerly as though it were a game. "I mean, if you tell a batter to hit a home run, that's not really a command. That's just encouragement. And if you tell someone to drop dead or go to hell, that's not really a command either; it's a—a curse."

"How about if you tell someone to be good?" suggested Joan. "That's not a command either, is it? It's more like a—"

"A pious hope," Aaron suggested, "like 'Drive carefully.' I'd say it had to be something specific. You agree, Rabbi?"

"Oh, yes, I'd say so. And I think it would have to be something that the person would not otherwise do, something he might even be unwilling to do."

"I don't follow you there, Rabbi," said Aaron.

"Wouldn't you want your subordinate to obey you willingly?"

"Of course. What I meant was that the coach who tells the batter to get on base is not really issuing a command because that's what he goes to the plate to do anyway. Similarly, when you tell your students to pay attention, you're not really issuing a command because presumably that's their reason for coming to school. On the other hand, when you assign ten problems to be done for the next class, that is a command, because while some might do them willingly because they enjoy doing problems, others will do them only because you have ordered them to do them."

"All right," said Aaron, "I get the distinction. What's the point of all this?"

"The point is that our commandments are all from a superior, God, to inferiors, us; they are specific and within our normal capacities; and we are expected to obey them whether we want to or not."

"I'm not sure that I understand that last part," said Joan. "It seems to me that if God ordered something done, and you loved Him, you'd be eager to do it, or you should be."

"Sure, but if it's a command, then you have to do it even if you're not inclined to. It's a question of attitude. One of our sages urged, 'Do not say, "I will not eat forbidden food because I do not like it." Say rather, "Although I yearn for it, I will not eat it because it is forbidden."' That attitude produces a sort of corollary to the effect that one may do what is not specifically forbidden. And in the same vein, if a commandment does not apply specifically, you are exempt from it."

"How do you mean?" Aaron asked suspiciously.

"Well, I have a distant relative who is jokingly referred to in the family as Simcha the Apicorus. That's Yiddish for Epicurean," he added in explanation.

"He goes in for gourmet foods?" asked Joan.

"No, with us the term means 'agnostic' or 'atheist' out of a mistaken notion of what the Greek philosopher actually taught. Now Simcha, while a devout and observant Jew, has original and unusual ideas about some of the commandments. Once, when I went to visit him, I noticed there was no mezuzah on the door frame. I assumed it had fallen off and mentioned it to him. To my surprise he said he had never put one up. Why not? He smiled slyly at me and explained, 'The commandment stipulates that it should be written on the door frame of your house. So it doesn't apply to me because it's not my house. I'm only renting.'"

They laughed. The rabbi went on, "Of course, if I had chosen to argue the point with him, he might have claimed that to do what has not been specifically ordered suggests that you think you know God's will when He has not actually stated it. Or he might have argued that it was only the Oral Law that was involved and not the Written Law, so he had some latitude for interpretation."

"What's the difference?" asked Aaron.

"Between the Oral Law and the Written Law? Well, the Written Law comprises the commandments that are in the Bible, in the five books of Moses. The Oral Law, according to tradition, was given to Moses at the same time and consists of the specific regulations by which the commandments of the Written Law were implemented. You might compare the Written Law to the American Constitution and the Oral Law to the interpretations of the Supreme Court. Take this matter of the mezuzah. As I explained, it contains a little parchment scroll on which is written a passage from Deuteronomy which says, 'You will love the Lord with all your heart and all your might—"

"Oh, yes, I remember," said Joan eagerly. "It says you are to remember the commandments when you're working and resting. And you tie it around your finger to remember—"

"Around your arm and your forehead," the rabbi corrected her, smiling, "'And you are to write them on the doorposts of your house and on your gates.' Well, if you were to read that in some modern text, you would probably regard all those separate instructions as serving only to emphasize the first clause, which calls for loving the Lord with all your heart and all your might."

"Like the old song, 'I'll love you always, in the springtime and the summer, in the winter and the fall,'" suggested Aaron.

"Exactly. Or, if you chose to take the passage literally and to write 'the commandments which I give you' on the door frame, you would write down the commandments themselves. That's what the passage seems to call for. Well, the Oral Law tells us to write down just the passage itself and enclose it in a little oblong box in a special way and then to attach the box to the door frame. And it tells us where and how to attach it. In other words, the Oral Law tells us specifically how the general commandments in the Written Law are to be applied and carried out. Sometimes it adds regulations to make sure that the Written Law is carried out. This is known as 'building a fence around the Torah.'"

"Can you give us an example?"

"Sure. Perhaps the most common example is the two sets of dishes that observant Jews use."

"Oh, I know about those," Joan said.

"You do?"

"Yes, you use one set of dishes for dairy products and an entirely different set for meat."

"That's right." The rabbi nodded approvingly. "Well, that's the regulation of the Oral Law, but there's nothing in the Bible, that is, in the Written Law, to that effect. There is a commandment, repeated several times, that 'Thou shalt not seethe the flesh of the kid in the milk of its mother.' It may be because it was a common practice among the Canaanite nations. More likely, it is because the idea itself is abhorrent and repulsive. So, to avoid the possibility of the one ever coming in contact with the other, the Rabbis ordained, and it is part of the Oral Law, that we erect a fence around that commandment and use two sets of dishes, two sets of cooking utensils, two sets of silver, one for meat and the other for dairy products."

116

"I should think that would be awfully hard to keep up," Joan said.

"Not at all. If you've grown up with it, or get used to it, you find the idea of eating meat from the same dish from which you've eaten cheese is repugnant, quite apart from any religious significance it might have for you. The stomach has its own laws. When I went away to college and first began eating in restaurants, the sight of someone at a nearby table buttering his bread as he was eating meat almost caused me to retch. After a while I got used to it, and it didn't bother me."

"What did you eat?" Aaron asked curiously.

"Oh, I'd have a salad or fish. Fish is *pareve*, that is, neutral, and can be eaten on either meat or dairy dishes." He smiled. "My cousin Simcha claimed that chicken was, too, since a chicken doesn't give milk, and hence her young couldn't be cooked in it."

"Hey, that's right," Aaron exclaimed. "Your cousin Simcha is a corker. I'd like to meet him sometime."

The rabbi smiled reminiscently as he thought of other notions that his cousin was wont to argue with great vehemence.

"Is that what you mean by kosher?" asked Joan. "The two sets of dishes?"

"That's part of it. The word *kosher*, or *kashere*, means 'ritually fit.' There are a number of commandments in the Bible, in the Written Law, amplified by various interpretations in the Oral Law, that constitute the law of *kashruth*. In general, it stipulates that only the flesh of those animals which have a cloven hoof, that is, that are herbivorous, and which chew the cud—both requirements must be met—may be eaten. All others are taboo. In the matter of seafood, only those which have scales and fins are permitted."

"No shellfish?"

"No shellfish. In the matter of birds, a number are listed by name as unclean. They appear to fall in the general category of birds having the curved beak and the talons of the bird of prey. Other birds, primarily domestic poultry like chickens, ducks, geese, turkeys,

117

may be eaten. All creeping and crawling things are taboo, as are all insects. The Bible does permit a variety of locust and grasshopper, but since we are not certain just which are referred to, we avoid all of them. Let's see, what else? Oh, yes, all fruits, vegetables, nuts, seeds, grains are permitted."

"Well, that's not too bad," Joan said. "I mean it's not too restrictive. What I mean is that in the matter of birds, for instance, nobody eats eagles or buzzards or seagulls, or—how about crows?"

The rabbi shook his head.

"Well, there you are," she said triumphantly. "We even have a saying about eating crow. It implies something you wouldn't normally care to do. And it's the same with the animals. They say that the Chinese eat dogs. I don't know if it's true or not, but I never heard of anyone else eating them, unless maybe it was Eskimos when they were starving. And oh, yes, the French, I understand, eat horse meat, but—"

Aaron laughed. "It's a regular article on the menu of the Harvard Faculty Club."

"Well, I've never eaten it. And I don't eat insects or creeping and crawling things either. The very thought gives me a shudder. So I guess that everything I eat is kosher, at least as far as the animals are concerned."

"How about pork products?" Aaron suggested. "Bacon?"

"Oh."

"Uh-huh, so there you are," Aaron said smugly. He addressed the rabbi. "How about it, Rabbi? Pork is even more taboo than any of the others, isn't it? It seems to me that we have a special attitude toward the pig."

"That's true. We tend to avoid even the living animal. We don't raise pigs, although we do raise other animals that are not to be eaten, like horses and camels and dogs and cats."

"Is it because it wallows in the mud and we think of it as dirty?"

"I don't think so. One view I've heard is that it is because the pig was an object of worship by some of the

118

pagan people in the area. Among the Greeks, Ceres was frequently portrayed with a pig beside her. My own idea is that it is repugnant to us because it is the one domestic animal which serves no purpose other than to be eaten. Don't you find the thought of raising an animal just to eat it distasteful?" he asked them.

"But we eat the other domestic animals, cows and sheep and goats—"

"But that is not the ostensible purpose for raising them," the rabbi insisted. "The meat of the kosher domestic animals we can regard as essentially a by-product. We raise the sheep for its wool, and the goat and the cow for the milk they give. And the cow was also used as a draft animal. As for the non-kosher domestic animals, we use the horse and the camel to provide transportation. The dog protects the house from intruders. The cat keeps the house clear of rats and mice. Only the pig serves no other purpose than to be killed and eaten, and that is abhorrent to us."

"That sounds reasonable," said Aaron.

"In France they use pigs to dig for truffles," Joan observed.

"How do they keep them from eating the ones they dig up?" asked Aaron.

"I don't know. I suppose they muzzle them."

The rabbi smiled broadly. "Then I'm afraid we would not be permitted to use them for that purpose on the principle implicit in the commandment 'Thou shalt not muzzle the ox that treads the corn.'"

"Is that a sample of Talmudic reasoning?" asked Aaron.

The rabbi grinned. "Come to think of it, it's not bad."

Not understanding, Joan looked uncertainly from one to the other and then asked, "Is that all there is to it? Not eating certain things and not mixing others?"

"Oh, no, there's more to it than that. The kosher animals are merely the varieties that we are permitted to eat. The individual animal must also be kosher."

"But if it's—I don't understand."

"The opposite of kosher is *trefe*. The word means

119

'torn.' An animal that is mutilated, or diseased, or has died a natural death, is *trefe*, even though it is one of the kosher species. To be kosher the animal must be slaughtered by a licensed slaughterer, called a *shochet*, who is pious and is familiar with all the regulations of his trade."

"Why does he have to be pious?" asked Aaron.

The rabbi looked at him in surprise. "Because we are forbidden to cause needless suffering to a living creature. Whereas an ignorant, irreligious man might take a sadistic pleasure in his work, the pious, observant man is aware of the principle and performs the necessary act with proper respect. So the method used is to pass a razor-sharp knife back and forth across the neck of the beast, thereby severing the windpipe and jugular vein so that the death is painless. If the animal suffers pain, it is *trefe*. This method also ensures that the greatest amount of blood will be expelled from the carcass, for we are forbidden to eat meat with the blood still in it."

"That's a funny one," Aaron said. "Why not?"

"Because according to the Bible, the blood is life and belongs to the Lord. The point is made again and again."

"But there's bound to be some blood left," Joan objected.

"True. So when the housewife buys her meat from the kosher butcher, she soaks it in cold water, which has the effect of raising the blood to the surface. Then she coats it heavily with coarse salt, which absorbs the blood. After which she washes off the salt. Only then can it be cooked."

"No rare steaks," Joan said sadly.

The rabbi shook his head. "No rare steaks. I might also mention that after the beast has been slaughtered, the *shochet* examines the viscera for traces of anomaly or disease, which would also render the carcass *trefe*. Let's see, that's about it, except—"

"There's more?"

"We don't eat the hindquarter."

"You don't? Not of any animal?" Joan stared her disbelief. "But that means no rump roasts or rump steaks or—"

"Uh-huh. And no leg of lamb or kidney chops."

"But why not?"

"Because when Jacob wrestled with the angel, he was struck on the hip muscle so that he limped afterward. It's in commemoration of that."

"You know, Rabbi," said Joan reflectively, "it's hard to be a Jew."

He smiled. "It's a common saying with us, but believe me, not for the reason you have in mind. Those who observe don't feel inconvenienced, and those who do not are of course not bothered at all."

But Aaron was not convinced. "I'm bothered about this kosher business. I can understand about the clean and unclean animals. As Joan pointed out, it's not too much different from what other people eat. It may even be healthier. There is the danger of trichinosis from pork. And shellfish is one of the common causes of allergic reaction. And I'm all for killing animals as painlessly as possible. But that's standard procedure these days anyway. As I understand, they stun them—"

"I am told that our way permits the blood to flow more freely," the rabbi interjected. "The shock of the stunning tends to inhibit the flow of blood."

"Well, that's what I'm getting at. All the business of the blood. That's sheer voodoo magic. And so is the business of the hindquarter. And the two sets of dishes. I had no idea that the reason for it was to avoid cooking the flesh of the calf in the milk of its mother. I agree with you that the very thought is repulsive. But do you have any idea of what the chances are of its ever happening? Especially here in America? There is a much greater chance of being hit by a meteor. What I'm getting at is, here are people going to extraordinary lengths—two sets of dishes, two sets of silver, two sets of pots and pans, I hear some even have two refrigerators—all to prevent something from happening that

121

wouldn't happen in a million years. You said you were a rationalist. Does that strike you as rational?"

"Let's consider it," said the rabbi mildly. "That the kosher diet is perhaps healthier than the prevailing one is not of overriding interest to the observant Jew. It is not the reason for his adherence to it. He follows it because he thinks it is commanded by God. If it were deficient, or even if it were severely limited, he might feel it necessary to cast about for additional justification. But it is obviously wholesome and adequate, so his certainty that it was ordered by God is sufficient reason to follow it. Sure, it calls for restraint. But restraint is inherent in religion, just as it is in civilization for that matter. The limitations that are imposed seem to him logical and reasonable. It may be that by the magic of biological chemistry the flesh of carnivores or even of scavengers is just as wholesome as that of the cud-chewing, grass-eating animals, but it would be hard to convince most people. His religion called for him to be clean and pure, so it seemed reasonable to him that he should limit his consumption of meat to that which he considered to be most likely to be clean and pure. I might also point out that it was a common belief, and to some extent still is, that we become what we eat. Primitive people may eat the flesh of the lion they've killed in order to acquire his strength, or deer meat to acquire swiftness. So, a peace-loving people may have acceded to a diet of the flesh of grazing animals for that reason."

"Oh, as I said, I'm not quarreling with that part of it—"

"All right, let's consider the rest of it." The rabbi settled back in his chair. "The regulations concerning the blood could be a kind of fence set up by God, similar to those set up the sages, to prevent transgression of an important commandment."

"How do you mean?"

"Well, I gather that the gourmet is scornful of meat well done. The rarer the better. Some even find raw meat a great delicacy."

"Steak Tartare—mmm," said Joan.

"Well, there you are," said the rabbi. "I gather that Joan likes it. But the next step could be eating the living animal."

"Aw, come on, Rabbi."

"Why not? There is a large tribe in Africa that maintains herds of cattle. They milk them and drink the milk, but they also bleed them regularly and drink the blood. It's how they get their protein. And how far is that from the abomination of eating a portion of a living animal?"

"We-ell—"

"Of course," the rabbi went on, "it may go back to some ancient taboo. There's no evidence of such a taboo among the ancient peoples of the area to be sure, but many primitives show a special attitude, either of respect or of fear, to blood. The Bible is quite explicit about not eating meat with the blood still in it, for 'the life is in the blood.' The various references to blood seem to suggest that while the flesh involves only the individual animal, the blood involves the entire species."

"Couldn't it be because the neighboring tribes did commonly ingest blood and bloody meat?" suggested Aaron. "It would be another way of differentiating themselves from the other peoples of the area."

"Quite possible," said the rabbi gratefully.

"And the taboo of the hindquarter?" asked Joan.

"I'll admit the ostensible reason is farfetched. It might be because it is the bloodiest portion of the carcass since it is farthest removed from the throat where the cut is made by the *shochet*. Actually it is only the sinew of the thigh that is forbidden. If that is removed, the rest can be eaten."

"But isn't meat that has been drained of all its blood dry and unpalatable?" asked Joan.

"Not if it's properly cooked," said the rabbi. "I don't know much about cooking, so I don't know how it's done, but I've never had cause to complain of either my mother's cooking or my wife's. I suppose they add things like—er—fat or gravy. Or maybe they cook it slowly. It comes out good."

"I don't care much for rare meat either," Aaron said. "Joan does, though. I suppose it's because my mother always prepared meat well done. Come to think of it, she used to salt the meat and wash it the way you said we were supposed to when my grandfather was living with us. I guess it's all in what you get used to."

"That's right. The stomach obeys its own rules."

"But the two sets of dishes have nothing to do with that," said Aaron. "Do you have a rational explanation for it?"

"The biggest mistake the rationalist can make is to exclude the irrational," said the rabbi. "When the rules were first promulgated by the sages, most people lived on small farms which were self-sustaining. They raised cows and sheep and goats whose milk they drank or made into cheese. On festive occasions they occasionally slaughtered calves and kids and lambs and ate the meat. There was a definite possibility of the flesh of the young coming in contact with the milk of its mother, if a slatternly housewife or servant neglected to scour the pots thoroughly. The easiest way to avoid breaking the commandment was to have one pot for meat and another for milk and milk products. So now the possibility is remote. What of it? The pattern has become ingrained." He pointed at Aaron's arm. "Do you ever turn back the sleeves to form a cuff?"

"Of my jacket? Of course not. What's that—"

"That's what those three little buttons are intended for. I'm told that in expensive, tailor-made suits there are real buttonholes to correspond. I imagine that making that little slit at the end of the sleeve and sewing on the buttons, especially if there are also corresponding buttonholes, must add materially to the cost of manufacture. But custom tailors and clothing manufacturers go on doing it even though the reason for it has disappeared. Styles and customs change so slowly as to be barely perceptible. The early automobiles had sockets for buggy whips even though there were no longer horses to whip. A bosun in the navy still communicates with a special whistle, and in the army they still use bugle calls, even though all naval vessels and all army posts have public address systems."

"Yes, but—"

The rabbi was not to be interrupted, however. "A custom that is associated with a group takes on special significance. Quakers were characterized by simple clothes of sober colors. So when one of them began wearing gay bright colors, it symbolized that he was cutting himself off from the group. It was like an announcement that he was opting out of the society. A practice or custom may be irrational, but when it becomes a symbol it may take on great significance. And giving up the irrational for the rational may have unforeseen results not always desirable. A friend of mine who is a Catholic priest was telling me that in giving up their traditional habits, not only did nuns lose a good deal of the respect that had always been accorded them, but many even lost their sense of vocation. He's convinced that it was one of the contributing factors in so many giving up their vows in recent years. And another friend of mine claims that tennis stopped being a gentleman's game when players gave up the traditional white flannels and began to play in the more sensible, more rational, shorts."

"And you think not having two sets of dishes is like giving up Judaism?" asked Joan anxiously.

"No, but it's an act of dissociation. Dining can be merely a matter of ingesting food for the necessary energy to carry on one's activities. And it can be a matter of ceremony, intended perhaps to manifest one's difference from the lower animals, which eat merely to satisfy their hunger. You can very sensibly eat off paper plates with plastic knives and forks, or with your fingers from a communal bowl for that matter. But most people prefer china and silverware, even though it involves the trouble of washing them afterward. With us, eating has always been something of a religious ceremony. The viands we see on the table before us are

125

a manifestation of God's bounty, and we are grateful for the opportunity to thank Him for them. Many Jews who do not normally wear the *kippah*, the skullcap, put it on to eat just as they do when they pray or enter a synagogue."

"Like the Englishman who dresses for dinner even when dining alone in the jungle?" suggested Aaron.

"Something like that. We think the extra trouble and expense of two sets of dishes is worthwhile, all the more for the feeling of satisfaction we get from knowing that we have taken extraordinary precautions not to transgress a commandment."

The rabbi added with a chuckle, "Curiously enough, Reform Judaism, in a high fervor of rationalism, discarded the whole business, not only the two sets of dishes but the restriction to the kosher animals as well. And they found they had to bring it all back; the restaurants and cafeterias at the Reform seminaries, I understand, are kosher."

"Reform Judaism is a separate sect, isn't it?" Joan asked. "Are there many different sects in Judaism?"

"Only three," Aaron said, "Orthodox, Conservative, and Reform. Right, Rabbi?"

"Pretty much," the rabbi said, pleased that Aaron had undertaken to answer.

"I suppose that's bound to happen in any religion, splitting up into different sects," Joan said. "I'm surprised there are only three. There are dozens in Christianity."

"Hundreds," said the rabbi, smiling. "Literally. And ours are not really sects, at least not in the sense that yours are."

"No?"

"Well, can you imagine a Protestant, say a Methodist, who is also a Roman Catholic at the same time?"

"Of course not, because—"

"But a Jew can be a member of both an Orthodox

127

synagogue and a Conservative one. And I've known young men with political ambitions who have joined all three. I know Reform rabbis who go to Orthodox synagogues to recite the Kaddish on the anniversary of the death of a parent."

"But how can they?" Joan said.

The rabbi considered for a moment. "You see, Christianity involves faith, a mystical belief in the divinity of Christ. That belief, that faith, is the test of a Christian. On that there is general agreement. But there is a wide difference of opinion on the specifics of that basic belief, differences as to the nature of Jesus, as to his relationship to God, as to his mission, as to any and every possible aspect of him. And since the religion is based on belief, these differences take on tremendous importance because it is the correctness of your belief on which your future in the afterlife depends. Now these beliefs are embodied in creeds, short statements of the essentials of the belief. The adherents of each creed constitute a separate sect, and since the differences are naturally many, there are many sects."

"Then why isn't it the same with Jews?" Joan asked.

"Because we don't have a creed as such. That is, our faith is not a test. Our basic principles we take for granted. With us it's a matter of deeds, of actions. We have been given commandments by God as to what we must do. So the breakdown with us is pretty much what you'd expect: those who are extremely observant, those who observe little or not at all, and those who are somewhere in between."

"I see. So the Orthodox are the most traditional and—"

The rabbi laughed. "The most observant," he corrected her. "We all claim to be the most traditional. The Orthodox give practically the same authority to the Oral Law as they do to the Written Law, and since their practices and services are almost identical with those of their fathers and grandfathers, they claim they are the most traditional. We Conservatives do not feel that the Oral Law has quite the same authority as the

Written Law because it consists of the interpretations of men—sage rabbis to be sure, but men. We contend that the basic tradition includes a recognition that changes and adjustments must be made from time to time to meet changing circumstances. And since we make such changes, we feel that *we* are in keeping with the tradition. Reform Judaism asserts that in the face of cataclysmic events such as the destruction of the Temple, for example, Jews have always revised their practices completely to conform to the new situation. So from that point of view, they claim *they* are the true traditionalists."

"But what sort of cataclysmic event took place that was comparable to the destruction of the Temple?" Aaron asked.

"The emancipation of Jews throughout the Western world in the nineteenth century," said the rabbi. "The Reform movement started in Germany back in the early part of the nineteenth century and was originally concerned with merely westernizing the service—by curtailing the liturgy, introducing choral singing accompanied by an organ, and having the sermon and some of the prayers in the language of the country instead of in Hebrew. At first the German rabbis who led the movement tried to find justification for the changes in Talmudic law, but gradually, in England and even more in America, they tended to make changes largely on what they regarded as a rational basis, which was usually in accordance with prevailing religious practices."

"You mean in accordance with Christian practices," Aaron said.

"That's right. They discarded the prayer shawl and the skullcap. The entire service was now in the vernacular, and as I mentioned, it was held on Sunday rather than Saturday on the rational grounds that in that time of the six-day work week it was the one day that the majority were free, and it was also the day when the Christian sects held their services.

"They discarded the Mosaic law, both the written

and the oral, on the ground that it was proper only during biblical times in the land of Israel, and announced that they accepted only the moral and ethical principles of the Bible. They even took the ultimate step of announcing that they no longer considered themselves part of a Jewish nation, but merely a religious community."

"Wow!" exclaimed Aaron. "I see why my grandfather always referred to them as *goyim*—Gentiles," he added for Joan's benefit.

The rabbi nodded. "And there was some justice in your grandfather's characterization, because unlike Christianity, Judaism is a code of practices followed by a particular people. The two are inextricably bound together—practices and people. And that, not merely in their own minds, but in the opinion of the rest of the world. To drop the practice is one thing, but to separate themselves from the people was regarded by many Jews as apostasy."

"But Reform Judaism is not that way now, is it?" Aaron asked. "The ones I know are all strong for Zionism and Israel."

"That's right."

"What happened?"

"They couldn't maintain it. They couldn't live up to their own declared principles. It's like a father who disowns a son. Can he fail to be concerned when he hears that his son is seriously sick or in great trouble? Can he feel no elation or pride when his son is supremely successful? They couldn't cut themselves loose. It's one of the faults of rationalism that it doesn't take into account the force of the irrational. By 1937, in their Columbus Platform, the leaders of the Reform movement repudiated much of what they had announced back in 1885 in their Pittsburgh Platform. They called for a return to the Torah, both written and oral, the preservation of the traditional customs and symbols, and the use of Hebrew along with the vernacular in the services. Most important, they admitted that there is a bond which binds Jews, even those estranged from their religious tradition. Whatever reservations any of them may have had about that last were no doubt dispelled by the Holocaust on the one hand and by the establishment of the state of Israel on the other."

"So how is it now?" asked Aaron.

"I would say that what we see now is a spectrum or band extending from the most meticulously observant Orthodox through the more liberal Orthodox to the more traditional Conservative through the less observant Conservative to Reform Judaism which also has its traditional and liberal wings."

"Then the Orthodox are the only ones who didn't change?" asked Joan.

"Oh, I wouldn't say that. They were influenced by the changes that took place, and that in both directions. My father tells me that when he was a youngster, and of course he attended an Orthodox synagogue, it was unthinkable for a young man, or even an older one, to wear the *kippah*, the skullcap, on the street. Nor would he have had the fringe of the small *tallis* that he wore under his shirt dangling outside his trouser leg. It would have been regarded as presumptuous in a young man and an affectation in an older man. Nowadays it's quite common. That, of course, is by way of reaction to liberal Judaism. On the other hand, whereas it was usual for women to be separated from the men in the synagogue by having them seated in the balcony, frequently behind a screen, in most modern Orthodox synagogues there is no balcony and men and women sit on the same floor, although there is some sort of partition between them. The reading desk is not in the middle of the sanctuary, but is in front of the Ark as in the Conservative synagogues. About the only observable difference between the Orthodox and Conservative synagogues is that in the former the cantor always faces the Ark instead of the congregation as with us. And oh, yes, we are apt to have an organ and female voices in the choir."

"Is that all?" asked Aaron.

"There are other differences, of course—in the liturgy, in the priorities in the training for the rabbinate—but none that are apparent to someone coming into the synagogue for a service."

"Would I notice the difference?" asked Joan.

"Aaron might, but I don't think you would, especially if it were a modern Orthodox synagogue. You might, though, after you had visited a number of each. You would perhaps notice, even before you entered, that the Conservative synagogue, especially if it is in the suburbs, would have a parking lot. The Orthodox synagogue probably wouldn't."

"You mean they don't ride in automobiles? They're not allowed to?"

"Not on the Sabbath or the holidays. They can during the week, of course, but not enough come during the week to create a parking problem."

"But on the Sabbath they all walk, even if they live at a distance?"

The rabbi laughed. "Not by a long shot. They drive, but they park around the corner or on the side streets."

"But isn't that hypocritical?"

"Those who do it think it is better to go to the service, even though it is a breach of the commandment, than not to go at all. That is, the fulfillment of one commandment overrides the breach of another. That's the point of view that the Conservatives take. The Reform synagogue does not recognize the commandment at all."

"I see."

"Once inside," the rabbi went on, "you would notice that in the Orthodox synagogue men are separated by a barrier."

"You mean husbands separated from their wives? But that's awful."

"You think so? Personally, I never could see any reason for making a fuss over it. In our synagogue men and women sit together, but it wouldn't bother me if they were separated. I can't believe that men are so uxorious that they can't stand being separated from

132

their wives for the length of the service. If the matter were put to a vote, I'd probably vote to have them sit together because it has become the custom of the country."

"Well, I think it's a sign of male chauvinism," said Joan flatly.

The rabbi shrugged. "In the Orthodox congregations I know about, the most active members are the women, as they are elsewhere. While the rabbis of those congregations may have halachic, that is, Talmudic, reasons for the separation, my guess is that the members favor it merely because that's the way it has always been and they are reluctant to make a change. All right, so what else would you notice? You might find that there would be more long woolen prayer shawls in evidence. The Conservatives tend to go in for narrow silk ones. The Reform don't wear any. The Orthodox synagogue will be a little less orderly and more relaxed with people coming in and going out, seemingly whenever they feel like it. During the reading of the Scroll, there will be a lot of whispering in the congregation, and very few will appear to be paying attention to what is taking place in front of the Ark, almost a kind of recess. It may strike you as warm and friendly and informal, whereas the service in the Conservative synagogue will strike you as being a lot more decorous, more the sort of thing you'd expect in a house of worship."

"That's really the big difference, isn't it?" remarked Aaron. "The Conservatives go in for decorum in their services."

"I suppose," said the rabbi. "I sometimes think we are a little too concerned with decorum."

"But a service should be orderly, shouldn't it?"

"Why?"

"Well, gee, when you come together to do something, you want it orderly so—so you can transact your business, whatever it is."

"Did you ever see our Congress or Senate in action?"

"What's that got to do with it?"

"They come together to transact business."

"Oh, well..."

"But they argue and walk out and talk among themselves. On the other hand, when a parliament in one of the dictatorship countries meets, there is perfect order and decorum, with everyone seated on time, with no one leaving the assembly no matter how long or tedious the speeches, with all applauding in unison at the appropriate times. The point is that the synagogue is a place where people come to pray as individuals but together. They are individuals praying in public. They are not performing as a chorus."

"Then why pray together at all?"

"Ah, because it is a public service replacing the public sacrifices that were made in the Temple in biblical times. We pray as a group or congregation, and when we refer to ourselves in our prayers, it is always in the plural. And of course, some prayers *are* recited in unison, and some are recited only in a public service. I suppose the real point is that the synagogue is not a holy place like a church or a cathedral which imposes a special somber and solemn mood on the worshiper. It's a meeting place. The service could be held in a home, as indeed it is when someone is confined to his house because he is in mourning."

"But how about the altar? Doesn't the synagogue have an altar?" asked Joan.

"An altar? No. There is a table on which the Scroll is unrolled when we read from it, and there is the Ark, the cabinet in which the Scrolls are kept, with a lamp above it which burns continuously, the eternal light. And oh, yes, there is a menorah, a candelabrum, for the candles we light in the evening at the inception of the Sabbath and holidays."

"Then the decorum of the Conservative and Reform services—" Aaron began.

"Is something we copied from the Christian Church services," said the rabbi promptly, "probably under the mistaken notion that the lack of decorum in the traditional service was due to the social ignorance of the *shtetl* Jew of Russia and Poland with whom it was identified rather than because it was inherent in the nature of the service."

"You mean that the order and decorum are no more necessary in the Jewish service than they would be at a—at a football game?" Aaron said.

"Something like that."

"How is it in Israel?" Joan asked. "I suppose they have big synagogues there—" She broke off as the rabbi shook his head.

"There are a couple of biggish ones, but none that would compare with our big synagogues, or even with our medium-sized ones. There are several hundred in Jerusalem, but most of them are little one-room affairs where a couple of dozen people crowd the place. There, by the way, the Orthodox are in complete control, and Reform and Conservatism have practically no standing."

"I would assume so," said Joan. "It's like Rome, isn't it? Jerusalem anyway."

The rabbi laughed. "No, it's not like Rome. The supremacy of the Orthodox in Israel is a lot more like the supremacy of the AFL-CIO among labor unions. In fact, it's very much like labor union jurisdictional politics, with the Orthodox extremely vigilant to prevent Conservatism or Reform from gaining a foothold. They make it difficult for Conservative or Reform groups even to acquire land for synagogues. They have complete control of marriage and divorce, and even of citizenship. That is, they decide who is a Jew and who is not."

"Well, they're in the majority, aren't they?" Aaron observed.

"Very far from it," said the rabbi. "The religious parties total less than fifteen percent of the population. The overwhelming sentiment of the country is nonreligious, if not actually antireligious. It's a semisocialist state, you see."

"Then how..."

"Because there are so many political parties, all governments are of necessity coalition governments. To get a majority, the Labor party, which ran the country up until the last election, found it politic to take as coalition partners the religious group, primarily because they were not particularly interested in either economics or foreign affairs, and hence the Labor party had a comparatively free hand. But they had to pay for the cooperation of the religious parties, and giving them control over marriage and citizenship was the price exacted."

"That seems like a pretty big price to pay," said Aaron.

"Well, there was a certain justification for it, even from the point of view of a nonreligious government. There was the danger of two nations developing—"

"How do you mean?"

"Because many whom the rest of us would accept as Jewish might not be so accepted by the Orthodox. So they would tend to restrict marriage of their young people to their own group, whose ancestry they were sure of. In a few generations two ethnic groups that did not intermarry would develop. A similar logic decreed that the food in the army should be kosher since it was mandatory for the observant and constituted no hardship for the unobservant."

"Yeah, I can understand that," said Aaron, "but do the Orthodox approve of the idea of a Jewish state at all?"

"Some don't," the rabbi admitted. "The Naturei Carta, a sect on the extreme fringe, don't even recognize the state. But there are only a few hundred of them. Their reason is that it represents an interference with what they regard as God's will. From their point of view, the Jews should return to the Holy Land only when God indicates, presumably when He sends the Messiah. So it is presumptuous to set up a state when He has not yet indicated that it is time. There are other Orthodox Jews who hold similar views, but they are now reconciled to the idea of statehood. Nevertheless, the extremists tend to exercise a strong influence on all the religious parties far out of proportion to their numbers. Extremists always do."

"Are they the Chassidim?" asked Aaron.

"They're the ones with the fur hats, aren't they?" asked Joan.

"They don't wear them all the time," said the rabbi, "only on the Sabbath and on holidays. They are a splinter group, or more properly several groups under an umbrella that might be called the Chassidic movement, which is Orthodox and highly observant."

"I thought they were just those who were most observant," said Aaron. "When my grandfather used the term *chassid*, it was to denote someone who observed every little regulation. He'd refer to someone as a 'regular *chassid*' as though he were a saint or something. Sometimes he'd use the term sarcastically to denote the opposite."

"It does have that meaning as a common noun. But nowadays it refers to someone who is a member of a sect that was founded in the eighteenth century. You remember I said that study is a religious obligation with us, one of the most important. Well, that can be overdone, too. And at the time Torah and Talmud study had become a highly involved, not to say pedantic, exercise which had the effect of excluding the great mass of simple folk. To aggravate the situation, the idea developed that these unlearned were therefore not engaged in the full worship of God. In effect, in the heavenly kingdom they were second-class citizens."

"Like the difference between the laity and the clergy in the Middle Ages?" Joan suggested.

"A little like that, although the similarity never occurred to me. Well, anyway, a religious leader came forward, the Baal Shem Tov, which means 'master of the good name,' who preached that God was to be found not only in the synagogue and the yeshiva, but everywhere—in the fields and the forest and the highway. And one could worship Him not only by pedantic study of the Talmud, but in joy and gladness by singing and dancing and eating and drinking. Soon he gathered

137

around him a number of followers, Chassidim, and aroused the enthusiasm of thousands throughout Russia and Poland. He was regarded as a saint and miracle worker by his simple, unsophisticated followers. It was assumed that he had special contact with the Almighty, and that his prayers had special power. In time this attitude was applied to each of his pupils, all of whom were assumed to have acquired this special power. Moreover, it was thought that this power was transmitted to their male descendants. So a number of dynasties were developed, each consisting of the descendants in the male line of one of the pupils of Baal Shem Tov. Some of them, perhaps most of them, were learned men and were officially ordained rabbis. But many were not. And some were indeed saintly men, but some were out-and-out rascals who were supported, and that lavishly, by the Chassidim of their dynasty on the assumption that as descendants of one of the pupils of Baal Shem Tov they had inherited the spiritual power and authority of their illustrious ancestor. The Chassidic leader, the Zadek, that is, the Saint, was called 'rebbe' rather than 'rav,' which is the title of the ordained rabbi. But even those who were officially ordained rabbis usually didn't function as such. That is, they did not advise on legal matters or sit in judgment in legal cases. The advice they dispensed was usually on personal or family matters. In other words, they went in for what we now call counseling. They also taught a special interpretation of the Scriptures, usually from a mystical point of view, for they were heavily involved in mysticism and the Kabbala, the esoteric interpretations of Judaism current in the Middle Ages."

Aaron drawled, "Somehow, Rabbi, I get the idea that you don't approve of the Chassidic movement."

"I don't," said Rabbi Small. "I am not unmindful of its service in freeing us from a slavish devotion to dryasdust scholarship and the hope it gave a downcast and depressed people living in great poverty and in constant fear of the hatred and prejudice surrounding them. Nevertheless, I feel that it is contrary to the basic

Jewish tradition. Although the saintly character is common in our history, we have no room for saints as such. The respect and devotion and awe that surround the rebbe transcend that which we accord even to Moses. Judaism has no place for the kind of authority that the rebbe exercises over his followers by virtue of his birth. And if you say that he is not responsible for the superstitious regard of his Chassidim, I can only say that since they are so obedient to his wishes, he could stop it by simply telling them that he disapproved."

"This superstitious regard, how does it manifest itself?" asked Aaron.

The rabbi looked off into the distance. "I told you about the man who went to the rebbe because he was childless."

"Oh, yeah. And the rebbe told him to go home and check the mezuzah. I remember."

"Well, here's another. In Israel I met a man from Australia. He had an unmistakable Brooklyn accent, however, and I remarked on it. He admitted that he was from Brooklyn originally, but when he lost his job he went to see his rebbe, who told him to go to Australia. 'So I went, and I prospered almost immediately.' I questioned him closely. Did he discuss it with the rebbe? Did the rebbe explain what he could do in Australia that he couldn't do in America? No, the rebbe simply told him, 'Go to Australia.' He didn't question the rebbe; he didn't ask anyone else for advice. He just obeyed."

"That's really something," Aaron commented.

"At the festive gatherings they hold regularly, the Chassidim struggle with one another and scramble for the *sheraim*, the remainders, the scraps from the rebbe's plate, not because they are famished, but because his leavings are regarded as holy." The rabbi laughed. "The Chassidim of the famed Nachman of Bratislava did not install another Zadek when he died because they felt that no one could take his place. They kept his chair in their synagogue, however. I understand that recently they managed to smuggle it out of Russia, piece by piece, and reassemble it in Israel, where it now stands, roped off, in their synagogue in Jerusalem, like the chair of Mary Baker Eddy in the Christian Science Mother Church in Boston."

"Wow! But if Judaism is as rational as you say, how does it tolerate Chassidism?" asked Aaron.

"Good question," said the rabbi. "I suppose in part because the movement has changed. What began as a reaction to pedantic scholarship and meticulous observance of the regulations, both beyond the capacity of the ordinary people, is now most ardent in the espousal of this same kind of scholarship and the observance of every jot and tittle of the rules. So, because they are devout in the observance of the externals, there is a tendency to assume their adherence to the basics. But most of all, since ours is not a creedal religion and we have no hierarchy, who is to say that they are wrong?"

"I suppose. But on the other hand you've got to admit that they've brought a lot of young people back to Judaism, many of them alienated kids who had been involved with drugs. I should think that would count for a lot with you, Rabbi," said Aaron.

The rabbi nodded. "Yes, I know. But I've heard the same claim made for Synanon, and the Reverend Moon, and Hare Krishna, and a host of other sects that have proliferated over the country. The parents of these youngsters have come to me for counseling—counseling? Huh—more for support and approval."

"They expect you to approve their kids' joining the Hare Krishna movement?" Aaron asked, incredulous.

"Uh-huh. Their children were involved with drugs and casual sex. Perhaps they were in trouble with the police. And now they are in some kind of religious movement. The parents are bewildered and distressed, and what they hope for from me is assurance. Don't I think it's a good thing because they live regular lives now and are off drugs? Isn't it an improvement? Doesn't it show that they are at last settling down? Sure, it's not our religion, but isn't an interest in religion in general, any religion, a good sign?"

"And what do you tell them?"

The rabbi spread his arms in despair. "What can I tell them? That I approve? Obviously not. I suggest that it is a good sign that their children are maintaining contact with them."

He smiled wanly. "It doesn't increase their regard for me. It's even worse when they come to tell me that their son has joined a Chassidic sect and is planning to go to Israel and spend the rest of his life in Talmudic study. They don't like it and they are uneasy, but they are certain I will approve, at least, and they will feel better for it."

"And do you?"

The rabbi shook his head. "No more than they do. It may be an improvement, but it's not a cure. It's not the appeal of the rational argumentation of the Talmud that draws them, but the mystic appeal of the rebbe, the guru, who knows all and can resolve all their doubts."

"You don't approve of mysticism at all?" Joan asked.

"It's dangerous," said the rabbi simply. "It takes the person out of the world. Whether the mystical state is achieved by asceticism, or special exercises, or drugs, the effect is to withdraw from the everyday world of one's fellow man in order to achieve a kind of ecstatic union with God. From what I've read, I have the feeling that the result is not that one merges with God so much as that one tends to absorb God into oneself and then to admire the thus enhanced ego. The glory of Judaism is that it is a rational religion, centered in this world, the real world we were born in and must live in.

"Mysticism also tends to slide off into magic. One constantly hears of the special powers of the mystic, of his power to withstand physical pain, his power to heal, his power to see into the future—magical powers. It is this magical aspect of mysticism that appeals to the disillusioned young. They want to know—they want to know everything. But not through the normal discipline of study and thought. That's too hard and takes too long. They want some magic that will give them an understanding of life and the universe all at once, instantly, intuitively. So they try drugs and fool around with Tarot cards and I Ching and other magical nonsense. And when they've had a bad trip or two, or when they begin to worry about the police or about the society they're involved in, they turn to the Eastern cults, to Zen Buddhism, or to Sufism, or to this guru, or that one. Then some of them come to Chassidism. The rebbe is another guru, although perhaps one more acceptable to their folks, who may feel that in coming back to their tradition, they have given up their former ways. They may tell themselves that they are happy as they spend long hours in Talmud study, just as they thought they were happy formerly when they spent long hours in Zen meditation."

"But how do you know they're not happy?" Aaron persisted.

"Because mysticism is usually escapism. It is the refuge of the defeated and the despairing. When life is bitter, or dull beyond endurance, without direction and without hope, one yearns for a superman, a savior, in whose service life will again have meaning. They attempt to transcend the real world of experience. They try to focus their minds on the universe, ultimate reality, the Godhead, because from that dizzy eminence the worst evils are but scarcely noticeable irritations, as mountains when seen from an airplane seem to be mere wrinklings of the surface of the earth.

"But the whole thrust of Jewish tradition is against it. When we are subjected to pain and hardship, we resent it as Job resented his sufferings. We do not accept it as our fate, Kismet, as does the Muslim. Nor do we delude ourselves that we will be compensated in another world as does the Christian. And we certainly do not pretend as does the Christian Scientist that the pain itself is a delusion and does not exist. Nor yet do we attempt to cultivate a mental serenity that will minimize the awareness of the pain as do the adepts of the Eastern religions. No, we face reality. We recognize pain and suffering and evil for what they are, and we resist them and try to improve or change things in order to eliminate them."

"Well, I guess that's the attitude of most people these days," said Joan, "regardless of the doctrines of their respective religions."

The rabbi smiled. "True, but there's one other thing that is basic to Judaism. If the suffering was caused by men in power and authority, we try to remember how it felt so as not to inflict it on others when we have the power and authority. That's the lesson of the Passover."

"How about the Arabs in Israel?" asked Aaron.

"That's a good example of it," the rabbi replied promptly. "Those who are citizens have equal rights with the Jewish citizens, except that they are not subject to the army draft. Although one sect, the Druse, serve in the army, and in the recent wars served with distinction."

"And how about those in the occupied territories?"

"There, too. If there ever was a more considerate, more reasonable, less repressive occupation, I can't think of it."

"The Arabs don't agree," Aaron remarked dryly.

"I wonder. I'm inclined to believe that much of the trouble in the occupied areas is due to the unusually kind and decent treatment given them. It is so at variance with what they expected and what they would normally have received from their fellow Arabs in similar circumstances that they can't understand it and assume it must be a sign of weakness in the occupying authority."

"How about the American occupation in Japan and Germany?" suggested Joan.

"Ah, but those countries had surrendered and signed a peace treaty. In theory the people of the occupied territories are still at war with Israel and—" He stopped, sensing another presence.

An old man with a cane, but nattily dressed in a

chocolate brown leisure suit, had stopped in front of the cottage and was looking at them curiously. But it was evidently only to catch his breath. He waved to the three on the porch and continued on his way.

CHAPTER

9

"This Oral Law you keep referring to, it isn't really oral, is it?" asked Aaron. "I mean, it's not handed down by word of mouth, surely?"

"At one time it was," said the rabbi. "According to the tradition, and the Orthodox still accept it, when Moses came down from Mount Sinai, he had the complete Law. The general principles were written out by Moses, and that constituted the Written Law, the Bible, or that portion of it which is called the Books of Moses, or the Pentateuch. But again according to the tradition, God also told him just how these principles were to be carried out, and these were not written down, but were passed on by word of mouth. And this is the Oral Law. Of course, the likelihood is that the Oral Law was the body of customs of the people which had developed over the years. And they were not written down because presumably they were the common practice and everyone knew them. Eventually, about the third century of the Common Era they were codified in what we call the Mishna. The process was something like the rules of etiquette which were transmitted by parents to their children by word of mouth or by example until eventually someone like Emily Post thought to write them down and publish them in book form. Of course, the Mishna was more than just the manners and customs of the people. It embodied our whole system of jurisprudence for one thing. Naturally there were disagreements, and even in matters of liturgical procedure there were differences of opinion. Interestingly, the Mishna, unlike most law codes, gives both sides of the argument.

"Well, no sooner was it compiled than it became the subject of study, analysis, commentary, and debate. These, in turn, were codified as the Gemarah around the sixth century. The two together constitute the Talmud. Here, too, not only were both sides of the argument given, but there was also a lot of extraneous material in the form of legends, fables, parables."

"Like those that Jesus used?" suggested Joan.

"Precisely. So we have in the Talmud the Halacha, which means 'the way to walk,' which is the debates and discussions on the rules, regulations, and laws, and the rest we call the Aggadah, which means 'narration.' This codification of material in the Talmud did not close the book by any means. It has gone on in the form of numerous writings—analytical, argumentative—in the form of scholarly treatises, and particularly in the form of what we call Responsa, which are answers to letters written by various individuals to famous scholars asking for an interpretation of a regulation, usually governing some specific community problem. Those have continued."

"You mean it's still going on?"

"Responsa? Oh, yes, and the study of the Talmud is still going on, of necessity, when you think about it. The assumption is that since it is presumably the word of God, it continues to be valid. To go back to that broadcasting station idea, think of a message garbled

146

by static. Naturally it is subjected to study and analysis, and various attempts are made to fill in the blank spaces. Is it surprising that the original evidence should be studied by generation after generation when it is believed that it contains directions for every aspect of life? The records and pictures of Mars and Venus sent back by the rocket will be studied endlessly, perhaps until we finally land survey teams who will be able to make inspections on the ground."

"I see what you mean."

The rabbi smiled at Joan. "The sages who were engaged in the study of the Law, starting from a couple of centuries before the Common Era, were the Scribes and Pharisees who are referred to in the New Testament."

"How did they get the reputation of being hypocrites?" asked Aaron.

"They didn't with us. That's a Christian idea."

"All right, so where did the Christians get it?"

"They didn't so much get it as cause it," said the rabbi.

"Why would they do that?"

"Well, the Church as we know it is essentially Pauline rather than Christian—"

"You mean St. Paul?" asked Joan.

"That's right, Saul of Tarsus, who changed his name to Paul, and who changed the orientation of the movement from the Jews to the Gentiles. Jesus, himself, and his disciples were, of course, Jews and remained Jews. Zealous Jews. You might even call them chauvinist Jews."

"Chauvinist?"

"Sure. Not only did Jesus insist that the Law of Moses was to be obeyed in the smallest detail, but when a Canaanite woman came to him asking that he cure her daughter, he spurned her because she was not Jewish, saying that he had been sent only to the people of Israel and that it was not right to take the children's food and throw it to the dogs. That, I submit, is chau-

147

vinism, especially when you consider that it was contrary to normal Jewish doctrine.

"After the death of Jesus, the movement with headquarters in Jerusalem continued under the supervision of his brother James and Peter. It was a Jewish movement, and whatever proselytizing was done was directed toward the Jews. Some thirty-five years later, Paul came along. Although born a Jew, he evidently opted out. I presume that was the significance of his changing his name from the Jewish Saul to the Roman Paul. Now, *his* activities were primarily directed to the Gentiles, and his teaching was frequently contrary to the Mosaic law. In fact, he urged Jews to give up their adherence to such basic religious practices as circumcision, the observance of the Sabbath, and the laws of *kashruth*."

"Did the Christians back in Jerusalem go along?" asked Aaron.

"Not at all. There was controversy, and eventually a split. The gentile Christian Church that Paul had started became *the* Christian Church, and the Jewish segment finally disintegrated and disappeared. The sayings of Jesus in Aramaic, the language he and his disciples spoke, were translated, edited, amended, and when they were eventually published in Greek as the Gospels several hundred years later, the Church was completely gentile and the original anti-Jewish bias of Paul became established as the official attitude, and has remained so down to the present."

"Let me get this straight," Aaron interjected. "Are you saying that the whole thing was a ghastly mistake? That Jesus didn't start anything new or different? That he didn't think he was the son of God or the Messiah or whatever? That in his own time back then, his followers didn't think he was divine and rose from the dead?"

The rabbi pursed his lips as he took thought. Then he said, "We know the historical figure of Jesus only through the Gospels written several centuries after his death, so we can't tell what his own perception of himself and his mission was. But even in the Gospels we see a difference between the Jesus at the beginning of his ministry and the Jesus near the end of his ministry and his life. You must realize that Israel was under Roman domination and it was a time of great trouble and misery. As frequently happens in such times, people yearn for a miracle, some magic that will reverse the situation, perhaps a superman to come and take charge. There is something of the sort going on right now, although the problem is not with an external enemy so much as with a malaise caused by modern technology. Consider the popularity of Superman, and Batman, and Wonder Woman, and all the rest. Of science fiction in general. And the sudden interest in mysticism, in various mystical religions, in the mystical turn that some of the established religions have taken. Think of the new psychologies that have sprung up, and the new messiahs, each with a band of true believers whose faith is such that they are willing to surrender their fortunes, their former lifestyles, their very lives for him. Recently we have seen a whole community undergo mass suicide at one man's behest.

"I suppost these movements are apt to coincide with shifts in the established religion, and that was happening in Israel at the time, too. The religion was shifting from a temple cult, presided over by a professional priesthood, to a more democratic form centered in the synagogue under the influence of the scholars, those same Scribes and Pharisees. The temple-oriented group, the Sadducees, were the rich and the powerful, the establishment, who tended to cooperate with the Roman authorities occupying the country. The Pharisees were anti-Rome and intensely nationalistic. Whereas the Sadducees wanted to keep control of the religion in their own hands, and keep it a religion of ritual and animal sacrifice, the Pharisees were in the process of converting it to a religion of study and prayer in which all would participate. The two parties disagreed on various matters of ritual, but the most important difference was that the Sadducees either downgraded or refused to accept the Oral Law, whereas the Pharisees gave it almost the status of the Written Law. Now since the Pharisees tended to be highly observant, the natural result of working out precisely how each commandment was to be obeyed, I can see how a Sadducee might call them hypocrites, because that epithet for the more observant comes naturally to the lips of the less observant. But Jesus was certainly no Sadducee."

"What was he?" asked Joan.

"He may have been of the radical wing of the Pharisees. His arguments with the sages in the synagogue were in the Pharisaic tradition. He may also have been one of the Essenes, an ascetic, mystical sect that probably had close relations with the Qumran Cave people. We don't know too much about the Essenes, except that they were an extreme religious group who may have practiced an ascetic and communal way of living. There is some evidence that they were celibate, which may account for the fact that Jesus, although thirty years old when he came on the scene, was not married, which was most unusual at the time."

He paused as he considered how best to make them understand the situation. Then he said, "Think of the modern political spectrum. The Communists level most of their attacks not against the Right, but against the Socialists who are also on the Left. Similarly, Jesus did not attack the Sadducees, who were the establishment, but the Pharisees, who were also anti-establishment. You would think that parties of the Left would make common cause against the Right, and I suppose sometimes they do, but more often they are most bitter toward the party most like them. That peculiar psychological quirk may also help to explain the greater antagonism which the Church has displayed over the years to the Jew than to the Muslim, the Hindu, or the pagan for that matter."

"I thought you said the Pharisees were the establishment," Joan objected.

"I did. And they were, but it was after the Sadducees had lost power."

"Then you're saying that the position of Jesus was the same as that of the Pharisees?" said Aaron. "Except that he thought they didn't go far enough? But wasn't there anything different in his doctrine?"

"Oh, sure. The point is that the Pharisees were engaged in working out rules, carefully defined procedures, which if followed would ensure that God's commandments were carried out. These, like the commandments themselves, were rules to live by in this world. But Jesus was concerned not with specific actions, but with how men thought. In the modern phrase, what mattered was if their hearts were in the right place. Then he was willing to overlook infractions of the rules. That's what he meant when he said, 'It is not what goes into a person's mouth that makes him ritually unclean; rather what comes out of it.'"

"But didn't he mean that the spirit was more important than the letter?" asked Joan. "And if the Pharisees were concerned about the letter, he might consider them hypocrites because they might be flouting the spirit that the letter stood for."

"Good point," the rabbi admitted. "But let me get a copy of the New Testament so that we can see the whole passage."

He went into the cabin and reappeared a moment later, shuffling pages as he returned to his seat. "Ah, here it is. It's in Matthew and also in Mark. I see I quoted the original line correctly. Then his disciples ask him what it means and he says, 'Don't you understand? Anything that goes into a person's mouth goes into his stomach and then on out of his body. But the things that come out of the mouth come from the heart, and these are the things that make a person ritually unclean. For from his heart come the evil ideas which lead him to kill, commit adultery, and do other immoral things, to rob, lie, and slander others. These are the things that make a person unclean. But to eat without washing the hands as they say you should—this doesn't make a person unclean.' End of quote."

"But that seems to do away with all the food taboos,"

Aaron objected, "and those are in the Bible, aren't they? I mean, they're in the Written Law. They're not interpretations of the sages."

"Uh-huh. On the other hand he said"—again the rabbi flipped pages—"'Do not think that I have come to do away with the Law of Moses and the teachings of the prophets, but to make their teachings come true. Remember that as long as heaven and earth last, not the least point nor the smallest detail of the Law will be done away with, not until the end of all things.'"

"But that's in flat contradiction of the other," said Aaron. "Did he change or—"

"I don't think so," said the rabbi, "if you're thinking of the gradual evolution of a philosophy. There wasn't time for one thing. His life as an itinerant preacher was only about three years. I think that seeming contradiction was due to two things. One, that he spoke extemporaneously to crowds. His sermons were not carefully prepared texts stating his position. He would begin talking, and as the crowd responded, he would get caught up in his own rhetoric and pile it on, so to speak. It's a common phenomenon in public speaking. That would explain some of the extreme things he says in the Sermon on the Mount, like being guilty of adultery if you see a woman and want to possess her. And plucking out your right eye if it causes you to sin, that is, by looking at the woman. And loving your enemies. And not worrying about the food and drink you need to stay alive because if God takes care of the birds, He will certainly take care of you. Well, now, all that is rhetoric."

"Why is it rhetoric?" Joan challenged.

"Because it obviously can't be intended as practical instruction. What good would it do? You could still see out of the left eye and lust just as sinfully. And birds that make no provision for food and drink aren't taken care of by God; they die."

"Oh, all right. And what's the second?"

"The second?"

"Yes, you said there were two reasons for the contradiction between what he said about the Law of Moses and what he said in the Sermon on the Mount. One was rhetoric, and the other?"

"Oh, yes. Well, the other I think was that Jesus believed that the end of the world was indeed imminent. The times were out of joint. Gog and Magog were in the ascendant and Armageddon just around the corner. Conditions were ripe, as they usually are, according to various prophecies, for the world's destruction. The idea that the world was soon coming to an end because of its immorality has been a common concept throughout history. In the last century, the Millerites sold all their possessions, and dressed in white sheets and ascended a hill—right here in America—to await the end of the world and their own elevation to heaven. The modern evangelical preachers whom I hear on TV refer to it constantly. In the passage I quoted, you remember, Jesus said that the Law of Moses would apply 'until the end of all things.' From that point of view, from the assumption that the end of the world was likely to occur soon, the Sermon on the Mount makes even practical sense. Not worrying about the future is eminently practical if there is no future. You might say that whereas Pharisaic Judaism is a religion for living, Christianity is a religion for dying—understandable if you think of this world as only a temporary stopover on the way to the real world, the world to come."

"Do you believe Jesus was sincere, though?" asked Joan.

"Oh, yes, I think so. He was aware that he was preaching a new doctrine and he probably regarded it as an inspiration from God."

"And when he began thinking of himself as the Messiah and the son of God?" asked Aaron.

"He did not claim to be either at first. He referred to himself as the Son of Man. But then he asks Simon what he thinks, and when the answer is 'You are the Messiah, the son of God,' Jesus accepts the nomination, as it were, but cautions his disciples not to tell anyone."

"But the son of God!"

153

"Well, the concept of man as god was not so unusual in those days. The Roman emperors made the claim almost as a matter of course, and there is every reason to believe that the great mass of people of the time accepted it as reasonable. Only a few years ago, there was a cult leader in America called Father Divine whose followers thought he was a god."

"But look here," said Aaron, "wasn't the Messiah supposed to be just a man according to Jewish tradition? So how could the disciples think of him as both the Messiah and the son of God?"

"I suppose because fine distinctions, especially in the realm of the supernatural, or of theology, are made by trained, sophisticated minds. The Pharisaic rabbis evolved the idea of the Messiah as a man. But simple folk—and the disciples were all humble, uneducated people—were apt to confuse heroes with supermen and gods. When Jesus first asked them, 'Who do people say I am?' they answered, 'Some say John the Baptist. Others say Elijah, or Jeremiah, or some other prophet.' Which would seem to indicate that they had no clear idea of what form the supernatural or the superhuman might take. So here we have a young man in his early thirties who has in the space of a year or two become what we would now call a celebrity. Large numbers come to hear him when he talks, and he is able to cure the sick, the lame, and the blind."

"You believe he really effected all those cures?" asked Aaron.

"Oh, it's quite likely. We don't regard them as miraculous these days because we know about hysteria and functional disorders and the psychosomatic nature of many diseases. But in those days it would certainly have been regarded as miraculous."

"How about those he raised from the dead?" asked Joan.

"With all the controversy these days over pulling the plug, we know that it's not so easy to determine when someone *is* dead. In any case, his effect on large crowds and the occasional incidents of healing the sick made

154

it clear to his disciples that he was not an ordinary young man of thirty, and it's quite obvious from his general style that he, too, was aware that he was someone special. Once it was suggested that he might be the Messiah, he might very well have come to believe it, like the celebrity who believes his own press notices. Yes, I think he was sincere."

"But his death," said Joan, "that seems to have been willingly accepted by him. Why would he if he really thought he was the Messiah, or the son of God?"

The rabbi nodded. "Well, in many of the mythologies and religions of the time, the death of the god was a common belief. It was used as a means of explaining the seeming death of the world in the winter and its revitalization in the spring. It was the central theme of the Eleusinian mysteries, for example.

"Even if you are convinced you are a god, though, there is always somewhere in your mind the knowledge that you are only human with the normal human limitations. A pebble in your shoe will bring it home to you. So while with one part of your mind you are certain that you can summon the hosts of heaven to your aid with a flick of a finger, another part of your mind knows very well that you can't. In the matter of dying, however, the tradition of the death and resurrection cycle is sustaining, especially if one goes willingly, at least until the very end, when one finally realizes the awful truth and cries out, 'My God, why have you forsaken me?'"

"But how about his appearance afterward?" asked Joan.

The rabbi shrugged. "Well, of course, that was necessary, or the whole story collapses. That is, if there had been no appearance after the death, then even the events of his life would have been subject to doubt and question. The basic difference between men and gods is that gods don't die and men do. But the death of Jesus had been witnessed and no doubt recorded. The Romans were meticulous about records. So it had to be shown that the death was not a real death but rather a transfiguration."

"You mean that the disciples just made it up?" Joan asked.

"No-o. But if you have invested so much of your intellectual and emotional life in an idea, it's hard to give it up when it appears you have been mistaken. When you hear a rumor that tends to confirm your original belief, you are inclined to accept it because you want to."

"Yeah, but why was it all necessary in the first place?" Aaron asked. "I mean, what was supposed to be God's justification for having him die, especially if he was going to be resurrected afterward? For that matter, why would He have him born in the first place?"

"Why, he came to save," Joan said. "That's why he's called the Savior."

"To save whom, and from what?" Aaron demanded.

"To save the world, mankind. Because Adam sinned when he ate the apple. So all his descendants are born in sin. Isn't that right, Rabbi?"

"M-hm. 'In Adam's fall, we sinned all' is the way the old rhyme has it. So sinning man could be restored to grace only by the supreme sacrifice of Jesus. In effect the Church accepted the story in Genesis of Adam and Eve and the forbidden fruit as historical fact. That's why it was so hard for the Church to accept Darwinism. Obviously, if man gradually evolved from some other species, there was no Adam, no Eve, and no Tree of Knowledge, and the foundation of Christian theology was badly undercut."

"And how is it for the Jews?" asked Joan.

"Oh, our religion is grounded primarily in the commandments. The stories of Adam and Eve we regard as myth and fable, serving perhaps to explain death. Of course, nowadays all but the most fundamentalist Christians also interpret the story symbolically. The modern rationale for Christ is that he is necessary as an intermediary between finite man and an infinite

156

God. We Jews have never felt that need." He smiled. "Maybe because He made a Covenant with us."

"How do you account for the phenomenal success of Christianity?" asked Aaron.

The rabbi spread his arms wide. "How can one tell what ideas will suddenly take hold and sweep a nation or the world? Think of the spread of Marxism. Or for that matter, think of the spread of other religions like Islam and Buddhism."

"But not Judaism," Aaron interjected.

"No, not Judaism," the rabbi agreed. "As I said, it's hard to be a Jew."

"You mean because of anti-Semitism?" asked Joan.

"No. I was thinking that it is psychologically hard. The virtuous Muslim, when he dies, goes to Paradise; the Buddhist assumes he will be reincarnated at a higher level; the Christian goes to heaven. When the virtuous Jew dies, he just dies. As for the Christian's misdeeds, there is the comforting feeling that his faith will secure absolution for him. If he is a Catholic, he can also count on the prayers and the accumulation of grace of the entire church. He receives the benefit of the pleadings and good offices of Mary and all the saints. And in any case, one appears for judgment not before some remote, ineffable being, of a grandeur and power beyond imagination, but before His son who lived on earth and knows at first hand the temptations to which men are susceptible. What else? For the evangelical Christian even the trials and tribulations of this imperfect and unhappy world, the pain and the sickness that flesh is heir to, can be mitigated or removed entirely if one's faith is strong enough. It's a hard combination to beat—an all-inclusive insurance policy for the price of faith." He smiled wistfully. "Too bad I can't buy it."

"Why do you say that Jews don't have a creed?" asked Joan. "It's just a statement of what you believe, isn't it? And there are definite things you believe in, aren't there?"

"Well, yes, of course. But a creed is something more. It is binding on the adherents of the sect. In fact, it is by virtue of the acceptance of the creed that one is a member of the sect. We don't have anything like that. With us, it's not so much what you think as what you do. In one Midrash, or homily, for example, God is imagined as saying, 'Would that they abandoned Me, but observed My commandments.' The prophet says, 'What does the Lord require of you but to deal justly and walk in His way,' which suggests that we are concerned with actions rather than protestations of belief. Nevertheless, from time to time our sages have tried to embody the essence of our religion in a statement of principles. The best known are the Thirteen Articles of Faith of the Rambam—"

"Rambam? Is that a title or a name?" asked Joan.

The rabbi laughed. "It's a proper name, one of those abbreviations I think I told you about. It stands for Rabbi Moses Ben Maimon, sometimes known as Maimonides, a twelfth-century philosopher."

"Oh, yes, like Katz."

The rabbi smiled approvingly. "That's right. Well, anyway, those articles of faith were even incorporated in some prayer books, but there is and was considerable disagreement on them, and in any case, they weren't binding."

"What's wrong with them?" asked Aaron.

"Well, there are certain specific articles on which there is disagreement, but I guess mostly it's the general idea of setting down a list of beliefs rather than actions. We're not too comfortable with the comparatively few commandments that can be transgressed by thought."

"Like what?"

"Well, the commandment 'Thou shalt not covet' for one. The thought comes into the mind unbidden; it is not an act of the will. The sages had difficulty interpreting that one, and for the most part they waffled. Another is 'Thou shalt love thy neighbor as thyself.' They debated that one at length. How can one? How is it psychologically possible to love one's neighbor as oneself? The hypothetical question was posed: if two companions were walking in the desert, and one had only enough water to save the life of one, and the other had none, what should the first do? One rabbi held that in keeping with the commandment he should share the water and they should both perish."

"That doesn't make too much sense to me," Aaron remarked.

"No more did it to most of the sages," the rabbi agreed. "In addition to which it would mean that the one accepting the water would be breaking the commandment. In general, the Jewish attitude was best expressed by the great sage Hillel. When a potential convert asked him for the essence of Jewish ethics, he said, 'Do not do unto others what you would not have them do unto you. The rest is commentary. Go and study.' That's frequently referred to as Hillel's Golden Rule. It has the merit of being a realizable goal."

"You know, that's not bad," said Aaron admiringly. "That's not bad at all."

"But it's merely the negative of the other," Joan protested.

"Sure, but that makes it a principle you can live with."

"But if it's the same thing—"

"But it isn't," Aaron insisted. "Take a millionaire. I'd like him to give me half his earnings. That's what I'd like to have done unto me. But I couldn't do unto someone else in the same way. If I gave someone half my earnings, I wouldn't have enough left to live on. Anything I did for someone else would give me no satisfaction, because I'd realize it was always less than what I'd like someone to do for me. All I'd get for my pains would be guilt feelings. My guess is that after a while I'd say to hell with it. By putting it in the negative, this guy Hillel changed the focus to something I can accept because I can follow it. What he says in effect is because I don't want you to bother me, I won't bother you. I go along with that. He strikes me as a smart man."

"He *was* a smart man," said the rabbi, "and he said many wise things. One was 'If I am not for myself, who will be for me? And if only for myself, what am I?' Another was 'Don't think too poorly of yourself, for there are none who are without sin.'"

"That's pretty modern psychology," Joan admitted. "This Hillel—I knew a boy once by that name—was he a philosopher?"

"Not in the sense that Plato was, or Aristotle. Unlike their Greek contemporaries, the Jewish scholars were not too concerned with such things as the nature of ultimate reality."

"Why not?" Aaron demanded.

The rabbi hesitated. "I suppose it's because a people, or their wise men, tend to focus their thinking on what concerns them most. The Jewish sages had no interest in these questions because they felt they already knew the answer: it was the one God. He had given them commandments on how to conduct themselves and it was important to understand them. So their intellectual concern was mainly ethical and legal, just as that of the Christian sages was mainly theological. Hillel, like his colleagues, was a student of jurisprudence, engaged in amplifying the basic commandments into the specific regulations which would control man's conduct from day to day. Most were derived from a few fundamental concepts that govern our thinking."

"What concepts?" asked Joan.

"That the one God who created the universe was a God of justice; that He endowed us with mind and will so that we can choose freely between good and evil; that He taught us the extreme importance of freedom by taking us out of slavery in Egypt. Practically all of our laws as well as our code of ethics are grounded in those few concepts. Take our labor laws—"

"Labor laws? They had them in those days?" asked Aaron.

"Of course. And they were as advanced as any modern labor code. For instance, the laborer could stop work at any time as an expression of freedom from servitude to his fellow man."

"Well, I guess that's implicit in labor law everywhere."

"Is it? How about the totalitarian countries? Does a laborer in Russia have the right to drop his tools and walk away from the job in the middle of the day if he chooses? And how about the logical extensions of the principle?"

"What extensions?"

"The rabbis held that inasmuch as each laborer had the right to stop work whenever he wanted to, and since they all had minds and wills, they could come to an

161

agreement and all stop work at the same time. In other words, they could form unions and strike. How long is it that labor has had that right even in the democracies?"

"Okay, that's pretty modern, I guess."

"What's more," the rabbi went on, "his wages and his hours of work had to conform to local custom. The employer could not take advantage of a surplus of labor to pay less than the going rate, or to require his employees to work longer hours. And he had to pay them in money, not in kind. None of this business of 'I owe my soul to the company store.' If he were a day laborer, he had to be paid that day, before the sun set, because according to the rabbis, 'He is needy and depends on it. Else he will cry out to the Lord against you and you will incur guilt.' The implication is that the Lord is a God of justice who will see that justice is done."

"Yes, that seems pretty progressive for the time," Aaron admitted.

"Why do you say for the time? How about these times?"

"Well, we've got the forty-hour week and we've got a minimum-wage law, so rabbinic law or biblical law, or whatever it is, is no more advanced than ours in that respect," said Aaron. He hesitated and appeared troubled. "On the other hand, I'm not so sure that the migratory farm workers are covered by our labor legislation. And it seems to me that in some parts of the country the company store is still operating. Is there anything else?"

"Oh, sure. The employer could not change the nature of the work for which he had hired the laborer. If he hired him by the day for a specific job, and work was finished early, he could give him additional work, but it could not be more difficult than that for which he had been hired originally."

"Well..."

"Oh, Aaron, the strike at the turbine plant in Lynn last year took place because the company ordered the drill operators to do work that was different from what they had been doing," Joan pointed out.

"That was something else," said Aaron. "The men went out on strike because they claimed the time and motion people had not allowed enough time for the new job. They were on piecework so they felt they wouldn't be able to make as much as formerly."

"What's the difference? The principle is the same, isn't it, Rabbi?"

"I would say so. The contention of the workers in those cases is that they would have to work much harder on the new job to make the same salary they did on the old."

"I suppose," Aaron conceded. "Any other benefits for labor?"

"Sure. The rule was that although the master could discharge an employee because his work was inadequate, and even for reasons of immorality, nevertheless he could not discharge him because he could get someone who would work for less, or even for a better worker."

"And yet the employee could leave to go where the pay was higher?" Aaron said.

"That's right. Because he had the right to stop work at any time."

"But, gosh, on that basis the employer could suffer considerable loss," Aaron objected.

"Then he could bring suit against the employee," said the rabbi.

"The way the cards were stacked, he'd have a fat chance of winning though."

"Oh, I don't know. There's a biblical injunction that the judge must not lean in favor of the poor man over the rich man."

"You mean the other way around, don't you?" Joan asked.

"No. The point of the injunction is that justice must be evenhanded. It is expected that justice will be tempered with mercy, but first justice must be done. As it is, the law was weighted in favor of the employee. For example, in the case of a dispute between employer and employee as to whether the employee had been paid, the finding was for the employee if he gave an oath to that effect. Also, if he caused damage while working, he was not liable for it if he undertook to give an oath to the effect that it had not been intentional on his part."

Aaron nodded slowly. "That does seem pretty liberal. I don't think modern labor legislation goes that far. I'm not sure about the damage part, but it seems to me that a laborer who claimed he hadn't been paid would have to prove it."

The rabbi smiled. "I suspect that giving an oath was a much more solemn thing in those days. To give a false oath was to incur the wrath of the just God."

"If you believed in Him," Aaron observed.

"I guess more people did in those days," Joan said. "Didn't they, Rabbi?"

"I'm sure of it. Agnosticism and atheism are modern developments, functions of the scientific revolution."

"Well, naturally," said Aaron, "science offers an alternative. By the way, how much of all this labor law is still followed by observant Jews?"

"I don't know," said the rabbi, "because labor law these days is so complicated. The state has imposed all kinds of regulations that have been worked out in conjunction with labor unions and representatives of large corporations." He brightened. "But there's one Talmudic regulation that is still followed in Israel that is quite unusual. The Written Law required that a bondsman who was set free was to be given the wherewithal to earn a living, the tools of his trade perhaps. He was not just dismissed. His master was required to give him something to maintain himself for a while. Well, the rabbis felt that this same principle should apply to the free laborer. And to this day, severance pay, on the order of one month's pay for each year worked, is given the worker by his employer when he leaves. The point I'm making is that those laws and regulations are extrapolations of the basic principles I mentioned: a God of justice, free will, and freedom."

"But you spoke of bondsmen," said Joan. "Were they slaves? Did the Jews have slaves?"

"Slavery was normal to the period," the rabbi said. "The likelihood is that it played a very small part in the economy of the country."

"How do you know?" Aaron asked.

"Because there is so little reference to it in the literature of the period, for one thing. For another, slavery is usually a function of a large conquering empire, like Rome, where war produced numerous captives who then were enslaved. And Israel was not that even in its heyday under Solomon. And finally, the land itself was small and the economy consisted of small family holdings where slaves in large numbers were not economically feasible. There are indications, too, in the slave laws. A runaway slave could not be returned to his master. That in itself would tend to break down the system. Remember the Dred Scott decision? Also, a slave was to be treated kindly. If he suffered any permanent damage, the loss of an eye, or of a tooth, at the hands of his master, he was to be freed 'for his tooth's sake.' And again and again there are adjurations to treat the stranger kindly for 'you were a stranger in Egypt.' And finally, there was the law that he was to be freed during the Year of Jubilee, the fiftieth year which came after seven Sabbatic years."

"How about Jews?" asked Aaron. "Were there Jewish slaves?"

"Ah, that's something else again. That could hardly be called slavery since the Jewish bondsman was to be freed during the Sabbatic year, that is, every seventh year. So at the most he could serve only six years. And he was to be treated pretty much as a member of one's family. As one of the sages put it jokingly, 'He who acquires a bondsman, takes unto himself a master.' But so ingrained was the idea of liberty and freedom, that even this mild bondage was viewed with abhorrence. Occasionally, a bondsman did not want to be freed in the Sabbatic year. Then his master was supposed to drill a hole through his ear. And one of the sages suggested that instead of drilling the hole through his ear, it should be drilled in his head, so inconceivable was it to him that anyone would prefer bondage to freedom."

"You know, Rabbi," said Aaron, "there's something that puzzles me about all this."

"Yes?"

"I don't pretend to be much of a historian, but I've read some and I took a couple of courses in college. My general impression is that the laborer, the poor, the landless, didn't have very much in the way of rights, I mean legal rights, throughout most of the world. The only people with rights, that is, rights protected by law, were the upper crust. My impression is that up until practically modern times the ordinary laborer, even if he wasn't a slave or a helot or a serf, even if he was technically free but was just poor, was pretty much abused as a matter of course. Now are you telling me that things were different among the Jews?"

The rabbi considered for a moment and then said, "Being poor is never pleasant, anytime, anywhere. But, yes, there was and is a difference among Jews. I won't deny that the poor were frequently mistreated, because the main thrust of the diatribes of the prophets was against their mistreatment. On the other hand, it could be argued that this showed that they did not lack for spokesmen. But there were laws for the poor—"

"You mean those labor laws you just told us about?"

"No, in addition to those, laws for the poor, to give them food and sustenance."

"Oh, you mean charity," said Joan. "Christianity urges charity, too. You know, 'Faith, hope, and charity, and the greatest of these is charity.'"

"No, that's something else again," the rabbi said. "That kind of charity, giving out of the goodness of your heart, is urged by all religions. But we also have Tzedaka, which means 'righteousness,' and it is a *mitzvah*, that is, a commandment, and hence it is something one must do rather than merely what one ought to do. This gives it some of the connotation of a tax. The institution goes all the way back to biblical times and is the result of specific commandments in the Written Law amplified by interpretations in the Oral Law."

He gnawed at his lower lip as he wrestled with the problem of how to explain it to the young woman. "It's like this. When the Israelites settled in the Promised Land, the basic idea was that there should be no poor. The land was divided up equally so that everyone could maintain himself. Now of course it was realized that there is great inequality in character and ability between individuals, that while some are industrious, others are lazy, some are intelligent, and some are stupid. And it was realized that because of the inequality of ability as well as differences in luck, some might have to sell off their farms or their houses or portions of their land. To maintain the system, there was the law of the Sabbatic year. Every seventh year all property was returned to its original owner, all debts were canceled, and all bondsmen were freed. What's more, there was no planting that year; the land was allowed to lie fallow. The point is that poverty was considered intolerable and measures were taken to prevent it."

"And did it work?" asked Joan.

"Probably not even the first few years," said the rabbi promptly. "But there were other laws. The uncultivated crops of the fields and the vineyards of the Sabbatic year belonged"—he raised an admonishing finger and repeated for emphasis—"belonged to the poor. Every third year, a tenth of all one's harvest went to the poor. Every year, the produce of one corner of one's field was segregated for the poor, as were the gleanings of all fields and vineyards, the overlooked sheaves of grain and bunches of grapes, or those that had fallen while being harvested. These laws probably were kept. Remember the story of Ruth and Boaz? Now what is significant about these contributions to the poor is that they were not made out of the goodness of the donor's heart. They were not his to withhold, for 'the earth is the Lord's and the fullness thereof.' They belonged to the poor as a right, just as though they had deeds to that effect. Now, the attitude engendered by those laws is our general view of what you call charity."

"But you don't do it now. You don't return property or cancel debts on the seventh year nowadays, do you?"

"No, of course not. That system was possible only in a society of small farms. As soon as commerce developed, it was seen that the system could not be sustained, and all sorts of ingenious devices were developed to get around and nullify the law. But the attitude that the poor had a claim on society persisted."

"But how does it express itself?"

"It's hard to explain. Gentiles frequently say admiringly, even enviously, that we Jews take care of our own."

"Yes, I've heard that said."

"They are referring to our various social services, hospitals, homes for the aged, orphanages. Well, you don't suppose it is because we are naturally more generous than the rest of the population, do you? We have miserly people and generous in the same proportion as other peoples. The difference is that we don't merely ask for support for our charitable institutions; we insist on it."

"I don't understand. Do you tax people?"

"Hey, I can explain that," said Aaron surprisingly. "I was at my folks' house one Sunday last year, and a neighbor, a Mr. Goldstein, came over to collect for the Red Cross. My father wrote out a check and handed it to him. Goldstein didn't even look at it. He had a kit with envelopes and stickers that you put on your car, and little cardboard signs that you put in your window. He just checked my father's name off his list, inserted the check in an envelope, gave him a sticker and a cardboard sign, thanked him, and left. That was all there was to it. The whole business took maybe five minutes at the most."

"Well, of course," said Joan.

"Yeah, but listen to this. That same evening my father gets a call and it's from this same Goldstein. He wants to know if my father can see him. He's got him on his list for the UJA, the United Jewish Appeal. About an hour later he comes over, and he has another man with him, name of Shapiro. They take off their coats and come into the living room like they're planning to spend the evening. My father introduces me to Shapiro—I know Goldstein, of course—and he asks me what I do. I tell him, and we talk about colleges for a while. Mostly, how his daughter is worried about getting into a good college. Just like a regular social evening.

"But then they get down to business. Shapiro starts telling us about all the social services that are supported by the UJA, and about the special needs that each has. The home for the aged needs a new wing; the religious school needs a new bus because the old one is practically falling apart. And Goldstein chimes in that he's worried about the kids 'because that jalopy shouldn't even be allowed on the road.' I remember wondering if they took turns at it and if at the next stop Goldstein would do all the talking and Shapiro would occasionally add his two cents' worth. Anyway, after about half an hour of this, one of them says, 'So what shall we put you down for, Mr. Freed?'

"My father right away gets kind of wary. He asks casually what his contribution was last year. And when they tell him, he says all right to put him down for the same amount. Goldstein gives my father a hurt, sorrowful look and bleats, 'But Mr. Freed—' Shapiro, the talker, he's actually indignant, like he's been insulted. He becomes cold and formal and says, 'Mr. Freed, in these days of inflation and high fuel costs, we expect people to increase their last year's contribution by quite a bit. Our target is to get them to double their last year's pledge.' And Goldstein adds, 'That's right, Mr. Freed, that's what our projections show we're going to need.' So then my father points out that his costs have gone up, too, and how high interest rates are and how tough it is doing business with the banks these days. Well, they argued and they talked, and finally my father upped his pledge. When they left, I said, 'I don't understand, Dad, how you could let those two jokers talk you into giving more than you planned.' And he answered, 'You've got to, Aaron, you've got to.' Then he kind of smiled and said, 'Actually, I didn't do too badly. They hooked Bill Pasternak'—that's his partner—'into doubling his pledge.' I just couldn't understand it because my father is no pushover. But now, from what you said, Rabbi, I get the picture."

"What was your mother's reaction?" asked Joan.

Aaron laughed. "She wasn't there. She'd gone visiting, but my father told her when she returned. She told him he'd been had, but it was only to be expected since Goldstein was a professional *shnorrer*."

"*Shnorrer?*"

"The word means 'beggar,'" the rabbi explained. "In this case, since they were not asking for themselves, 'solicitor' would be a better translation. But even if it were for themselves, the term *beggar* does not really express the full flavor of the word *shnorrer*. The *shnorrer* frequently displays a kind of irrepressible cheek—our word is *chutspah*—"

"Oh, I know what that means," Joan exclaimed. "I heard it defined as the kind of nerve or gall that permits a man who is being tried for the murder of his parents to ask the court for leniency on the grounds that he is an orphan."

"Yes, that's the classic example," said the rabbi, smiling. "There are a number of mildly amusing stories which emphasize the *chutspah* of the *shnorrer*. The fact that the stories are in our tradition suggests a special attitude, that we admit that the poor and unfortunate have a claim on the community. The *shnorrer* is apt to be the victim of chronic hard luck of whom it is said, 'If he studied to be a shoemaker, children would be born without feet.' We feel responsible for them."

"But I don't see that it's so much different from the Christian attitude," said Joan. "Some Christian sects even require tithing."

"It's not quite the same," the rabbi insisted. "The

good Christian who tithes is responding to his feeling of a personal obligation to God by giving one tenth of his income to the church, which may indeed use it for helping the poor, or may use it to support foreign missions, or even to enlarge or improve church buildings. And if the minister or the committee of vestrymen decides to use the money for the last rather than for the first purpose, they can always justify it by the remark Jesus made that 'the poor you will always have with you.' He said that on the occasion when a woman poured a jar of expensive oil on his head and his disciples objected that it could have been sold and the money given to the poor. With us, the commitment is to the poor because they have a claim on us in accordance with the commandment which uses wording similar to that of Jesus, 'There will always be some who are poor and in need,' but it goes on to say, 'so I command you to be generous to them.'" He thought for a moment. "You know, it occurs to me that the difference between the two attitudes, the Christian and the Jewish, may be due in part at least to that Christian insurance policy we talked about. Where there is the feeling that the poor will receive just recompense for their sufferings in heaven, in the next life, there is no need to worry about them in this life."

He paused and pursed his lips as he considered. "There is considerable emphasis in Christianity on charity. And in Islam, too. Probably in most other religions as well. But the concern is with the giver. In Judaism it is with the recipient."

"I—I don't follow you, Rabbi," Joan said.

"Well, in reading the New Testament I get the feeling that charity is enjoined so that the donor may acquire merit or spiritual growth. And to some extent, so it is with us. But the emphasis with us is on the right of the recipient. Our law acknowledges the right of the recipient to what he receives. That's the significance of the law of the corner of the field and of the uncultivated crops of the Sabbatic year."

171

"You mean that there is a sense of his having been cheated out of it?" Aaron asked curiously.

"No-o. Because it did not come about through any act of the donor. It was due to circumstances, luck maybe. Nevertheless, we feel that the unfortunate have a claim, and in giving what you call charity, we are merely giving them their due." He grinned at Aaron and said, "That's a fine distinction for you, but as your own story of your father and the UJA shows, it is significant. Let's have some coffee."

CHAPTER

11

"With all this emphasis on law and justice," said Joan as she sipped her coffee, "isn't there any place for mercy and compassion in Judaism?"

"There are those labor laws, and the laws for the poor," Aaron pointed out.

"Yes, I know, but—I was thinking of—well, you know, between ordinary people. I imagine most societies have special arrangements for the poor." She tried again. "I guess what I'm getting at is, doesn't your religion say anything about having compassion for the weak, yielding to them, just because they are weak, if you know what I mean?"

The rabbi nodded. "I understand. Law consists of setting up lines of demarcation between right and wrong, proper and improper, lawful and unlawful. As I understand your question, is there anything in our religion which urges us or calls for us to bend those rules? Well, with us that kind of thing is built into the law. Or if the Bible gives us a general principle to that effect, the rabbis and sages tried to particularize it in regulations."

"Can you give us an example?"

"Sure. Take the law of Onaah, which says, 'Ye shall not wrong one another.' That was particularized to prevent overreaching, especially in the marketplace. It was established that one sixth constituted a fair profit, and that more than that was tantamount to fraud and could cancel the transaction."

"A sixth? Sixteen and two thirds percent?" said Aaron. "That's pretty slim, isn't it?"

"Perhaps by today's standards," the rabbi admitted. "But I don't suppose they had to figure on a high overhead in those days. In any case, it applied only if the seller concealed his margin of profit. If he stated it openly, the transaction was legal. It was also used against wounding someone's feelings, which was thought to be even worse than overreaching. An interesting extension of the principle was that it was regarded as wrong to price a merchant's wares if you had no intention of buying, since it raised his hopes only to dash them when you walked out of his shop. I always quote that one to Miriam whenever we're in town and she's attracted by something in a shop window. Not that it does me any good," he added ruefully. "She goes in anyway, and all too frequently buys."

"That's because she doesn't want to dash the merchant's hopes," said Joan.

"That's one way of looking at it. I'll have to keep it in mind in the future," said the rabbi with a grin. "Of course," he went on, "restraints or restrictions on profit margin in the marketplace are common in various societies. The point I wanted to make was that included in our law there was also some compassion for the merchant. I'll give you another example. In Talmudic law, as in common law, the finder of lost property is required to seek out the owner and return it. But in our law, while waiting for the property to be claimed, the finder was required to take whatever measures were necessary to keep the property from deteriorating. Procedures for different kinds of property were spelled out. For instance, if it was a parchment scroll that had been found, the finder had to unroll it every now and then to keep it from getting stiff and cracking."

"I wouldn't consider that compassion," said Aaron. "That's just carrying out that Golden Rule of Hillel you spoke of."

"Well, they do overlap," the rabbi admitted. "All right, consider this then. In Talmudic law, as in common law, when a man makes a will, it is binding on the heirs. The executor of the estate disburses it in accordance with the provisions in the four corners of the will, as it were. But in Talmudic law an exception is made if the will is drawn up when the testator is ill, more particularly if it is his last illness, in which case he may make changes orally, and these are binding on the executor and the heirs. The reason given for this exception to the general rule is 'that the testator may have peace of mind in his last days.'"

Aaron nodded. "I presume the oral instructions have to be given in the presence of competent witnesses."

"Of course."

"Well, it certainly is a nice touch. Can you think of any others?"

"There is the institution of contingency divorce," said the rabbi.

"Oh, that sounds interesting," said Joan. "Contingent on what? On whether they like each other? A kind of trial marriage?"

The rabbi smiled. "No, nothing like that. But when a man went to war or embarked on a long and hazardous journey, it was common for him to give his wife a *get*, a divorce. Then if he failed to return, or was missing in action, she could produce the divorce and was free to remarry instead of having to remain a grass widow because she couldn't prove he was dead."

"Are those procedures still followed?" asked Aaron. "I mean by the observant Jews?"

"Some of them are. There is one overriding principle,

however, referred to as Dina Malchuta Dina, which states that the law of the secular government under which we happen to be living takes precedence over Talmudic law when they are in conflict. The Jewish contingency divorce, or any Jewish divorce for that matter, would be useless to the woman if she could not obtain a secular divorce."

"But those, inheritance and divorce, they are sort of family matters," Joan objected.

"All right," said the rabbi. "Here's one that involves enemies. There is a commandment in the Bible which forbids cutting down the fruit trees of the enemy when laying siege to a city. Other trees could be cut down for the construction of the engines of war, but not fruit trees. That is to ensure a food supply to the enemy when the siege is over. By the way, the rabbis expanded that to forbid any senseless waste."

"Well, yes, I admit that's—"

"And if a woman was captured during the course of the war, the law required that she be permitted to spend a month mourning her family, after which her captor was expected to marry her. If he did not choose to marry her, he had to let her go free. She could not be sold into slavery."

Aaron turned to Joan. "How about it, Joan, that's pretty decent, isn't it?"

But the rabbi went on. "There are any number of laws and regulations to the same effect. One of the ways in which we address God is *El Molay Rachamim*, which means 'God full of compassion.' It is perhaps particularly manifest in our attitude toward the lower animals. For example, out of our respect for life, we are forbidden to hunt for sport. And consider the various commandments dealing with the lower animals. 'Thou shalt not muzzle the ox that treads the grain.' The poor beast has no way of knowing that the grain belongs to the farmer. To see grain at his feet and to nibble at it is automatic with him. To prevent him is a cruelty. It's interesting that that very commandment is referred to in the New Testament by Paul—"

"Really?" Joan was interested.

The rabbi nodded grimly. "But he quotes it to justify his use of church funds for his personal needs and expenses. He regards it as having only figurative significance. 'Is God concerned about oxen?' he asks rhetorically. Well, from our point of view, He certainly is. And He shows it in a number of commandments. 'Thou shalt not yoke an ox to a donkey.' The difference of strength in the two beasts constitutes cruelty to the weaker one. Again, if an ox or a donkey has strayed and is lost, we are commanded to return it to the owner, even if the owner is an enemy. This is not for the benefit of the owner, but rather for the poor beast that misses the warmth of his stall and will remain unfed. So, too, if he has fallen under his burden, we are commanded to help him even if his owner is an enemy. Also, if we come across a nest and the mother bird is sitting on her eggs or her young, we are forbidden to take her; and if it is the eggs we are after, we may not take them while the mother bird is there."

"The whole kosher slaughter bit was developed because it was thought to be practically painless, wasn't it?" Aaron asked.

"That's right. The knife must be razor-sharp, and the *shochet*, the slaughterer, must test it each time on his thumb and nail to make sure it is. If there is a nick in the edge which might catch on the throat of the beast and cause him momentary pain, the meat is thereby rendered unfit. What else? Oh, yes, there is the fourth commandment on keeping the Sabbath. You remember that it applies to animals as well as to humans. 'Your animals are not to be worked on the Sabbath.' In fact, compassion is such an integral part of our religion that Maimonides said that any Jew who fails to show compassion thereby casts doubt on his descent from Abraham."

"But isn't it the same with Christianity?" asked Joan. "The Church is always talking about charity—'and the greatest of these is charity.'"

"No, it's not the same. Christian charity is doing

177

something kind because you want to, out of the goodness of your heart. The obligation to be charitable is subject to your own interpretation. With us it's spelled out. It's a series of particular *mitzvoth* from which we acquire the general principle and proper attitude. With you, giving money to a beggar is charity. And it is with us, too. It is a *mitzvah*. But we consider it a greater *mitzvah* to lend money to enable a man to get on his feet, and because it is a loan which he can eventually repay, he does not suffer embarrassment."

He sat back in his chair. "You hear a lot these days of the Judeo-Christian ethic, but except for the basic principle of the sanctity of the individual as opposed to the doctrine of his subordination to the state or society, for example, the two are quite different. On the assumption that this world is the only world and not merely a portal to the next, our ethics is based on a code to live by. It takes into account man's essential nature as part animal and part something else—mind, soul, spirit. Christianity, on the other hand, tends to regard the dual nature of man as a kind of mistake on God's part. At least that part of him which is akin to the animal was regarded by the Christian as a defect, something to be extirpated, or at least suppressed or subdued by self-denial.

"Improvement? Reform? What need when this is merely a stopping-off place to the real world? 'The poor ye shall always have with you.' Why think of the future when there is to be no future? Hence, 'Do not store up riches for yourself here on earth.'"

"Well," said Joan, "a minister once explained that all that was an attempt on the part of Jesus to get us to change our pattern of thinking, to consider a new approach, a new way of relating to ourselves and our fellow men. Like when he said to turn the other cheek and 'judge not that ye be not judged,' he didn't mean really to turn the other cheek, or maybe he did. But what he was after was to break the old pattern where one person strikes another for some wrong that he did, and then he or his friends strike back because of the first blow, and then he or *his* friends have to strike back in revenge, and so on. It just goes on and on. What Jesus wanted was for the violence to stop, if not by mutual agreement, then by unilateral action. What's more, it works, as Gandhi and Martin Luther King proved."

The rabbi shrugged. "The lesson to be learned from both examples is that if you're planning to turn the other cheek as a matter of public policy, you should be very careful in selecting the one you're going to turn it to. Gandhi's movement had some measure of success because he was opposing a fairly civilized British administration. And Martin Luther King's because it was seen on television and gained the support of the rest of the country who were not immediately involved. What if Gandhi had tried the method against the Nazi regime or against Stalinist Russia?"

"And both movements ended up in considerable violence," Aaron added.

"It certainly has not worked for the Jews," said the rabbi. "Quite the contrary. Down through the Middle Ages, during the Holocaust in our own time, and the experience of the state of Israel in dealing with Arab terrorists, all seem to indicate that failure to resist evil does not automatically convert it to good; it merely increases it."

"I suppose the theory is that the guy that hits you is conscience-stricken and ashamed of himself if you don't hit back," Aaron said.

"Yes," the rabbi responded, "and it has fascinated a number of writers—Bernard Shaw, Victor Hugo. And I daresay it happens occasionally. But the Jewish attitude, like that of the world in general, is that assault is wrong and should be resisted rather than condoned. I might also point out that if the assault is not with a hand or a fist but with a bullet, the victim may not get a chance to exercise his option. He may be dead."

Aaron chuckled, and Joan said tartly, "I wasn't thinking of it as a matter of practical behavior so much as an ideal to aim for."

"Well, even an ideal should be practical," said the rabbi, "at least in the sense that it should be possible for normal humans to achieve it. Otherwise it can have the opposite effect of what is intended."

"I'm not sure I follow you, Rabbi," Aaron said.

"It's simple enough. Suppose you set up an impossible goal. Naturally you fail to achieve it."

"Sure, by definition."

"So what do you do? If there is no great intellectual or emotional involvement, you may discard it as unrealistic, or you may congratulate yourself on your progress, however little. But if you are convinced that the goal is all-important, then your failure may result in a variety of forms of behavior, most of them irrational."

"Such as?"

"Such as giving up entirely, or blaming your failure on someone else, or redefining the nature of those you're contending with. The Pilgrims could justify their outrageous treatment of the Indians by considering them not human. The same advice has been used to justify the mistreatment of the blacks." He sat back in his chair. "When I was teaching, I saw a lot of it, and you probably do, too, Aaron."

"How do you mean?"

"A student who was on the honor roll in high school, all A's perhaps, comes to college, expecting to make the same grades there. But in college the competition is much harder. The other students were also honor students at their respective high schools. That's usually how they got there in the first place. Our student works hard and when the grades are announced, finds he has received—B's."

"Yes, I know what you mean," Aaron said. "And the next semester, instead of working harder, he lets go and just gets passing grades."

"But how does that apply to Christianity?" Joan asked.

"One of the most peculiar characteristics of the Christian world is the violent religious wars that have

180

been waged all through its history. There's one going on right now in Ireland. Even when it hasn't been one sect against another, there has frequently been the most cruel and vicious punishment for seemingly minor deviations from orthodoxy. All this in the name of the Prince of Peace! I am not speaking now of the massacres and pogroms of non-Christians. I am thinking of the bitter enmity between Christian and Christian. The history of every Christian country is stained with the blood of its religious martyrs. This violence, so curiously at variance with the professed compassion of the religion, must be one of the great paradoxes of human behavior. I can only suggest that it may be due to trying to achieve an unnatural and impossible ideal. In the face of certain failure, while one may compromise and settle for a somewhat lower and more readily attainable peak, another reaction might be to give up and go in the opposite direction, so that an unachievable love can turn to irrational hate."

"Well, all that is in the past," Joan objected.

"How about present-day Ireland?" asked Aaron.

"Oh, I don't think what's going on there is really religious," Joan said. "As I understand it, it's ethnic and social and economic. The Catholics are Irish and the Protestants are of British ancestry, and because they are in the majority in Northern Ireland, they have been able to keep the Catholics from getting good jobs or decent housing."

"But it all started because of the difference in religions," Aaron said.

"That may be," Joan admitted, "but I was thinking—I mean, I don't see any difference here in America right now. What I mean is I know a lot of Jews. One year at college my roommate was Jewish, and I visited at her home all through the spring vacation, and we're still close. I went to her wedding and to the Brith when her son was born. Yes, and to that Pid—" She looked at the rabbi for help.

"Pidyon Haben," he supplied.

"That's right. The Pidyon Haben. And I've never noticed any difference in the way we think or act or—"

"How about it, Aaron?" asked the rabbi. "You have Christian friends. Do you see no difference?"

Aaron chuckled. "The only thing that comes to mind is that Christians seem to drink a lot more than we do."

"That could be genetic," said the rabbi. "It's a peculiarity we seem to share with Italians and Chinese. Or it may have something to do with the mores of the three peoples. There are certain similarities. Nothing else?"

"Well, I've never lived with a Christian family, just visited of an evening, so I—Oh, here's something. I was visiting at a friend's house. It was during the football season and my friend's kid brother who was on the Salem High team had broken his collarbone the week before in a game. His mother was talking about it and she was pretty upset. Understandable, right? A mother's heart—her youngest injured? Wrong! What upset her was Jerry's terrible disappointment at not being able to play in the Peabody game. What's more, neither my friend nor his father seemed in any way surprised at the mother's attitude. Gosh, when I think how my mother reacted when I said I was going out for the basketball team..."

The rabbi chuckled. "I know what you mean. Of course, you can't generalize from one case, but I'm inclined to agree that Jewish mothers are still overprotective of their children. I think that's changing, though."

"All right then, here's something. I know that my folks were a lot more concerned about my doing well in school than were the folks of my gentile friends. And it wasn't only for grades. They were always pushing me to go to the public library."

The rabbi nodded. "Yes, study has always been important to us. Nowadays the importance of study and learning is pretty generally recognized, but it's a relatively recent development and is due in large part to the demands of a technological society and to the importance of social upgrading. With us it was important from the beginning because it is a religious obligation. According to the sages, a Jewish father has four duties to his son: to circumcize him, to teach him Torah, to teach him a trade, and to get him married. Some add a fifth obligation: to teach him how to swim."

"By teaching him Torah, you mean religion?" asked Aaron.

"Ye-es, but it's a little more than that. Its true significance is suggested by our saying, 'One should not use the Torah as a spade to dig with.' It implies learning for the sake of learning. When you think about it, it's one of the things that distinguishes man from the lower animals. All animals learn what they need to know—where to find food, how to avoid predators, where to hole up for the night—all practical things. Only man seeks knowledge for no practical reason, but simply because it's interesting. It's the distinction between liberal arts study and professional study. But we also regard practical study as important in accordance with another saying to the effect that 'who does not teach his son a trade, teaches him to be a thief.'"

"But this business of not using Torah study for practical purposes, how does it affect rabbis? When you studied to be a rabbi, weren't you studying to—to—"

"To learn a trade? No, that came later. I suspect my motivation was probably like yours."

"How do you mean?"

"Well, you probably studied science in high school and as an undergraduate because you were interested in it, and only later decided to earn your living by it. I began studying Talmud with my grandfather when I was quite young, eleven or twelve, and found myself drawn to it and wanted to continue. Originally rabbis were not paid for their rabbinical work. They supported themselves by following various trades, some quite lowly like cobbler or woodcutter. That didn't change until sometime in the Middle Ages after the expulsion of the Jews from Spain, when economic conditions in the countries they fled to made it impossible for the many refugee rabbis to earn a living at their former trades. So the custom developed of paying them, not for their rabbinic work, but for the time they presumably were taking off from their secular work. At least, that's the rationale."

Aaron was inclined to argue the point. "Still—"

But Joan interposed with, "And this rabbinic work was not ceremonial, I think you said, but legalistic?"

"That's right. Advising and deciding on points of law."

"So Rabbi Small could earn his living as a lawyer," she said tartly to her fiancé.

"Could you?" asked Aaron impishly.

The rabbi chuckled. "Not without considerable study."

"Would it take much?" asked Joan. "Is our law so different from Jewish law? Oh, I know Congress and the different states have passed all kinds of laws and regulations, but I mean basically is it so different?"

"Yeah, how different are they?" Aaron asked.

"Well, they are similar in the sense that the same things that are considered wrong in one code are also considered wrong in the other. But whereas American law is based on English common law, which was essentially the practice and customs of the early Anglo-Saxons, Judaic law is grounded in the Bible, which means that it can't be changed since it is the word of God."

"But you do change it," Aaron urged.

"We don't so much change it as get around it," said the rabbi, smiling.

"How do you mean? What's the difference?"

"Well, for example, we are forbidden to charge interest when we lend money. That was all right in an agricultural economy when the loan was a temporary aid to someone who had had a bit of bad luck, but when we began to engage in commerce which involved loans on a long-term basis, the restriction on interest was paralyzing. Here in America what would happen would be that Congress would finally pass a law permitting the lending of money on interest. But with us that would mean contravening the word of God. So we got around it in various ways. One was by *heter iskah*, whereby lender and borrower form a partnership and one gets paid more for presumably more work done. Among the observant the form is still used. They simply include in the contract the phrase 'in accordance with *heter iskah*.' By similar devices we arranged to keep other laws up to date. The limitations of the Sabbatic year, when all private loans are automatically canceled, were avoided by the *Prosbul* of Hillel. By this device a creditor declared that all debts due him are hereby given over to a court of law for collection. This made it a public loan and hence not subject to the remission. If it had not been for the *Prosbul*, much commerce in the sixth year, say, would have been brought to a standstill."

"That's civil law, though," said Aaron. "How about criminal law?"

"We did the same sort of thing in criminal law. We adjusted procedures so as to give the accused every possible break out of a feeling of compassion, which is like a shining thread woven through the fabric of our law."

"Is there the same presumption of innocence as in our law?"

"Not expressly stated as such," said the rabbi, "but implicit in our criminal procedure. Two eyewitnesses were required to prove a crime, and they were subjected to rigid examination by the court. But the court could accept almost any evidence at all to prove innocence. Criminal cases were tried before a court of twenty-three judges and a majority of two was required for conviction, but only a majority of one for acquittal. Once the accused was acquitted he could not be tried again, but if he were found guilty, he could have any number of retrials. One major difference in the two codes is that many crimes like theft and robbery and assault are regarded as torts against the victim rather than crimes against the state."

"You mean assault and robbery and theft are not crimes? But that's terrible!" exclaimed Joan.

"Why?" asked the rabbi mildly. "A crime is an offense against the state. When you think about it, isn't it just a legal fiction that when A steals from B, he is really stealing from the state? When A is caught, he is tried by the state and if found guilty, is punished by the state. All well and good, he has done something wrong and deserves punishment. But how about B? What does he get out of it? He is not compensated for his loss if he has been robbed, or for his hurt if he has been assaulted. The perpetrator goes to jail, and I heard that it costs the state on the average of twenty thousand dollars a year to keep him there. And when he comes out he's usually worse than when he went in. Talmudic law calls for him to repay his victim, in certain cases several times over. You see, our law has compassion for the victim, too."

"The lights in the hotel have just gone off," Aaron remarked.

"Really? I didn't realize it was so late." As they rose to go, he asked, "Shall I see you tomorrow night?"

"We'd like to come," said Aaron, "but tomorrow is Friday, the beginning of the Sabbath. Will it be all right with you?"

"These talks are most appropriate for the Sabbath," said the rabbi with a smile. "I shall expect you."

CHAPTER

12

"I didn't know how they'd feel at the hotel if we drove up on the Sabbath, so we walked over," Aaron announced as the rabbi greeted them and motioned them to seats.

"I don't know either," said the rabbi. "It was thoughtful of you."

"Aaron and I were talking about what you said last night," said Joan, "about all this compassion you say Judaism has for the poor and bondsmen and animals and all. Yet it considers women as—well—like second-class citizens."

"Where'd you get that idea?"

"Oh, I know a lot of Jewish girls. In my senior year my roommate was Jewish and we're still very close. So I've heard them talking, and while I'll admit they didn't seem terribly concerned, and even kind of joked about it, there was no doubt that they regarded Judaism as male chauvinist and—"

"Precisely what did you hear?"

"Oh, you know, that a man can divorce his wife anytime he wants to, and she can't divorce him at all. And I remember they once talked about some law where a widow had to get her brother-in-law's permission to remarry, and—"

The rabbi raised a palm to stop her. "Let's start with those. That last, levirate marriage, marriage with a brother-in-law, is a good example of how a law, a good law, intended for one purpose, is perverted in the course of time to almost its opposite as a result of changing conditions. In a patriarchal society like Israel in biblical days, it was a tragedy for a man to die without issue. So a custom developed whereby his brother would marry the widow and the first child of the union would be named after the dead husband 'so that his name would not be lost to Israel.' Now, obviously, the obligation was on the brother-in-law. It was his duty to his dead brother. I say obviously because in the event of his refusal, the custom called for the widow to go to the elders and report that her husband's brother refused to do his duty. He was then summoned, and if he persisted in his refusal, she loosened and removed his shoe and spat on the ground in front of him, saying, 'So shall be done unto the man who does not build up his brother's house.' Since polygamy was legal at the time, the lady's ire was understandable. She had been repudiated. The term is *chalitza.* But once she had received *chalitza*, repudiation, she was free to marry whomever she chose. So while *chalitza* was seemingly insulting, it was also apt to be to her advantage, and I imagine was frequently the result of an accommodation between the two parties."

"You mean if she wanted to marry someone else, and her brother-in-law wasn't terribly keen on her, she'd pay him off, and he'd let her spit at him?"

"Something like that. I imagine so. Then when polygamy went out of fashion or was forbidden, the opportunity for the levirate marriage was curtailed considerably. The brother-in-law had to be single, for one thing. Furthermore, since intercourse with a husband's brother is interdicted in the Bible as an incestuous relationship—this was an exception, you see—the rabbis were not inclined to permit it, which meant that the widow *had* to accept *chalitza*. And that in turn meant that the brother-in-law had to grant it. So what had started out as a responsibility and obligation on his part now became a privilege which he could grant or withhold. And if he were mean, he could make things most unpleasant for the widow; he might demand money, for example. Usually the arrangement is made, but if he's obdurate and unconscionable, the rabbi can bring pressure to bear to force him to be reasonable. Nevertheless, it occasionally caused great hardship."

"So why didn't they change it?"

"Because in theory you can't. It's in the Bible, which means that it's God's word. The best you can do is try to interpret it into a nullity."

"But if it works obviously against the original intention..."

"My dear, all legal systems develop flaws. If they are minor and affect comparatively few, you overlook them. If many are adversely affected, you adjust the law by reinterpreting it, but you don't change the basis of the entire system, unless it's by revolution. Take the American Constitution. At one time the 'due process' clause was interpreted so as to prevent any child labor legislation. When the spirit of the times changed, it was interpreted the other way. But if you want to actually change the Constitution, you have to pass an amendment which then has to be ratified by two thirds of the states. And that's not easy. Think how much trouble the women's movement is having trying to get ratification of the Equal Rights Amendment."

"But isn't it foolish to be bound by a set of laws formulated a couple of thousand years ago?"

"No more than it is for us as Americans to feel bound by a set of laws formulated a couple of hundred years ago," replied the rabbi. "As our Supreme Court tries to determine the intentions of the Founding Fathers, so our rabbis try to determine the intentions of Almighty God. You might better ask why the intentions of a handful of eighteenth-century politicians should be of such concern to the two hundred and forty million Americans living today. I suppose the answer is that any framework is better than no framework at all. It's more important to know what you can do and what you can't do, what you'll be praised for and what you'll be punished for, than it is to know that the praise is reasonable and the punishment logical. If you know what is permitted and what is forbidden, you can at least arrange your life accordingly."

"The British don't have a constitution and they seem to do all right," Aaron pointed out.

The rabbi opened his eyes wide. "But they do have a constitution. It's not written down in a single document like ours. Rather it's a series of documents going back to the Magna Carta, and even beyond, because it was largely a reaffirmation of old custom. To fully appreciate the benefits of a constitution, I suppose you have to live in one of the dictatorships. There you are subject to the whim of the dictator or of any member of the ruling clique, and a crime is what they happen to think it is at the moment. They may even have a written constitution, sometimes quite an elaborate one, but it is only a scrap of paper, and to appeal to it may in itself be regarded as a crime."

"All right, I'll take your word for it that a constitution is a good thing to have," Joan said good-naturedly. "But aren't we getting rather far afield? We were talking about the marriage and divorce laws, remember? Or are the Jewish divorce laws like the levirate marriage business, something that started out good and then went wrong?"

"Oh, no, our divorce laws are among the most liberal in the world. Indeed, they are as modern as this minute; far more progressive than those which obtain in most of the states of the Union, let alone other countries. We recognized from the beginning that a marriage may

190

turn out unsuccessful and made provisions accordingly."

"Then it isn't true that only the husband can grant a divorce?"

"Oh, it's true enough, but it's—it's a kind of legal fiction."

"You've used that phrase before. What do you mean, a legal fiction?" she asked suspiciously.

"Look here: if I steal a purse, or if I assault someone, it is considered a crime against the state, or in England against the crown. It's the state or the crown that brings an action of law against me, not the person injured. It isn't his lawyer, but the public prosecutor, who appears in court against me just as though I had robbed the United States Treasury or assaulted the Queen of England. By a legal fiction a crime perpetrated on an individual is regarded as though it had been committed against the state. The law, any law, is full of such assumptions. They're necessary to make it work in the interest of an ordered society. Now back in primitive times, the man took a wife. Although she consented, the action was his. And this is implicit in our wedding ceremony down to the present day. The groom announces, 'Behold, with this ring you are sanctified to me according to the laws of Moses and Israel.' The bride says nothing. She indicates consent by permitting the groom to put the ring on her finger, which is why to the Orthodox a double-ring ceremony makes no sense."

"You mean he buys her? That the ring is the purchase price?"

"No, not at all. Because in those societies where there is a bride-price, the money is paid to the girl's father or family, and not to the girl. The ring, or it could be a small coin, is an earnest of his intention, and by taking it she indicates her acceptance. The fact that it can be the smallest coin in the currency would show that it is not a purchase price. Now since the man takes and she is thereby sanctified and reserved to him, then the logic of the situation demands that if for some rea-

191

son the marriage is unsatisfactory, he is the one who un-takes, that is, divorces."

"Well, I see the logic of it," said Aaron, "but it seems to me grossly unfair. And I can't for the life of me see how you can call it modern and progressive."

"Ah, but that was in the beginning. It was probably the prevailing mode among all the peoples of the area. And even then there were differences, for we required that notice of divorce must be given in writing, and not merely by telling the wife as is the custom in many Arab countries to this day."

"Big deal!" Aaron was not impressed.

"Yes, it is a big deal," said the rabbi, "because the notice had to be written in proper form, which was highly involved like legal forms today, so that it usually had to be done by a scribe or a rabbi. This meant that the husband could not divorce his wife in the heat of passion; there was some delay involved—"

"Not to mention that it enabled the rabbis to get in on the act," said Aaron.

The rabbi smiled. "Not to mention it."

"But how is it now?" asked Joan impatiently.

"Ah, now the husband who wants a divorce must go before a rabbinical board, and only if they find sufficient grounds will they grant a divorce."

"Is his wife there to question and cross-examine him?"

"No, but—"

"Then it's just a kangaroo court."

"But she doesn't have to accept the *get* as we call it. Ever since the decree of Rabbenu Gershom about a thousand years ago, the husband cannot divorce unless his wife consents. You see, marriage with us is a civil transaction, a contract of sorts, so it is within the logic of the situation that both parties have to agree if the contract is to be dissolved. As a matter of fact, a written contract called the *ketubah* is actually drawn up and signed in the presence of witnesses by the groom before the wedding and is read out as part of the ceremony, and then given to the bride to keep like a promissory note. Among other things it stipulates a sum of money which the groom undertakes to give the bride in the event of a divorce."

"Oh, I see," said Joan very much mollified. "Then if both parties want a divorce—"

"It is granted. It isn't necessary to prove that either party was at fault. Of course, the rabbinical court will counsel the couple in an effort to save the marriage, but if the parties insist, the rabbi will write out the *get* for the husband to give to his wife. He's the one who gives it."

"But what if she wants it and he doesn't?"

"Then the court will listen to her complaint, and if she has proper grounds, they will order him to grant her a *get*."

"How do you mean, order?"

"Just that. It's an order of the Rabbinical Court."

"And if he refuses?"

"Then the court will apply whatever sanctions are available to it. In Israel, where the Rabbinical Court has full authority in matters of marriage and divorce, they will send him to jail." The rabbi laughed. "When I was in Israel, a few years ago, the Rabbinical Court ran into a peculiarly frustrating problem. They had approved a *get* for a woman, but her husband was unwilling to grant it. And they could not send him to jail for contempt because he was already there. The newspapers were full of advice, from readers and from editorial writers, as to what measures could be taken."

"How did it end?"

"He finally yielded. As I recall, they threatened to deprive him of his normal time off for good behavior and make him finish his full sentence."

"You said she had to have proper grounds," said Joan suspiciously. "What sort of grounds?"

"Oh, the usual—failure to provide support, cruel and abusive treatment. Plus some that are not usual. A woman could get a divorce if she found her husband physically repulsive, perhaps as a result of his trade. The sages mentioned the tanner's trade, for example."

193

"What was wrong with tanners?" asked Aaron.

"I suppose in those days they smelled bad," said the rabbi. "It suggests that the wife was not regarded as a mere chattel or sex object, doesn't it? As a matter of fact, the burden of providing conjugal satisfaction rested with the husband. The rabbis even tried to spell out the frequency with which men in various trades were expected to perform their matrimonial duties. Just recently, a man was tried in Israel for raping his wife, from whom he was separated. In response to the defense plea that in common law it was the wife's duty to give the husband sexual gratification, the court pointed out that in Halacha, in Jewish law, there was no such obligation; that it was the husband who was required to give gratification to the wife.

"Nor was the purpose of sex regarded as solely for the purpose of producing children. While the rabbis favored many children in adherence to the injunction to 'be fruitful and multiply,' there was recognition that the health of the woman was paramount. The production of two children was regarded as sufficient to satisfy the commandment, a boy and a girl according to the accepted ruling."

"What if there were two girls?" asked Joan.

"I imagine an observant Jew would go on trying. Is it very much different in families, all families, today?"

"And what did they do once they had their two children?" asked Aaron. "Use contraceptives?"

The rabbi grinned. "They appear to have known about them. The problem is that it appears to contravene the injunction against 'spilling the seed.' There was division of opinion, and Rabbi Meir, at least, insisted that in certain circumstances it was not only warranted, but required, as in the cases of a minor, a pregnant woman, and a nursing mother—the first two because it was presumed dangerous to the health of the mother, in the third case because the pregnancy would stop the flow of milk and thus endanger the health of the nursing child."

"And what if she got pregnant nevertheless?" asked Joan. "Could she have an abortion?"

The rabbi shook his head. "Not because she didn't want the child, or even on purely economic grounds. But the rabbinic rule was that if she was having extreme difficulty in giving birth, the child in the womb was to be sacrificed to save the mother. And through the years, in various Responsa, the rabbis have held that abortion is warranted when there is a hazard to the mother's physical or even psychological health."

"That's certainly quite different from the Catholic point of view," said Joan.

"That's because Catholics regard the fetus as a person from the moment of conception," said Aaron. "Isn't that right, Rabbi?"

"That's right. So abortion even in the early weeks is the equivalent of murder. Logically, there should be an inquest whenever there is a miscarriage. Our doctrine is that the fetus is not a person until the greater portion of it has emerged from the womb, so obviously the life of the mother takes precedence over that of the fetus because the mother is a person and the fetus isn't." He smiled at Joan. "By the way, there is another legal fiction we use in that case to justify the abortion. The fetus is regarded as a *rodef*, which is the term for one who pursues with intent to kill. Our law holds that it is permitted to kill the *rodef* to prevent him from killing his intended victim. Now, in comparison with other codes, do you still think our religion is sexist?"

But she was not ready to yield. "Marriage and divorce are—well, secular things. I know that Jewish wives have it good, but I guess I was thinking of religious matters."

"With us they're not separate," said the rabbi. "Look here, to understand a society and how it feels toward one of its components, you should examine its literature. It has been argued, for example, that the common people had little standing or influence in ancient Greece because they are not mentioned in the Homeric poems, and that Shakespeare's frequent inclusion of the lowly, some of them cheeky and irreverent, suggests that England was a more open and democratic society than France, where the literature confines itself to the doings of kings and princes. Well, we have a literature—the Bible. And whether you regard it as the word of God, or as a bunch of legends finally edited into a single chronicle, the fact remains that none of the women who appear in the story is a mindless, spineless sex object with no will of her own. From Eve on down, through Sarah, Rachel, Rebecca, Miriam, Deborah, Esther, Ruth—they all show that they are individuals in their own right. Why? Because the people that read this chronicle and lived by it regarded it as believable and plausible. Then there are the laws, the commandments: 'Honor thy father and mother'—"

"Yeah, but the man gets top billing," Aaron remarked.

The rabbi smiled. "Maybe because he's usually older."

"That's silly," said Joan, but she laughed.

"Sure it is, both Aaron's remark and my answer. Besides, in Leviticus where the commandment is repeated, it is the mother who is mentioned first. And how about the passage that says, 'A man should leave his father and mother and shall cleave to his wife, and they shall be one flesh.' There the advantage seems to be with the wife."

"But a man could have more than one wife," Aaron objected. "What did he do, cleave to each of them?"

"Polygamy *was* legal," the rabbi admitted. "It was normal for the time and the area, but I'm inclined to think that there was very little of it. The High Priest, for example, was restricted to one wife. Of the couple of thousand rabbis who are mentioned in the Talmud, only one or two were known to have had more than one wife. When in the eleventh century Rabbenu Gershom by the threat of excommunication abolished polygamy, his decree was readily accepted, by the Ashkenazim at least, because monogamy was already standard practice with them.

"Let's see, what other evidence is there for the equality of women? In matters of this kind clues and symbols are more significant than actual laws."

"I don't follow you there, Rabbi."

"What I mean is—well, in Russia women have complete equality by law. But we know that they don't actually have it because so few of them hold the top jobs in either industry or politics. And that's true even here."

"Oh, I see. So what clues are there in Judaism?"

"One is that we derive our Jewishness from our mothers rather than from our fathers."

"How do you mean? That we learn it from the mother?"

"No, I mean that according to Halacha the child of a Jewish mother is Jewish even if the father is not. But the child of a Jewish father is not Jewish if the mother is not."

"That makes sense," said Aaron. "You can't always tell who the father was. But there's no doubt about the mother."

"It's unusual," Joan admitted.

"All right, how about inheritance?" asked Aaron. "When a man dies, is his estate divided equally between the sons and daughters?"

"Ah, that's different. The principal consideration is the preservation of the estate, so only the sons inherit."

"Aha!"

"Aha nothing, if you mean that it indicates male chauvinism. The eldest son receives a double portion. Does that mean firstborn chauvinism? The estate, it was assumed, would be land, a farm. The intention was to keep it from being split up into uneconomic segments. The British did the same kind of thing by entailing an estate. Remember the situation in *Pride and Prejudice*? Besides, it's as broad as it is long. The first call on the estate, taking precedence over everything else, is the maintenance of the females, and the necessity of marrying them off with dowries commensurate with their social rank. By the time all the daughters are married off, there might be nothing left for the sons to divide."

"Well..."

"Here's another: a child born out of wedlock is not considered illegitimate."

"You mean there are no bastards among us?" demanded Aaron. "Isn't that what the word *mamser* means? Seems to me I personally know half a dozen."

The rabbi managed to grin at the witticism. "A *mamser* or bastard is a child resulting from incest or adultery. If the mother is merely unmarried, the child is legitimate."

"They stone the adulteress, don't they?" asked Joan. "I saw it in one of those epic Bible movies."

"I didn't see the movie," said the rabbi, "so I can't say how authentic it was. The Bible does stipulate stoning as the penalty for adultery, but"—and he held up an admonishing forefinger for emphasis—"it applies to the man just as it does to the woman. It was regarded as a terrible crime because it was destructive of the family, but both parties were equally guilty. I doubt if the penalty was frequently carried out, or if ever. Certainly not in Rabbinic times, because by then there had developed a great reluctance to apply the death penalty at all. The rabbis couldn't abolish it because it was in the Bible, but they did their best to nullify it as they did in all capital offenses. They stipulated, for example, that to arrive at a finding of guilty in a capital offense, there had to be two eyewitnesses. Circumstantial evidence, however compelling, was not enough. And the two eyewitnesses had to warn the parties that what they were about to do was against the law, quoting chapter and verse." He grinned. "It's hard to imagine a couple performing the sex act in those circumstances."

"Yeah, but suppose they saw this couple going into a motel, say, and they gave their warning. And then they saw them come out the next morning—"

"It would still be only circumstantial evidence," the rabbi interrupted Aaron.

"But suppose they admitted it?"

"Self-incrimination is not permitted under Jewish jurisprudence."

"You mean a man doesn't have to testify against himself, but—"

"I mean he is not permitted to," said the rabbi. "A defendant cannot confess or plead guilty to a crime."

"Well..."

The rabbi took advantage of the temporary lull to say, "Would you like some wine? I happened to mention that I was expecting company, and the supervisor of the dining room suggested I take the bottle that was on my table for the Sabbath meal. It's quite sweet."

"Oh, I like sweet wine," said Joan.

"And I can tolerate it," Aaron said.

CHAPTER

13

Aaron drained his glass and set it on the table. He shook his head as the rabbi raised the bottle to refill it. "Not just now," he said. He leaned back in his chair. "Doesn't it strike you, Rabbi, that there is a peculiar anomaly in the Jewish treatment of women?"

"How do you mean?"

"Well, I'll go along with the equality of women in the home and the family. Judging from my own family, maybe they are even a little more equal. Which makes it all the more curious that in the synagogue they are nothing—zilch."

"Nothing?"

"Sure. They stick them up in a balcony behind a screen as though they weren't there and—"

"They do this in the synagogue your folks go to?"

"Well, no. Theirs is Conservative, but they do it in the Orthodox synagogues."

"Well, as you realize, it isn't done in Conservative

synagogues, or in Reform congregations. But even if we consider Orthodox practice, what's so unusual about it? I'm not much older than you, and yet I remember that in the public schools it was customary to have the girls sit on one side of the room and the boys on the other. One of my teachers in the grade school used to punish the boys who were naughty by making them sit with the girls. The college I went to was an all men's college. I daresay most of the private colleges at the time were either men's schools or women's schools. Why? Because it was assumed, rightly or wrongly, that one sex would have a disturbing influence on the other; that young men at that emotional age would be unable to concentrate on their studies if there were attractive young women around.

"It was probably true in those days because women were not so much in evidence in daily life. They stayed home. When women were more visible, in stores and offices and on the streets, probably as a result of having to replace men during the wars of this century, coeducation became more common. The same thing happened in the synagogue. Separation of the sexes was no longer necessary because the sight of the other sex no longer distracted the worshiper from his or her devotions. So the Conservative synagogue gave it up. The Reform never had it. But even in the Orthodox congregations where they are very reluctant to make any changes at all, they gave up the screened balcony. In the newer Orthodox synagogues, at least, all they have is a railing about waist high, between the men's section and the women's."

"You mean that's all there is to it?" asked Aaron heatedly. "Then why aren't they included in the minyan, and why aren't they called to the reading of the Scroll?"

The rabbi was not in the least put out. "Again, in the Reform synagogue and in some of the Conservative ones, too, the women *are* part of the minyan and are also called to the reading. But not with the Orthodox.

The rationale of the Orthodox practice takes a bit of explaining."

"I bet it does," said Aaron.

Ignoring the sally, the rabbi continued. "Inasmuch as they are responsible for the home and the care and feeding of the family, women are exempt from those *mitzvoth*, commandments, that have to be done at a particular time. So, since the daily prayers have to be said at specific times of day, they are not required of women. Now, our thinking is that to perform a *mitzvah* that is not actually required of you is to perform it somewhat less than completely."

"I should think it would be the other way around," said Joan. "Isn't it better to do something because you want to than because it is required?"

"That's because you're not giving full weight to the definition of a *mitzvah* as a commandment, that is, as something that has to be done because it is an order from a superior. If you do it even though you don't have to, then you're not really obeying a commandment; you're merely being good-natured."

"I can follow your reasoning," said Aaron caustically, "but it's the most hair-splitting casuistry I've heard in a long time."

"I agree with you."

"You do? But then—"

"Oh, I'm not opposed to splitting hairs. It means making fine distinctions. But in this case I'm prepared to admit that it is adduced to justify the control of ritual and ceremony in masculine hands which has been common to all cultures since the dawn of history. I think it is significant that in Judaism a rationalization is offered other than the inferiority of women, either explicitly stated or generally assumed in other religions. However, I'm inclined to believe that in Judaism, at least, women have been quite willing to leave it to their menfolk, because I suspect they're not particularly interested in it. Besides, in a rationalist religion like ours, what difference does it make?"

"I don't follow you. What's rationalism got to do with it?"

"All right, compare it with a mystical religion like Roman Catholicism. Consider the mass. It is a miracle whereby bread and wine becomes the body and blood of Christ. But only the priest can do it. It is a magical act which brings him closer to the Godhead. He even ingests the god. To be sure, the laity participate in the ceremony, but at one remove. If the priest should fail to perform the ceremony properly, if he failed to say the magic words, then all they would be taking into their mouths would be a wafer, a bit of unleavened bread, and nothing more. He officiates at the altar which is not merely a table or a reading desk. It contains the relic of a saint, and is therefore holy. The laity do not approach it, but receive communion at the railing which separates them from it. As with magic in general, proximity is of the essence. The closer you are, the stronger the force, like the force of gravity which varies inversely as the square of the distance. Pilgrimages are made to the shrines of saints because that's where the miracles take place. Thinking about the saint at a distance evidently won't do it.

"You might say that the whole structure of the Church is based on the importance of proximity. Jesus appeared on earth so that man could bridge the awesome gap to God, the Father. The saints are a bridge to Jesus, and so on. Vatican II demonstrated, I think, that many of the laity resented their exclusion from the ceremonial of the service. They were indeed missing something, an opportunity for propinquity to the Godhead that was vouchsafed to the priesthood and not to them. Of course, the priest could argue that his special privileges were justified because of the sacrifices he was making. He had taken vows of chastity and obedience, and if he were a monastic, then also a vow of poverty. And to the great mass of the laity, I'm sure that seemed eminently reasonable. But how about the female religious, the nuns? They had made the same vows and their lives were even more restricted than the priests'. Yet only the priest could perform the mass for them, or hear their confessions and grant them absolution. Now *they* can argue that they are discriminated against because of their sex."

"And in the synagogue?"

"There is no mystery and no magic. And no chiefs and no Indians. You gain nothing by being nearer the Ark, except that you can hear better."

"The cantor?"

The rabbi shrugged. "He is merely someone with a good voice. He is employed on the holy days to enhance the appeal of the services and, to tell the truth, to mitigate some of their tedium. For the daily services anyone may be asked to lead the prayers, and it is customary to offer the honor or privilege to any stranger who might be present. The reader of the Scroll? He is merely one who is versed in the cantillation in which it is read."

"But those who are called up to the reading, aren't they getting a special honor?"

"It's an honor, to be sure, but it's—it's more of a social honor than a special religious opportunity. It is customary for the one receiving the honor to make a contribution to the synagogue. You can be sure that the ritual committee which distributes the honors has this well in mind when they make their choices. The result is that certainly on the High Holy Days the honors are apt to go to the wealthier members of the congregation. Perhaps the vast majority of the congregation never receive an honor from the time they are Bar Mitzvah until the Sabbath before their wedding day. What I'm getting at is that if there were some special rite which bestowed grace, that increased one's chances of getting to heaven, or reduced the time one might have to spend in purgatory, or enabled one to get a little nearer to the Godhead, then women would indeed have a grievance if it were forbidden then. But we don't have anything like that; ours is not that kind of religion."

"But if women have no part in the service, isn't that

a clue to how they are regarded by their menfolk?" Joan persisted.

"If it weren't for all the other things I mentioned that point in the opposite direction."

"Then how do you explain it?"

"As I said, I suspect that they weren't interested," said the rabbi quietly.

"Weren't interested?" she echoed.

"Uh-huh. I know it's not fashionable to mention it these days, but there *are* differences between men and women. Perhaps you've noticed. And I suspect that the differences are not merely of body and biological function, but also of mind. While I am prepared to accept the contention that women can do practically anything that men can do, I am not convinced that they want to, unless perhaps it is to prove that they can."

"You're saying—"

"I'm saying that there are things that men are interested in and are drawn to, and that women are not, even though they can do them as well as men. There is no hard evidence, but there are hints, suggestions, indications that certain areas do not particularly interest them. There is an indication in the Israeli kibbutz, which has had a continuous existence for over fifty years. The original idea was to have complete equality of the sexes where the women would do the same work as the men. They would work in the fields, planting, harvesting, operating tractors. They would dig ditches to drain swamps; they would construct the necessary housing alongside their menfolk. It was very advanced thinking for the time. It was for this reason that the children's houses were set up, so that the women would not be saddled with the care and feeding of their children. Community dining rooms were established so they would not be burdened with preparing meals and washing dishes afterward."

"Well, they were successful, weren't they?"

"Eminently successful. But a curious thing has happened over the years. Although the rules haven't changed, and women are free to do all these things, they have gradually drifted into the traditional women's occupations, nursing, teaching, cooking. There may be all sorts of explanations for this reversion to the traditional occupations, but one possibility surely is that there is an innate preference for them on the part of women; that there is something in the mind or character or psyche of women that leads them to prefer taking care of a child to operating a tractor in the field."

"It could simply be because it's easier," Aaron observed.

"Then why wouldn't some of the men bid for it? I don't know of any men who are in charge of the children's house. No, I think these occupations are basically sex-linked. And I make so bold as to suggest that the interest in ritual is also sex-linked; that women have no great interest in it, and that men have."

"What's your evidence for that?"

"Oh, nothing conclusive, although perhaps indicative. First of all, there is the curious circumstance that all religions are male-dominated and male-oriented, even primitive religion and ritual. I'm no anthropologist, but from what I've read and seen in documentaries, ritual seems to be the province of the male. The men wear the masks and the costumes and paint designs on their faces and bodies. The women watch. Or when they do participate, it is without special costumes or masks. Any decoration the women go in for seems to be to enhance or improve their appearance in accordance with tribal ideas of beauty. They don't do it for magic or religious reasons, to mimic or symbolize a god or an ancestor, as do the men. It may be that the men have preempted the function because they consider it a great privilege. On the other hand, it may be that the women don't share in it because they don't care to. Because they are amused by it, or are scornful of it. Because they think it silly or childish."

"Or it may be that they do participate and you don't happen to know about it," suggested Aaron dryly.

"True. I admit I'm talking from small knowledge. An expert on the subject might have all kinds of evidence to the contrary. But that's the picture I get which suggests that as a broad generalization, it's correct. Here is another bit of evidence in the same direction. Here in America, not so much now as a few years back, secret fraternal societies were popular—Masons, Odd Fellows, Elks, Red Men, Knights of Pythias, Knights of Columbus. All went in for grandiose titles, elaborate regalia, and complicated rituals. I think most of them, if not all, were also engaged in good works of one sort or another, like hospitals and summer camps for poor children. Now, there are women's societies, too, some of them spin-offs of the men's organizations. And they also go in for various charitable causes. But I've never heard of any that went in for elaborate ritual and regalia. Why not?"

"Oh, for pity's sake, who needs all that nonsense? Lord High Keeper of the Seal? Grand Worshipful Master of the Inner Temple? If you're going to help out the local hospital, why do you have to—" Joan stopped as she saw the rabbi's amused smile, his eyes, twinkling behind his glasses, fixed on her. "Oh, you!" she said in annoyance, and then she laughed.

Both men joined her, and Aaron, still laughing, said, "It doesn't prove a thing, you know."

"Of course not," the rabbi readily admitted. "But it's strange. Here's another. In our synagogue we have both a sisterhood and a brotherhood. The sisterhood is active all year round. They give shows, run bazaars and rummage sales, hold dances and dinners, all in order to raise money for the synagogue. And at the end of each year they hand the president of the synagogue a handsome check running to several thousand dollars, the result of their activities. The brotherhood on the other hand holds a series of Sunday bagel-and-lox breakfasts, usually with a speaker, and they either just meet their expenses or run short. About every other year they decide to compete with the women and run some sort of moneymaking affair. It's usually a grandiose project like a formal dance at a fancy hotel. Invariably they lose money and have to tax the membership to make up the deficit. The president of the brotherhood once tried to explain it to me. He said, 'The women don't hold jobs so they can be on the phone all day long, from the minute they get the kids off to school, twisting arms to sell tickets. Who's got time for it? Then they put out a program book and sell ads. They practically blackmail you into taking an ad. Men can't do that sort of thing any more than they can force contributions from all the local merchants for decorations and refreshments by hinting at reprisal in the form of a boycott. No wonder they make money. Nothing costs them a dime.'"

"The men seem to do all right when they go out collecting for the UJA," said Aaron.

"Yes, they do. It seems to be a matter of different interests, or different styles. Different something anyway."

"*Vive la différence*," Aaron murmured.

"I agree," said the rabbi, smiling.

"But what if the *différence* is artificial or accidental, or imposed to establish superiority by one party over the other?" asked Joan.

"Then of course it should be changed," said the rabbi promptly. "But you've got to be sure that the change reflects the actuality of the situation; that it isn't just being made to prove that you're able to make it; that it isn't change for the sake of change."

"You think that's happening or is likely to happen?" asked Joan.

"I think so. The Bat Mitzvah is a case in point.

"Bat Mitzvah? Is that different from—"

"It's a Bar Mitzvah for girls," Aaron explained.

"Oh, I didn't realize girls had it, too."

"It's a recent development," said the rabbi. "As I explained to you, the Bar Mitzvah is automatic when a boy reaches the age of thirteen. No ceremony is necessary—"

"Hey, I don't remember your saying that."

It was when I first came to see Rabbi Small, Aaron," Joan said. "Bar Mitzvah just means that you become

208

an adult, and it happens even if you don't go to the synagogue. Right, Rabbi?"

The rabbi nodded approval. "Right. It's no different from becoming eighteen. You can then vote, sign contracts—"

"Just a minute. You mean that I didn't have to learn all that stuff and make a speech, that I would have been Bar Mitzvah anyway?"

"I'm sure you're none the worse for your experience," said the rabbi soothingly, "and you probably got lots of presents."

"Sure, but gosh, I had to go to the cantor's house a couple of times a week for about half a year. And when I got up there, in front of the Ark, I was scared half to death, and my voice cracked just as I finished the blessings, and—" He grinned sheepishly. "No, I guess I suffered no permanent injury. But if I didn't have to, why was I made to?"

"Because it's one of the rites of passage. In Arab countries, and among other peoples who practice circumcision, that's when it's done, at puberty around the age of thirteen. Since it is painful at that age, it is thought that the youngster thereby proves his manhood. You see, he's not supposed to flinch or cry out during the process. I'm sure you prefer our way to that. And it's not a bad idea that a Jewish boy should demonstrate his manhood and prove he is an adult by reading from the Torah.

"The trouble is that it got out of hand. A celebration afterward is understandable, but the parties got more and more lavish, each family trying to outdo the other, until the party became the principal thing, and some people avoided the ceremony entirely because they couldn't afford the expense of the celebration they assumed had to follow."

"But you say they were Bar Mitzvah anyway."

"Certainly, but many of them didn't realize it. You hear of middle-aged Jews going through the ritual because they had missed it when they were thirteen, usually, they say, because their parents couldn't afford it. One came to me last year, a man of great wealth who had just moved into the area and had been invited by our president to join our congregation. He had hesitated because he thought that not having been Bar Mitzvah he wasn't really a Jew. Our president had grandiose plans for a congregation-wide party to celebrate the event." He smiled in satisfaction. "I soon put a stop to that."

"But don't some regard it as a kind of confirmation?" asked Aaron. "As sort of recommitting themselves to Judaism? I read about a whole bunch of old men, all over seventy, from California I think, who were planning to go to Israel for a mass Bar Mitzvah at the Wall."

"Yes, I read about that, and I'm sure the tourist or travel agencies did not discourage them. But it's not a confirmation. They became Jews, not when they were Bar Mitzvah, but when they were circumcised. It would make more sense if they had themselves circumcised again."

"That's silly," said Joan.

"Of course it is," the rabbi agreed. "Although when a man is converted to Judaism, he is circumcised even though he underwent the surgical procedure as an infant. He is required to undergo ritual circumcision, which consists of making a slight incision sufficient to draw a drop of blood."

"But what's wrong with considering it a confirmation?" Aaron persisted.

The rabbi pursed his lips as he marshaled his thoughts. "There is a basic sociological principle, a law you might say, that you can't change just one thing. That is, when you change one thing, automatically something else changes. We made a pact with God to carry out His commandments, and it was sealed in the flesh by circumcision. When you make a long-term business agreement, and sign and seal it, do you hold periodic meetings to renew the seals? We do have the concept of *tshuvah*, which means 'return.' It is a commitment which an individual makes to himself. What does it mean? Well, presumably one has strayed by failing to obey the commandments. So *tshuvah* means repentance for having failed and the determination henceforth to keep them. What is confirmation to us? We have no state of grace. With us it is a constant day-to-day matter. Every time we obey a commandment, we are confirming our faith.

"Now what is my objection to the Bat Mitzvah? And by the way, the girl is Bat Mitzvah at twelve rather than thirteen. Because it repeats the error which had developed with the Bar Mitzvah. The rationale is, 'If my son can have a party and get a bunch of presents and be the center of attention when he is thirteen, why shouldn't his sister get the same deal?' But it's even less reasonable for the girl. The boy is at least demonstrating that he's an adult by obeying the commandment to recite the morning prayers, by ceremoniously becoming a member of the minyan. But the girl is exempt from that commandment by reason of her sex. So what's the point of it?"

"With her it's confirmation that she's a Jew, I suppose," said Aaron. "After all, she can't undergo circumcision."

"That's right," said Joan. "A boy can be circumcised, but a girl can't."

The rabbi shrugged. "It's not uncommon among primitive peoples, and is even done today in some Arab tribes. It's thought to have the effect of reducing her desire and interest in sex, thereby limiting the likelihood of her disgracing the family later on."

"You mean they actually— How awful!" exclaimed Joan.

"Uh-huh." A sudden thought occurred to the rabbi. "Gosh, I hope the idea never occurs to these militant women."

"You know, Rabbi," Aaron began hesitantly, "this whole business of circumcision—" He broke his train of thought to ask, "All three segments of Judaism practice it?"

"That's right. Reform Judaism no less than Conservative or Orthodox."

211

"Well, I know it's supposed to be healthy; that the incidence of cancer of the uterus is much less among Jewish women than among women in general, and all that. But doesn't it strike you as a peculiar way of confirming an agreement with God, or of dedicating yourself to His worship? For one thing, it's not normally seen. And for another, it leaves out half of the principals of one side of the deal, the women. It would seem to me that a mark or a tattoo on the face or the forehead would be a lot more reasonable."

"Oh, certainly. Obviously, this is a case of cultural adaptation. The practice of circumcision no doubt goes back to the earliest primitive times, long before the time of Abraham. It was practiced by most of the tribes in the area, as it is today in Arab countries, and among African tribes as well. Curiously, not among the Philistines. 'Whisper it not in Ashkelon, tell it not in the streets of Gath, lest the daughters of the Philistines be gladdened, lest the daughters of the uncircumcised make merry.' Doctor friends tell me that in about ten percent of the general male population the foreskin is so tight as to make sexual intercourse painful. So primitive man solved the problem by removing the foreskin, probably first only for those who were seriously handicapped, and then subsequently for all males of the tribe. It would naturally be done at puberty when the need would arise. Since at that age it is painful, tolerating it without flinching would be a test of manhood. It is easy to see how it would develop into a rite. We continued the practice, I suppose, out of a superstitious fear of dropping an old custom. But we gave it new meaning. In the same way the Christian Church changed the pagan celebration of the winter solstice into Christmas and made it the date of the birth of Jesus. We circumcise in infancy, when the child is only eight days old, too young to feel pain, or at least to remember it."

Joan was still not satisfied. "Would it make any difference—I mean, do you really and truly think it would make a difference if women had exactly the same status in the synagogue as men?"

"I don't know. From the experience of the Reform synagogue we have found that it is wise to make changes slowly. If you move too quickly, you may have to backtrack."

"But how do you know, at the time I mean, if you're moving too quickly?"

"Ah, well, the important thing is to be sure that the change reflects existing conditions and is not merely a response to the pressure of a group. Take the matter of men and women sitting together, which is one of the main differences between Conservative and Orthodox. It came about, not because of any demand for equality, but because it had become the norm in everyday life."

"Then why are you opposed to women being part of the minyan or being called to the Torah?" asked Aaron. "I assume you are."

"Because I feel it is being urged as a means of demonstrating equality, rather than because women have come to feel the same way about these things as men do."

"So why not let them have it if they want it?"

"That's just the point. I don't think they do want it; not for itself, at least, but as another step up the ladder of equality."

Aaron pressed him. "You don't think they are equal?"

"Oh, yes, but different. They have different interests, different enthusiasms—"

"I see, 'separate but equal,'" said Aaron sarcastically.

The rabbi was not in the least disconcerted. "A cliché discredited in one area doesn't mean that it can't be valid in other areas," he said mildly, and then added, "It works perfectly well in public toilet facilities, for example."

"Bravo, Rabbi!" exclaimed Aaron, his eyes glinting with surprised pleasure. "You're right. They're separate and even different and still equal."

The rabbi nodded his appreciation. "Did you ever stop to think of the ultimate irony of this drive for

213

equality? By aspiring to all traditional male activities and interests, women are thereby deprecating their own interests and instincts. Women have ways of thinking and feeling that are different from men's—"

"But equally valid?"

"Certainly. Maybe even more so."

"Then why when you say your morning prayers, Rabbi, do you thank God for having been born male?"

"Do you?" asked Joan. "Really?"

"It's in the prayer book," said Aaron smugly.

"And what do women say?" asked Joan.

Aaron looked inquiringly at the rabbi.

"'According to the will of the lord,'" the rabbi replied.

"But that's awful."

"Why? Do you regret having been born female? Do you regret being a woman?"

"No, of course not. I'm quite happy the way I am, thank you, but—"

"So am I," said the rabbi. "The rabbinic rationale of the difference between the two prayers is that the male has more opportunities for obeying the *mitzvoh* because he has more to obey, starting in infancy with the *mitzvah* of circumcision. But the obvious explanation is probably the more likely one. Seeing how women were burdened during pregnancy and the pain involved in childbirth, men were quite naturally aware of the disparity in the life cycles of the two sexes. Since they were naturally grateful for their easier role, why shouldn't they thank God for it? Isn't that pretty much the view of the women's lib people? That men have it easier than women? Of course, it doesn't take in the compensations."

"Like what?" Joan challenged.

"Like the greater sensitivity of women, the sense of achievement in bringing forth a child, the special relationship between a mother and her children, and in modern times her better health and greater longevity. How do you weigh these one against the other?"

"You know," said Aaron, "I thought it was all supposed to be because of what happened in the Garden of Eden."

"Well, of course that was the rationale. It was like three conspirators sentenced by a judge. The snake, as the instigator, got the worst sentence. He was condemned to walk on his belly and eat dust. The woman, because she had seduced the man into sin, was condemned to bear her children in pain and suffering. She accepts the verdict and says, 'In accordance with the will of the Lord.' The man, condemned to earn his bread by the sweat of his brow, feels that he got off with the lightest penalty and thanks God for having made him a man. We don't know what the snake says. The story, like all fables, was developed to explain observed phenomena." He glanced curiously at Aaron. "How does modern science explain it?"

Aaron grinned. "Since ours is the only species that brings forth its young in pain, I suppose science would have to blame God for it because He gave us mind and will which enlarged the head of the fetus to the point where it is painful for it to pass through the normal pelvis."

The rabbi nodded. "All right, I'll accept that. And since God is just, I'm sure it's a fair trade-off." He noticed that their glasses were empty and asked, "More wine?"

"No, thanks," said Aaron. "I can drink just so much sweet wine."

"How about tea then?"

"Oh, I'd love a cup," said Joan.

"You brew tea on the Sabbath?" asked Aaron in mock reproval.

The rabbi smiled. "I thought Joan might do the honors."

She jumped up. "Of course." And as the rabbi started to rise, she said, "Don't bother, Rabbi. I'll find the cups and things."

CHAPTER

14

No sooner had Joan served the tea when the phone rang. Startled, Rabbi Small jumped up from his seat, almost upsetting the steaming teacups. It could only be from Miriam, and it had to be something serious for her to call on the Sabbath.

It *was* Miriam, but her voice, when he answered, was obviously cheerful. "I'm coming home, David. I'm taking a bus Sunday morning. I'll get to Grenardsville around noon."

"That's swell." Then he asked cautiously, "Your father, is he all right?"

"He's coming along nicely. He'll be in the hospital for another week, but he's doing fine. No complications."

"Then..."

"Oh, Aunt Sophie is coming up from Philadelphia to stay with Mama." She laughed happily. "I told Mama about your attractive convert, and she began to worry.

So she called Aunt Sophie and she was insistent. She said if I could leave you alone for a few days, in a hotel, mind you, she could leave Uncle Phil for a few days, especially when they have a married daughter just around the corner where he can get his meals. So I can come back to protect you from the fascination of your convert and from any predatory females that everyone knows hotels are full of."

He chuckled. "Very good."

"Er, David—"

"Yes?"

"Is she there now?"

"Yes, they are here."

"I'm looking forward to meeting them. Why don't you invite them to have dinner with us at the hotel when I return?"

"Sunday night?"

"Sure. Why not?"

"All right, I'll ask them."

When he returned to the porch, he announced, "That was my wife. She's coming back here Sunday. She suggested I ask you if you would care to take dinner with us here at the hotel, Sunday evening."

"Oh, we'd love to, but—"

"But we're leaving tomorrow," said Aaron. "Joan has to go back to work Monday."

"Oh. She was eager to meet you both."

"Couldn't we take a rain check, back in Barnard's Crossing, I mean?" asked Joan.

"By all means. I'll phone you when we get home."

"After Labor Day?"

"Oh, no. We had arranged to stay only for another week. Miriam might want an additional week, but we'll be home the rest of the summer."

"Oh, then I can come to see you?"

"Anytime, Joan," said the rabbi, obviously pleased at her enthusiasm. He looked curiously at Aaron. "And you? Will you be in the area during the summer?"

"I live in Cambridge," Aaron said, "but I usually come out to visit my folks weekends."

"Weekends? You come out Friday afternoon?" The rabbi showed interest.

"Yeah, around four o'clock usually. Why?"

"Well, I thought you might care to come to our Friday evening service, and then to the morning service the next day—with Joan, of course."

"Oh, I don't know..."

"Oh, that's wonderful," Joan said.

"Well, maybe we could do it one week."

"When?" the rabbi pressed him.

"Oh, sometime..."

"When the Messiah comes?" asked the rabbi sarcastically.

Aaron chuckled. "That's what my grandfather used to say, and my grandmother, too, come to think of it. But they said it in Yiddish."

"I'll arrange it," Joan offered.

Aaron canted his head and looked at the rabbi askance. "You believe in the Messiah?"

"Of course. I have to."

"Because you're a rabbi?"

"No, because of the logic of the situation," said the rabbi.

"What's logic got to do with it?"

"If you think of the universe as having been created by God, then it's fair to assume that it was for some purpose. And that suggests an ultimate goal."

"All right."

"So then you ask yourself what this goal can possibly be."

"Since you're dealing with an infinite intelligence," said Aaron, "the possibilities would be infinite, which in effect makes it pointless."

"Sure," the rabbi agreed. "Conceivably His plan might be to have the human race superseded by some other creature. Or this section of the universe, the sun and its planets, destroyed. One can imagine any of the possibilities one reads in science fiction. But inasmuch as we have posited a God who created man in His image, naturally we have to think of a goal that is some-

218

how connected with humans. In Christian theology the plan calls for a culmination in the End of Days when Christ reappears on earth and judges all men, who are then assigned to enjoy or suffer their just deserts in the world to come. The time of his coming is associated with a cataclysm which destroys the planet, a proper punishment for a wicked world. It will be preceded by wars and pestilence and a complete breakdown of all social order—"

"According to some of the preachers you hear on radio and TV," observed Aaron, "the time is about ripe for it."

"Oh, that's been going on for years," said Joan scornfully.

"Even back to biblical times," said the rabbi. "The prophets were always inveighing against the wickedness of the people and threatening them with the wrath of God. Their diatribes, however, were directed largely against the Jewish people, and not against the world as a whole. There was no suggestion of the planet being wiped out. I suppose because there was no concept of another world to come. And by the way, the concept of the Messiah doesn't appear in the Old Testament either. That doesn't come in until about the time of the Second Temple. The important thing to keep in mind is that if you assume a plan, you imply a goal. Since we have minds, we try to figure out what the goal is. Naturally it will be related to our view of the plan and the planner."

"That's still a pretty tall order," said Aaron.

"Not really. You can almost spell it out. If we assume that God created man in His image, you discount the likelihood that we are to be replaced by a race of superants, for example. The plan must involve us, humans. Then if you assume that He is a God of justice, it follows that the goal is a society of men where justice and righteousness prevail. And this, not enforced and imposed on man by a celestial agency, but resulting from an increase in wisdom and understanding. Certainly not by divine fiat, or He would not have created

219

us with mind and free will. This world of justice and righteousness is something we have to work out on our own. So what comes to mind is the perfect political system. But that suggests a leader, a king, or a president. And that's what the Messiah is. He is, first of all, a man, and not an angel or a spirit. And because we believe that we were chosen to lead the way, our tradition holds that this leader will be one of us, a descendant of our most revered king, David."

"Doesn't the tradition call for the prophet Elijah to come in on the act?" asked Aaron.

"He is part of the folklore and mythological embroidery that developed around the basic concept. Why Elijah? Because he was presumably wafted up into heaven instead of dying. So he's been in a kind of cold storage and is presumed to come down to earth every now and then, at the Passover, for example. At the Seder, you may remember, we set out a special cup of wine for him in the event that he should drop in. One view is that he will precede the Messiah and come to Jerusalem where the resurrection of the dead will begin."

"But I thought you said you don't believe in a second life," Joan objected.

"I said 'one view.' We have no theological hierarchy, no final arbiter to establish an official creed. We are enjoined, as a religious obligation mind you, to study and think about our religion. So there are any number of opinions as to God's intentions. For many, the Messiah was a daydream hero who would right all wrongs. But how about those who were dead? What about the wrongs they had suffered when they were alive? So something had to be worked out for them, which called for bringing them back to life. However, the rabbis set certain limits to our thinking about the Messiah. One is that the Messiah is a man of men. That implies that his coming will produce a political and social revolution of some kind. It could come as the result of a constant improvement in human affairs. Or it could result from a reaction to great trouble and misery."

"But in either case that could come about through some organization like the United Nations," said Aaron.

"It could," the rabbi agreed. "But an organization, or a committee, that actually gets anything done is usually dominated by one man."

"And according to your thinking, this one man would be the Messiah?" asked Joan. "And he would be a Jew?"

"Or a convert," said the rabbi good-humoredly. "You remember that King David was the descendant of a convert."

"He was?" Joan exclaimed, wide-eyed.

"Uh-huh, the descendant of Ruth, whose story is told in the Book of Ruth and was presumably included in the canon for that reason. 'Whither thou goest, I will go, and thy people shall be my people.'" The rabbi looked at her quizzically.

"What do you think of that, Aaron? One of our kids could make it."

"Don't hold your breath," said Aaron. "If the coming of the Messiah caps a long march toward universal peace and justice, we've got a long way to go."

"It could come from a universal revulsion of what we have now," said the rabbi. "It's possible. From what I read in the daily press and various magazine articles, I get the impression that there is enough food and necessary raw materials to take care of the present world population. And we now have the technical capacity to keep the population static. So we could eliminate the main causes of war, at least. It's a question of willingness."

"Yeah, but everybody would have to be willing at the same time," said Aaron.

"True," the rabbi admitted, "and that would call for a unanimity which up till now has been all but impossible. But in recent years there have been developments which might make it possible."

"What developments?"

"Well, I've already mentioned a couple—the capacity to produce food and goods in sufficient quantity, and

221

the capacity to limit population so that it never outruns the food supply. It's been the need for food that has probably been the basis for most wars. Now, both those developments are recent, too recent perhaps to have had full impact on the world's thinking. Another new development is the capacity to communicate with the entire world almost simultaneously. A plan that is worked out by some central world body can be communicated to everyone all over the world almost immediately, and everyone can know what is expected of him so that the plan can be implemented. That's new. And so is the capacity to move goods from one part of the globe to any other part in a matter of hours. We demonstrated it in the Berlin airlift and many times since when there has been some natural disaster like a flood or an earthquake. That's new. Then there's the nuclear bomb—"

"You're not suggesting that would help?"

"It could. It's a new element in the history of man. For the first time man is capable of destroying the planet, at least as far as his capacity to live on it goes. Up until now what could the most ruthless tyrant of a victorious army do? Kill off the entire population, level all habitations, destroy all industry, remove or kill off all livestock, burn all crops, and how long would it be before there were people living on the land again? Two years? Ten years? Certainly no more. But now the land can be rendered uninhabitable for centuries with all living things either killed off or rendered sterile."

"And how does that help bring about the golden age?"

"It gives the people a clear-cut choice. War is always a gamble. Even when a powerful country attacks a weak one, there is no certainty that another powerful country won't come to the aid of the country attacked, or maybe take the opportunity of their preoccupation to launch an attack on *them*. Nevertheless, the gamble was not a bad one. Even if one lost, the loss was not permanent. The bombed city could be rebuilt, treasure once again accumulated, and the area repopulated by a slight increase in the birthrate. So up till now, the gamble has been worth taking, judging by the number of wars that have been launched in the course of history. But now a war can be nuclear. Which means that the city, founded and developed because it was strategically located—on a harbor or at the confluence of several rivers—once leveled by nuclear bombs, cannot be rebuilt. The area will be radioactive perhaps for generations. A nuclear war is not a gamble; it is a certain loss because the planet iself is thereby diminished. The point is that for the first time in history we not only have the capability of waging a final war, but also the knowledge and capacity to remove the causes of war."

"And you think this would stop it?"

"I am only saying that whereas before we couldn't, now we can because the machinery is available. As to when the world will realize it and act upon it—" He shrugged his shoulders expressively. "It could be in fifty years, or five hundred, or five thousand. Once war becomes unthinkable, the coming of the Messiah becomes foreseeable."

"And then what?" asked Aaron.

The rabbi smiled and shook his head. "To tell the truth, I haven't done much thinking about it. My feeling, though, is that the function of the Messiah is not to bring everything to an end, but rather to inaugurate a beginning. When war becomes unthinkable, man will finally have a chance to grow to his full potential. Fear of one's fellow man that has obtained throughout history has held us back. It has been like a low-grade fever that has never permitted us to be truly alive and vital. Once we're rid of it, who can tell what we'd be capable of? In recent years science and technology have made enormous strides, but morals and ethics haven't budged. You could make out a good case that they've retrogressed. The most primitive peoples have guns and radios and gas engines and electricity as a result of the scientific and technological explosion of the last few years. What would happen if morals and ethics were to make similar strides?"

"Yeah, but political philosophers have been saying the same thing for years," Aaron pointed out. "It was thought that the League of Nations and the United Nations would implement it. What is it that makes it Jewish?"

The rabbi opened his eyes wide in surprise. "Many of our ideas and concepts have been accepted by the world. Does that make them any less true? Our religion is centered in this world, and all we have in the Bible on the distant future is the vision of the prophets of a time when swords will be beaten into plowshares and there will be peace among nations. They see also the return to Zion of the exiled Jews and the rebuilding of Jerusalem."

He smiled. "Many Protestants, especially the evangelical sects, sympathize with our yearning to return to Zion, for which we are grateful, even though mindful that their concern is due to the belief that it is a necessary preliminary to the second coming of Jesus Christ."

"The return to Zion—you believe that's important?" asked Joan.

"Oh, yes."

"But why?" asked Aaron. "From a rationalist point of view, I mean, why should Israel be important to you?"

"Because it's a package deal," said the rabbi promptly. "You might say it is part of the *quid pro quo* of our compact with God. The agreement was that we would be a nation of priests, His special people, who would be held to a higher standard of conduct, and in exchange we were to receive, among other things, the land of Israel in perpetuity. That was the bargain. According to our tradition, we sinned by not maintaining the high standard expected and agreed to. In punishment we were temporarily expelled from our inheritance, but we were assured that it was only temporary and that we would return. We have never doubted it. Over the

224

centuries we have said, 'Next year in Jerusalem' at the end of the Yom Kippur service and at the end of the Passover feast. In the synagogue, the Ark is set up against the wall that faces in that direction. We recite prayers for rain and dew for the times they are needed in Israel, even though they might be useless in the countries in which we happen to be, and even though others occupy the land for which our prayers are intended."

"But look here, Rabbi," Aaron protested, "according to what you yourself have been saying, the Jews received a set of commandments and instructions by which they have been able to lead more productive and more successful lives. It would seem to me that this yearning for a bit of land in the Middle East, and not a particularly rich piece of land—no oil, no minerals—is, well, it's childish. I can see where Jews might want a piece of land that they could call their own, if only to give them national status. But why *this* piece of land? In any case, it seems to me more intelligent to pray that more countries would be like the United States, where Jews could feel that they had the same rights as everyone else, than to want this bit of land, plunk in the middle of the Arab world which has been fighting with them about it ever since."

"Because it is our belief, the belief of Jews everywhere, all over the world, that this piece of land was given us by God. So it is the one place on earth to which we have a claim and a right. You may say that it is all delusion on our part, that God made no such contract, or even that there is no God to make it. But we believe it and have believed it for millennia. That is historic fact. And from a practical point of view, what if we had accepted the alternatives that have been offered us, Uganda by the British, or Birobidzhan by the Russians? Suppose that after a while the British decided to slam the door on further immigration to the country as they did indeed to the Holy Land during their mandate. How much resistance could we have mustered, knowing that the land was a free gift to which we had no legitimate claim? Britain was a world power then. And now it is a second-class power. Could we even depend on its active support if one of the superpowers were to decide that it was in its interest to expel us? That the deed of the country from Britain was worthless since it was not Britain's to give? And could we have been more certain of the good faith of the Russians if we had accepted Birobidzhan from them?"

The rabbi leaned back and interlaced his fingers behind his head. "Let's see if I can give you an analogy that might clarify it for you. You have your doctorate?"

"Yes."

"All right. Suppose your father had told you when you entered graduate school that if you completed your course of study successfully, and got your doctorate, he'd give you a present, perhaps a car. I'll assume you enjoyed your studies, and you received your degree. Now you've not only had several years of enjoyable study, but also you now have a degree which gives you academic and social status and even enables you to earn your own living. Nevertheless, assuming your father could well afford it, wouldn't you expect the promised reward?"

Aaron laughed. "As a matter of fact, my father did give me a car. How'd you guess? But it wasn't when I got my doctorate; it was when I got my bachelor's. But even though you call it a package deal, I still don't see why you have to take the whole package. Why can't you just take what's obviously important and good—"

"Because it doesn't work," the rabbi interrupted. "Reform Judaism tried it, and they had to give it up. They eliminated those practices that came about through fable like the Sabbath as a day of rest because God rested on that day, in favor of Sunday; all that they regarded as primitive tribal taboos like the food laws; all separatist customs like the wearing of the fringed garment; all claims and interest in the land of Israel because that was ancient history and had as much justification as the claim of the Indian to the American continent; they denied any connection with their fellow Jews other than the coincidental one that they derived their ethics from the same source. And what happened? It soon became a temporary stop on the road to assimilation. In all fairness, I have to admit that there may be some justice in their contention that it tended to keep Jews from assimilating who otherwise would. But that is only another way of saying the same thing; halfway in is also halfway out."

"But it's not that way now, is it?" asked Joan.

"Oh, no. Reform Judaism has done an about-face from the stand they announced in 1885 in the Pittsburgh Platform. In 1937 in the Columbus Platform they proclaimed their return to the Torah, both the Written Law and the Oral Law. What's more, they announced their loyalty to the group and called for their members to aid in the establishment of a Jewish homeland in Israel. They called for the preservation of the Sabbath and various Jewish customs and symbols, and even for the encouragement of the use of Hebrew. All that in little more than half a century. And right now, many of the leaders of the Zionist movement in the United States are Reform rabbis."

"But I still don't see where devotion to Israel has to be part of the package," Aaron objected. "I mean, we've been out of there for almost two thousand years, and in all that time, Jews continued to practice their religion and kept their beliefs. Now we're scattered all over the globe, and at least in the democratic countries we have freedom and equality. Maybe we don't in the dictatorships, in countries like Russia, but then no one is really free there. So why is it now important to Jews of America and Canada and England and France?"

"Because it's the goal we've been aiming for all that time. I suppose that from the traditional religious point of view, inasmuch as we were expelled for our sins, our return is a sign that we are back in God's good graces again. Obviously, for this purpose going to Uganda or to Birobidzhan would not do at all. If we did not go back

227

to the Promised Land, then it was not a return at all but merely another place of exile."

"But I understand that many of the Orthodox were opposed to the Zionist movement," said Aaron.

"Yes, and some few still are. But it was not the place or the return to it that they objected to; it was the method. They felt that it was presumptuous to try to go back on our own, that we were thereby seeking to dodge the just punishment that God had meted out to us. From their point of view, if God wanted us to return at this time, He would arrange it for us, perhaps transport us there by some miracle."

Aaron grinned. "Well, then you'd be sure it was His doing."

The rabbi shook his head slowly. "No-o, not for us. We believe that God works through men. You remember that in getting the land in the first place, Joshua had to fight his way almost inch by inch, and then under the Judges and the Kings they had to continue to fight to maintain themselves there."

"You said that was the view of the traditionalists," said Joan. "How about the others?"

"For many, like the survivors of the Nazi Holocaust, and the Jews in Arab lands, and in the Communist world today, it is a haven of refuge. No other country will do. It has to be our country, ruled by us. And what other place on the face of the earth do we have claim to? But even for Jews living securely in one of the democracies with no fear of having to flee from a hostile regime, the establishment of the state of Israel was a tremendous thing. It's hard to explain why it should be, but it is.

"It's true that many Jews in the democracies thought it could be only a token state, a sort of Jewish Vatican City whose stamps might be interesting souvenirs. They didn't even think it would help the refugee problem. 'Where will they put them all? How would they earn a living?' But as stories of the quite extraordinary accomplishments of that little country began to emerge, stories of the kibbutz, of the democratic army where soldiers called their officers by their first names, of their absorbing Jewish communities from the Arab countries in numbers almost as great as the existing population at the time, they began to take pride in the country. And with the Six Day War, the pride became sheer jingoism."

"But there's nothing religious about that," Aaron objected. "That's just hooray for our side."

"For many it begins that way," the rabbi admitted. "But then it's apt to take on a religious flavor. You see it in their behavior when they visit Israel. They go to the Western Wall and join a minyan and participate in the service. They buy fancy skullcaps and wear them as they walk in the street, something they would never think of doing at home. Even though it frequently puts them to some inconvenience, they glory in the city's closing down for the Sabbath. They don't think of it as just another small state like Denmark or Switzerland. For them it's a religious institution. I asked one visitor if he was planning to go to the synagogue on the Sabbath, and he said, 'To tell the truth, Rabbi, I feel that just being here is like being in a synagogue.' And he was not what would normally be considered a religious man."

"I'll bet Israelis don't feel that way," said Aaron. "Those I've met at M.I.T. are pretty darn secular."

"It's hard to tell," said the rabbi. "In a religion like ours, where there is no separation from what is usually considered the secular, the practices that are obviously religious have less significance. Is the soldier on guard duty at the border engaged in a secular activity or is he fulfilling a religious obligation?"

"Maybe the rest of the world would be more supportive of Israel if they thought of it as a religious institution," Joan suggested.

The rabbi smiled. "I imagine most Israelis would object. They consider themselves citizens of a modern state. What they find hard to understand is why the statesmen of the world are not more supportive. Here is a small country with little in the way of natural resources other than its people. It is a new political entity established on what had become barren soil through centuries of misuse. And yet in a surprisingly short time it has done some remarkable things and has given indication of being able to do many more. It would seem that it offers the world a wonderful opportunity to observe a unique experiment in the art of government. I should think there would be tremendous interest in seeing what kind of civilization they could produce if their boundaries were assured by international agreement and they didn't have to worry about their security."

"It's possible that they'd tear themselves apart," said Aaron cynically.

The rabbi smiled sadly. "That, too, would be worth knowing."

Joan rose and said, "Let me clear the tea things. We'll have to be going soon."

"Oh, that's very kind of you," said the rabbi. "But you can leave them—"

"It won't take me but a minute." Before he could protest further, she had gathered up the cups and saucers and retreated into the cabin. When she came out, she said, "You know what puzzles me, Rabbi? That a religion that is so sensible and practical should have had so little influence and attracted so few converts."

"You could argue that it had tremendous influence through its offshoot, Christianity, and Islam too," said Aaron. "I guess between them they converted the entire Western world to monotheism."

"But that's not what I mean. I'm not thinking about pagans and tree worshipers. I'm thinking of modern times. Or even right now. People are searching for some belief that will give their life direction and meaning. In California they say a new cult is formed practically every day. And yet very few become Jews."

The rabbi nodded. "That's true. I don't know what the figures are, but I don't imagine there are many converts to Judaism. On the other hand, without trying to we appear to have converted the Christian world to many Judaic ideas."

"You have?"

"Well, let us say that whether we've done it or not, at least the Christian world seems to have adopted many ideas that are similar to ours."

"Like what?" Aaron demanded.

"First, I'd say our concept of this world as the real world and not merely a testing place for the world to come. What's implied is that we must make this one as just and happy a place for everyone as possible. The Church is no longer inclined to assuage its feelings of guilt over the wretched and the poor with the comforting thought that they will get their proper reward in heaven."

"Well, yeah, but—all right. Anything else?"

"Oh, lots. The equality of women for another."

"Equality?"

"Yes, as seen in our treatment of them. We never locked them up in harems as is customary among the Muslim nations, nor did we ever regard them as chattels which was their legal status in English common law. Wife beating was unknown among us. English common law, on the other hand, stipulated that a man could not beat his wife with a stick thicker than his thumb. We treated them as equal partners in marriage, which with us is an essentially secular arrangement, so that if it didn't work, it could be dissolved. We did not regard them as breeding machines, or as sex objects. The shoe was on the other foot, in fact, and it is the wife who has the right to sexual gratification rather than the husband. In the wedding ceremony it is the husband who makes all the promises, and makes them in writing. I would say that much of what women's lib is fighting for has always been common practice among us."

Joan looked questioningly at Aaron, who nodded slowly. "Yeah. I didn't know the legal or doctrinal background for it, but from what I've seen in my own family, and I mean cousins and uncles and aunts, I'd be inclined to go along with the rabbi. In fact, I'd say that in most Jewish families the women are a little more equal than the men. Does that do it, Rabbi, or is there more?"

"Oh, sure. There is our respect for life as represented in our concern for the lower animals. It was only around the middle of the last century that the Society for the Prevention of Cruelty to Animals was established. There is education, which is a religious obligation with us. Illiteracy has been practically nonexistent among us for two thousand years. But it's only recently that the rest of the world has come to think of it as important. There is our concern for the poor and unfortunate, not as objects of charity but as our equals who have God-given rights to share in the good things of the world. There is the growing feeling that human rights must have a share in international relations. But most of all, there is the Jewish concern for liberty and freedom, ingrained in us by constantly recalling our experience in Egypt, which the peoples of the world are only now beginning to realize are among the necessities of life like food and water and air."

"But is all that the result of Jewish influence, or is it a natural development?" asked Joan.

The rabbi shrugged. "Who knows? Who cares? 'The Lord moves in mysterious ways His wonders to perform.' Jewish theory holds that God is the God of all, but that He chose us to be an example to the nations. Well, we have followed His commandments to the best of our ability, and for the most part have lived our lives on the basis of His ethical teachings. Some of them have been transmitted to the world at large through Christianity and Islam, frequently by force, which is not our way. We have felt that both these offshoots of Judaism were wrong in other respects, too. But they were also right in many respects. All right, now Christianity is working its way toward purging itself of these errors. I suspect that the Church is aware of the source of the change it is undergoing. It shows up in the frequent use of the phrase 'Judeo-Christian tradition.' It's a new phrase, one that would have been unthinkable in the Middle Ages or even as late as the last century. But suppose it is purely accidental and signifies nothing. Suppose Christian theologians, and Christians generally, merely regard the changes in their thinking as the result of normal growth, perhaps in response to the discoveries of science. What difference does it make? True, we remain a small sect, but truth is not established by the majority. Suppose the rest of the world gradually adopts our views on all moral and ethical concerns, but continues to differ from us in the externals, slight differences in religious ceremony and ritual; could we then not stand before God and claim that we had done our duty as He commanded us?"

"I wouldn't hold my breath waiting for it to happen," said Aaron cynically. He rose and held out his hand to the rabbi. "I want to thank you for these few evenings. They've been most stimulating."

Joan, too, extended her hand. "It's been a wonderful experience, Rabbi. I'm planning to arrange to go to that conversion class you mentioned."

"It's been pleasant and stimulating for me, too," said the rabbi. "And I hope you'll look me up in Barnard's Crossing."

He stood at the open door and watched them as they walked down the path together.

CHAPTER

15

When Miriam stepped off the bus, she tilted her head to be kissed, and then eyed the rabbi critically and asked, "Did you eat regularly, David? Are you all right?"

"Of course I did," he answered with asperity. "I think I may have even gained some weight. How's your father?"

"Cranky, but coming along nicely. And how is your lovely convert? Will I get to see her?"

"They went home yesterday. I invited them to call when we get back to Barnard's Crossing, and she said they would. But you know how these things go..."

"You really aren't very much interested in her, are you?"

"Not terribly. We are not engaged in competing with other religions in numbers of adherents. When there is a marriage involved, conversion may have some practical value, although a Jew going outside his faith for a spouse is usually already lost to us since it is so contrary to our custom and tradition. And that is what hurts. In this case now, it is Aaron I'm interested in rather than Joan."

"And how did you make out with him?"

The rabbi shrugged. "When I suggested that they might like to spend a Sabbath with us, come to the evening service, have dinner, come to the morning service Saturday—we were talking about their looking us up in Barnard's Crossing, you understand—he showed a singular lack of enthusiasm to the point where it was even a little awkward."

"Then you think they won't call?"

"Oh, I rather think they will. It was going to the synagogue that he objected to. I think he enjoyed our talks, as a kind of intellectual exercise, but I doubt if I convinced him that it was important."

"Well, maybe when he's had time to think about it..." she offered soothingly.

The Smalls returned to Barnard's Crossing on a Sunday, and the next day the rabbi slipped back to his regular routine of driving to the temple for the morning service at seven, returning home for a leisurely breakfast, after which if the weather was fine he would saunter back to the temple to spend the rest of the morning in his study, to take care of his correspondence and to see anyone who might happen to drop in.

Miriam had suggested that perhaps he ought to call Joan Abernathy, but he had said, "No, I don't want to appear to be pressuring her."

"But how will she know that you've returned?"

"Oh, I said we'd be coming home around this time. I suppose she'll call one night on the chance we've arrived."

Sure enough, when he appeared at his study a little after nine on Wednesday, the secretary greeted him with "A Miss Abernathy called a few minutes ago and asked if she could see you. I told her you were usually here until noon. She said she'd be in around eleven. Is that all right?"

He wondered idly why she had not called him at home rather than at the temple. His number was in the book. Was it because she thought Miriam might answer and she was perhaps reluctant to speak to her until she had met her? And why was she coming to see him in the morning? Had she given up her job? Or was the job one that gave her considerable freedom during working hours? He resolutely put his speculations aside, knowing that shortly he would be able to get the real answers, and immersed himself in his work.

A couple of hours later there was a knock on the door and the secretary opened it just wide enough to stick her head in to say, "Miss Abernathy is here."

"Have her come in." He rose expectantly to greet her.

But it was not the attractive young woman he had expected. This was a much older woman, in her late fifties. She was tall and angular with frizzled gray hair which had been lightly tinted with lilac. She had a prominent nose with deep lines on either side which had the effect of making her cheeks appear pouchy. Her mouth was small and the lips were pursed as though she disapproved of what she saw.

"I—I thought—" he began.

"I am Jane Abernathy," she announced.

"Joan's aunt? Won't you sit down, Miss Abernathy?"

She sat very straight, her back not touching the back of the chair. "I heard you preach once," she said. "It was a couple of years ago at our church."

"Oh, yes, during Brotherhood Week."

"I thought you spoke very well, very sensibly, and I thought you were sincere and..." Her voice trailed off. She took a deep breath and began again. "I am not just Joan's aunt. I'm more her mother. I've had the care of her since she was six months old. I've brought her up."

"Yes, Joan told me. She thinks of you as her mother."

She gave a snort of satisfaction and said, "So you

236

can imagine how I felt when she told me she was planning to take instruction in order to be admitted to your religion. She told me all about going to see you at Grenardsville and how you brainwashed her—"

"She said brainwashed? That was the expression she used?"

"Of course not," she answered contemptuously. "The victim is never aware of what's happening."

Although he reddened, by an effort of will he maintained his composure. When he spoke, his voice was gentle. "Your daughter—er—niece came to see me, asking to be converted. I told her that I do not do conversions. She then asked if she might talk to me about it. Should I have refused? So we talked and I tried to discourage her."

"Discourage? Why?"

"Because we're looking for understanding from non-Jews, not converts. Even her fiancé has no interest in her conversion. Do you also object to the marriage?"

Somewhat mollified, she said, "He's a nice boy, I guess, but I'd rather she would marry a Christian boy."

"So would I, and that Aaron would marry a Jewish girl. But these things happen, and then perhaps it's best for the marriage if both partners are of the same faith."

"Then why doesn't he change?"

"I presume because he doesn't want to, whereas she does. Tell me, Miss Abernathy, does her father feel as you do?"

"My brother has no interest in these things. He regards them as women's concerns. If it weren't for me, and if it were left up to him, Joan would never see the inside of a church. And if it had been a son that his wife had left him instead of a daughter, he probably wouldn't have permitted me to take him to church."

"And Joan's mother, was she a religious woman?"

"I didn't know her." As she noticed his look of surprise, she hurried on to explain. "My brother and I didn't see much of each other after our parents died. He was out of the country most of the time working for

General Electric. I'd get a card at Christmas, and that was about all. Even when he came back to the States, I didn't see him because home base for him was here in Boston and I was in Cleveland. Sometimes, on his way to the west coast maybe, he'd stop in Cleveland and we'd have dinner together. He married in England and didn't bother to tell me until he got back to this country. And then it was by letter. News like that you'd think would be worth a long-distance phone call, but no, just a letter with a snapshot of the two of them. She was a little bit of a thing, barely up to his shoulder. There was an invitation of sorts. He said he'd like me to come and visit with them, but that Sarah was having a difficult pregnancy and wasn't up to it now. I didn't hear from them until Joan was born. Then I got a card."

"You resented your brother's—er—coldness?"

"No-o. We had never been close. We didn't have the same interests."

"I see. But when your sister-in-law died—"

"He called to tell me. He said he had a practical nurse taking care of the baby for the time being. It was just a temporary arrangement and he thought he might have to give the child up for adoption. So I quit my job and came right away."

"He asked you to come?"

She shook her head. "He didn't have to. I wasn't seeing a child of my family given over to some stranger."

"There was no family on the mother's side he could have appealed to?"

The corners of her mouth drooped disparagingly as she shook her head. "She had no kin at all. She was an orphan. My brother didn't talk about her much, but he did tell me that she had been a refugee from Holland. She was a clerk of some sort, maybe a stenographer in this company he was doing some work for. He didn't know anybody in London, and I suppose she took advantage of his loneliness and got him to marry her."

"That's how most women get married, Miss Abernathy," the rabbi interjected.

She smiled sourly. "Is it? I wouldn't know. My

238

brother took me to England a few years ago. He was going on business and Joan was in school at the time, so I was free. We walked around London a bit, and he showed me where she had lived. It was a slum, a place called Whitechapel."

"It may not have been when she lived there," said the rabbi. "Neighborhoods can deteriorate very rapidly."

"Well..."

The rabbi leaned forward. "What is it you want me to do, Miss Abernathy?"

Quite suddenly she crumpled. "I don't know," she wailed. "I'm so unhappy." Tears came to her eyes and ran down her cheeks. She sniffed and searched in her purse for a handkerchief, and then nodded gratefully when the rabbi slid a box of tissues across the desk to her.

He waited for her to regain her composure, and then said, "Believe me, Miss Abernathy, it is not of our seeking. We know all too well how traumatic conversion can be, even more for the family than for the principal. Let's hope that in this case it turns out for the best."

When he came home for lunch and told Miriam what had happened, she said, "Oh, that's too bad, and I'm afraid it's not the end of it. Mrs. Freed called up and asked if she and her husband could come to see you. I suggested they come over this evening."

Although he was not given to making snap judgments of character, Rabbi Small decided immediately when the Freeds arrived that he would find Mr. Freed more understanding and sympathetic than Mrs. Freed. Unfortunately, she did most of the talking, and it soon became obvious that Aaron had spoken no more than the truth when he had said that in his family the women were a little more equal than the men. Although by the rabbi's reckoning she had to be in her fifties, her hair was a golden blonde and she looked surprisingly young. Mr. Freed, a tall, balding man, looked very much like his son, but was of a quite different temperament. He spoke little, but every now and then made silent comment by a gesture of the hand or a slow smile.

After the preliminary amenities, Mrs. Freed embarked on a long diatribe beginning with the rhetorical question "Who needed it? Aaron is a brilliant boy. You don't have to take my word for it. Ask any of his teachers, his professors in college. But then, you've met him so you know. So of all the nice Jewish girls he's met, he has to go and pick this *shicksa*. I suppose you as a rabbi will say I'm being punished for not keeping a kosher house—"

"Oh, no."

Mr. Freed smiled and made a deprecating gesture. His wife hurried on. "All right, so *you* wouldn't say it, but there are others who do. My own aunt, I'm sure, when she hears about it. Never mind. The point is..."

But it took her a long time to get to the point, and the rabbi was not sure that she ever did. She ended up with "If my Aaron gives up this wonderful opportunity, I'll never forgive her as long as I live." And having delivered her ultimatum, she sat back in her chair, her lips compressed, her jaw determined.

Mr. Freed said, "It's like this, Rabbi. This job in Israel at Rehovot, it really is quite an opportunity. He'll be doing research without being distracted with class work or committees. And he'll be working in his own field instead of his department head's field as he is now. You might say his whole career hinges on this. And he refuses to go without Joan."

"She refuses to go to Israel?"

"She won't go until they're married. Rabbi Bernstein says it'll be several months before she can be converted, and according to Aaron, they won't hold the place open. I guess there's some politics involved."

"Well," said the rabbi, "they could get married in a civil ceremony, and she can continue her conversion in Israel."

"She won't hear of it," Mrs. Freed exploded.

Mr. Freed nodded his head in confirmation.

"I see." The rabbi leaned back and smiled at them. "So what do you want of me?"

Mrs. Freed was about to speak, but her husband silenced her with a look. "We spoke to Rabbi Bernstein, but he won't budge. So we thought maybe you..."

"Convert her in the next few days? Perform the marriage ceremony?"

"You have the authority, haven't you?" demanded Mrs. Freed. "Bernstein isn't your superior. He doesn't have exclusive right to convert, does he? Can't any rabbi do it?"

The rabbi shook his head. He faced Mr. Freed. "You can see that it wouldn't do, can't you?"

Freed nodded sadly. "I knew you wouldn't, couldn't, but I figured it was worth a try. Joan is a nice girl, and about this business, I kind of admire her. It proves she's sincere, doesn't it? She's young though, they're both young, and young people have no give to them. But maybe it'll turn out all right. Aaron is sure he'll miss out on the Rehovot thing if he doesn't take it right away, but maybe they'll hold it for him, or maybe next year."

When they had gone, Miriam remarked, "He seemed rather nice, but she...She may have been a blonde years ago, but that shade comes out of a bottle. Still, she's Aaron's mother and...Isn't there *anything* you can do?"

"Sure, I can convert her and get Bernstein and every other rabbi on the North Shore sore at me for years to come," he answered with unwonted sarcasm, thereby betraying his own concern. Then he went on in a milder tone, "I don't really think it's as bad as they represented. It's hard for me to believe that the sort of position they were talking about wouldn't be held open for a few months. Aaron probably received a letter from the authorities telling him he was appointed and indicating the date on which they expected him to take up his duties. The chances are that a transatlantic phone call would straighten out the matter."

She did not continue the discussion, but the next evening at dinner she brought it up again. As she served coffee, she said, "You know, David, I feel sorry for those young people."

"You don't even know them."

"So what? I can still feel sorry for them. Isn't there something you can do?"

"What, for instance?"

"I don't know. Maybe you could talk to Joan, or Aaron, or—"

"To someone," he finished for her. "You have an exaggerated opinion of my powers of persuasion. And yet..."

"What is it, David? Have you got an idea?"

"I think I'll talk to Joan's father. Maybe you could call him for me and ask if I can come over and see him, tonight if possible."

"But why Joan's father?"

"Because he's the only one involved in this that I haven't spoken to yet."

The porch light was on, and Mr. Abernathy was at the open door as the rabbi walked up the path from the sidewalk. He was a tall man in a rumpled seersucker suit, stretching tightly across broad shoulders. He had a craggy face with a prominent nose, jutting chin, and pale blue eyes.

"Rabbi Small? Come in, come in. Hot, isn't it? If my sister were here, she'd offer you some of her special iced tea, but she's gone to a movie. So how would a glass of cold beer do? You're allowed to drink beer, aren't you?"

"Oh, yes. We are not teetotalers. A beer would be very nice right now."

"Er—maybe you'd like to come into the kitchen, Rabbi. There's a little more air there from the breezeway."

"Fine." He followed his host and sat at a white Formica table as the beer was poured into tall glasses. Abernathy raised his glass in silent toast, to which the rabbi responded in kind, and they both drank.

"Now what can I do for you?" asked Abernathy.

"You can answer a question for me."

"Shoot."

"Was your wife Jewish?"

Abernathy's eyes opened wide. "Yes, she was. How'd you guess?"

"Would you mind telling me about your marriage?"

"What do you want to know?" Abernathy asked warily.

"Oh, where you were married, what church, I mean?"

"We weren't married at a church. We went to the Registry Office. You see, she wanted us to be married by a rabbi. I didn't mind. I was very much in love with her, and I wasn't at all religious. That is, being married by a rabbi didn't mean my giving up anything. But the rabbi wouldn't marry us unless I was Jewish. I didn't mind converting for her sake, but where it involved getting circumcised, at my age, well, there I drew the line. I mean I wouldn't do something like that unless I had a strong commitment, and I didn't have, except to her. She understood, and we went to the Registry Office."

"Where did you meet her?"

"She was a stenographer in the office where I worked. There were three of us who had been sent over by the company, and she was assigned to us. The other two had their wives along, but I was alone, and you know how it is, a bachelor in a strange town. So I invited her out and one thing led to another. She was a little bit of a thing. Came up to here on me." He gestured to a point just below his shoulder. "And thin, a regular bag of bones. Lack of proper food while she was growing up, I suppose, or enough of it." He looked off into the distance. "But the biggest eyes you ever saw, and dark like they were all pupil."

"You felt sorry for her?"

"Oh, no. I didn't know much about her past until we had gone together for a little while, but she wasn't a tragic figure if that's what you mean. She was awfully good company and a lot of fun. She was, you know, perky, like a sparrow."

"You knew she was Jewish?"

"Oh, sure. From the first day when she was assigned to us, I knew she wasn't British for all she had a British-sounding name, Admore. You see, she had an accent. So I asked her about it. She was a refugee from Poland originally. The family made it to Holland, but there the Nazis caught up with them. There was an organization that concentrated on saving the kids. She was about ten or eleven at the time, and they managed to get her out. Her folks never made it. And you know, when she landed in England, she had just the clothes she was wearing. She had a bag, but it turned out that it was her father's. There was some underclothing, a couple of shirts, and in a separate blue velvet bag, his prayer shawl and those little black boxes with the straps—"

"Phylacteries."

"Yeah. Well, you know, they shuttled those kids around to various places in England. You see, the blitz was still on, so they didn't want them in London. And finally, when it was over, they were sent to various foster homes. And through it all, she kept that blue bag. At first because she figured on being able to return it to her father when he got out, but afterward she thought of it as a kind of heirloom that she'd pass on to a son if she ever had one."

He smiled sheepishly. "I promised that I'd let her bring up our children Jewish. And I wasn't snowing her, you understand. But when she—she left me, and I had Joan on my hands and my sister bringing her up, how was I going to manage it? If it had been a boy, maybe I would have tried to work something out so that he could use those things his mother had kept for him. I still have them, along with the rest of her things, in the attic upstairs."

The rabbi nodded sympathetically. "I understand. How long were you married?"

"A couple of years all told."

"And you never thought to remarry?"

He laughed. "I didn't think I'd get married the first time. My job called for me to move around a lot. You can't do that if you're married. Some of the men take their wives with them, but it means living in some pretty awful places for months at a time."

"But you did marry."

"Ah, well, Sarah was different. She could live anywhere. Then when she left me, and Jane came down to keep house, well, I couldn't get married then. What would I do with Jane? I couldn't tell her to beat it, that I wouldn't be needing her anymore. And if she stayed on with a wife in the house, she'd become little better than a kind of servant. I couldn't do that to her. She's my sister. So I guess I never thought of it too seriously."

"Joan was born in this country?"

"Right here in Boston at the Boston Lying-In Hospital."

"And she was baptized here?"

"Baptized? You mean taken to some church to have somebody sprinkle holy water on her? What was the point? I never went to church, so why would I bring her just to give her a name? Sarah wouldn't have allowed it anyway."

"But Joan did go to church after your sister came to live with you."

"Yeah, off and on. My sister is an old maid. I guess she was born to be one." He guffawed. "She looks like me, and that's no way for a woman to look. Now old maids are kind of fussy. Things have to be just so. You got to go to church because that's the proper thing to do. Now we Abernathys never were much for church-going, and she didn't at home. But now she had the responsibility of Joan so she seemed to think she ought to, for Joan's sake. I didn't object much because when you live with a woman, it makes no difference whether it's your sister or your mother or your wife, you've got to sort of give in now and then, especially when she was keeping house for me and bringing up my child."

"Did she know that your wife was Jewish?"

Abernathy shook his head. "It didn't occur to me to mention it to her. What was the point?"

"And you never told Joan?"

Again he shook his head. "What was the point? It would only have complicated things."

"Well, you will be interested to know that by our law, Joan is Jewish."

"By your law?"

"That's right. By Jewish law, a child born of a Jewish mother who has not converted is Jewish, regardless of what the father is."

"You mean—what if the father is Jewish and the mother is not?"

"Then the child is not."

"That's funny, but come to think of it, it makes sense." A thought occurred to him. "Then these lessons she's taking in Peabody—she's there right now—you mean she doesn't have to take them?"

"That's right, but I hope she'll continue."

"My guess is she will. She's pretty keen on them. But she wouldn't have to go through the whole course before she could marry Aaron?"

"She could marry him tomorrow. Of course, I'd want to do some checking—your wife's papers perhaps. I'm quite sure they'd support my finding."

"Well, gosh, that's wonderful, Rabbi. Joan will be overjoyed when I tell her. I gather there was some sort of trouble. Joan didn't explain it to me, but I guess this would make it all right. How did you come to think of it, Rabbi?"

The rabbi smiled. "It was something your sister said that started me thinking of the possibility that your wife might be Jewish. She said you had told her that she had been a refugee from Holland. Well, many if not most of the refugees from Holland had been Jews. She also said that you had shown her the house where she had lived in London. It was in Whitechapel. I have never been in London, but I know that at one time that was a predominantly Jewish section. But it was her name that clinched it for me."

"Her name? Sarah?"

"No, her surname, Admore."

"What about it?"

"It's a Jewish name."

"It doesn't sound Jewish."

"But it is. You see, names like Goldstein and Fine-gold and Rosenzweig are not really Jewish. They were chosen, when Jews had to have surnames, because they sounded nice and meant nice things. But the names Cohen and Levy are Jewish. A *kohane* is a priest, a presumed descendant of Aaron, the High Priest of Israel, who was the brother of Moses. So the name Cohen, and its cognates like Kagan, Kahn, Cohn, all show that the person is a *kohane*. A *layvi* is a member of the tribe of Levi, and the name Levy and its cognates Levine, Levitt, show that."

"So what's an Admore?"

"Ah, that involves a peculiar tendency we have to abbreviate certain phrases into a single word. Or sometimes we do it with a name, more particularly if the person is famous. The name Katz, for example, is an abbreviation of the phrase *kohane tseddik*, which means 'righteous priest.' So it also indicates kohanic ancestry. Similarly, the name Segal is another name showing membership in the tribe of Levi because it is an abbreviation of *segan leviah*, meaning—"

"But Admore, Rabbi?" said Abernathy impatiently.

"Ah, that is the abbreviation of the phrase *Adonenu, Morenu, ve-Rabbenu*, which means, 'Our master, teacher, and rabbi,' and was a kind of title which Chassidic Jews occasionally accorded their great or saintly rabbinical leaders. And the Jews of Poland were largely Chassidic."

"Does that mean that Sarah's father was a great rabbi?"

"Possibly. But the title was also used occasionally by his sons and descendants as a surname. And some of them had a lot of sons."

"Still..."

The rabbi smiled. "Yes, it denotes what we call *yic-*

chus, which means lineage or status. You didn't do too badly." He got up.

Abernathy also rose and walked him to the door. He grasped the rabbi's hand and shook it effusively. "Thanks, Rabbi. Many thanks."

The party had been arranged on the spur of the moment, an exuberant Aaron explained over the phone to the rabbi. "Some cousins of mine came in from Philadelphia for the wedding Sunday, and some friends of mine and Joan's happened to drop in, and before we knew it, they decided we had to have a party, and my mother went out to buy the necessary refreshments. I know it's short notice, but we would be terribly pleased, and honored, if you and Mrs. Small could manage to come tonight. It's strictly informal and, well—I wish you'd come."

When the Smalls arrived around eight, it was Aaron who opened the door and then pumped their hands in greeting as he said, "Gee, I'm glad you could make it." It was evident from the number of used paper plates and crumpled paper napkins that the party had been in progress for some time. Aaron explained, "Word got around, or more likely my mother spread it, and people have been dropping by for the last couple of hours. Come on, let me get you a drink."

The rabbi and Miriam wandered about sipping at their drinks, nibbling the food, the delicatessen, the cakes, and the cookies, that had been laid out on the sideboard. They were constantly being introduced to people by people whom they had just met. There was a group of young people, Aaron and Joan among them, in one corner of the room. As the rabbi and Miriam drifted in their direction, Aaron beckoned to them.

"I want you to meet my friend Professor MacDouglas. Jim is an agronomist and has just come back from Israel. He was telling us about the terrorist raid at the kibbutz up in the Galilee a couple of months ago. He was there."

MacDouglas, a chubby, sandy-haired young man,

nodded. "I was telling how the Israeli officer in charge was dickering with the terrorists through a bullhorn. He spoke in Arabic, but every now and then he'd add a word or two in Hebrew, for the hostages, you see. All the while, he was maneuvering his men around the back of the building. Then, when he saw that they were in position—he was still haranguing in Arabic, you understand—he suddenly shouted in Hebrew for the kids to drop to the floor. And that was the signal for his men to rush the place. They got all four of them."

"Did any of ours get hurt?" asked the rabbi.

"One little girl was stabbed in the leg, but it wasn't serious. Still, for almost five hours it was touch and go, and pretty horrible for the kids and their parents. I couldn't understand why they didn't bring up a bunch of the terrorists they'd captured in the past, line them up, and announce to those in the building that they'd shoot them all down right then and there if they didn't surrender. And you know what my friend Yaacov Ben Avrom who was there with me said?"

"Sure," said Aaron, grinning. "He probably said, 'We Jews don't do that sort of thing.'"

MacDouglas looked his surprise. "Yeah, that's exactly what he said. But if you did it once or twice, I'll bet it would work."

"But then," Aaron replied, "we wouldn't be Jews."

Joan turned and caught the rabbi's eye. Beaming, he nodded approval.